PRAISE FOR *THE CURSE OF MOONSEED MANOR*

"a gothic masterpiece that will delight and thrill readers of all ages…*The Curse of Moonseed Manor* will leave you spellbound…From start to finish, you'll be drawn into a world of adventure, romance, and mystery that will leave you breathless." — Suzie Housley, *Midwest Book Review*

"An unexpectedly cozy tale of mystery and romance among a dynamic cast." —*Kirkus Reviews*

"a delightful modern-day Gothic novel written in beautiful language, evoking feelings of looming disaster…a gripping read for any lover of the genre. It has all the classic elements needed to evoke feelings of mystery and suspense. It also creates a gloomy atmosphere and highlights the fear of the unknown." —*Readers' Favorite*

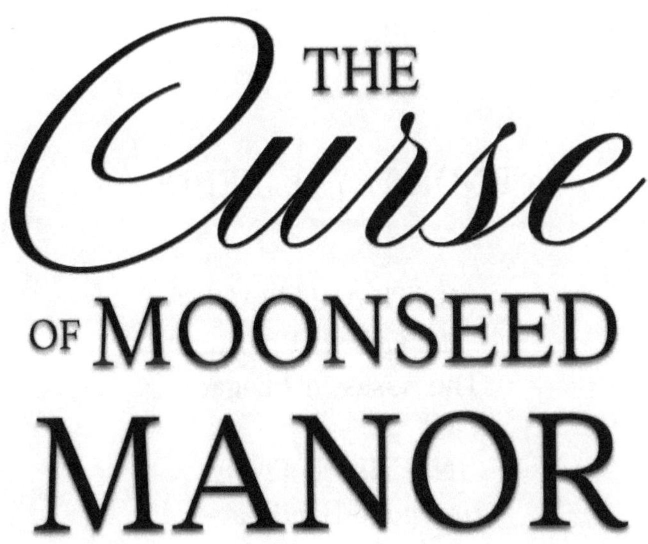

THE Curse OF MOONSEED MANOR

BOOKS BY D. LIEBER

MINTE AND MAGIC
The Exiled Otherkin
The Assassin's Legacy

INTENDED FATES
Intended Bondmates
Intended Strangers
Intended Enemies

COUNCIL OF COVENS
Dancing with Shades
In Search of a Witch's Soul

ALSO BY D. LIEBER
Conjuring Zephyr
Once in a Black Moon
A Very Witchy Yuletide
The Treason of Robyn Hood
The Curse of Moonseed Manor
The Goblin King's Mischief
The Winter Sorcerer and the Summer Witch
Bitten by the North Wind
The Glass Moth

THE *Curse* OF MOONSEED MANOR

By

D. Lieber

Copyright © 2023 by D. Lieber
First edition October 2023

Ink & Magick, LLC
Kenosha, Wisconsin
contact@inkandmagick.com

Hardcover ISBN: 978-1-951239-28-2
Paperback ISBN: 978-1-951239-29-9
Ebook ISBN: 978-1-951239-30-5

⚘ HUMAN AUTHORED

Reg #: 1744768, https://authorsguild.org/human

Edited by Samantha Talarico
Proofread by Julie Chyna
Cover art by GetCovers

SPECIAL THANKS

———

Thank you so much to all those who helped me make this book possible: John, Amy, Joyce, Laura, Aunt Debbie, Mary, Megan, and Kass.

CHAPTER I.

MY FATHER always said that a person is only as happy as they want to be. That isn't to say that one must always be happy. It was more to teach me that I was in control of my own emotions, that no one else had any power over how I was feeling.

I thought about this as I stared down at the camera in my hands. Melancholy pressed in on me. I embraced this feeling, comfortable in its familiarity. I had never been one to push my sadness away. It was just as important as its counterparts in my mind.

I ran my thumb over the crimson rose sticker stuck to the lens cap, the velvet, raised edges tickling my skin. I remembered the morning I'd awoken to find this camera, so shiny and new, on my bedside table. I'd saved for over a year to get it. But just when I'd saved enough, the very day I was going to purchase it myself, there it was—a bright red bow stuck to the top of the box.

I hadn't even had to ask who'd put it there; the grin on my dad's face as I scrambled down the stairs for breakfast said it all.

With a sigh I felt but didn't voice, I placed the camera on the glass case between me and the pawn shop owner. This wasn't goodbye. I would reclaim my most prized possession well before the loan expiration date.

The owner counted out my borrowed amount, a fraction of the value of the camera, and placed my pawn ticket atop the pile of cash.

"Thank you," I murmured, stuffing the bills into my wallet.

The old man smiled, his eyes soft and sympathetic. "I'll keep it safe for you. Don't worry."

I nodded, then thanked him again before turning to leave.

I passed all manner of things on my way out of the shop— everything from clocks and tea cups to cellphones and televisions. And each object my eye alighted on weighed a little heavier on my heart. These were people's dreams, the things they were willing to leave behind to just keep going.

As the bell above the door tinkled overhead, I stepped into the April afternoon, the sun bright but bringing little warmth as the still-cold wind whipped my face. I pulled up the hood of the sweatshirt I wore beneath my coat, stuffing my long hair in before putting on my helmet.

My well-worn sneakers made little sound on the cracked sidewalk when I took a few hurried steps to my bicycle. But I could feel the soles protest as I knelt and quickly unlocked the chain that tethered the bike to the lamppost. Hopping astride, I glanced to the left before pulling into the street.

Traffic wasn't bad this afternoon, lunch hour already over while the city settled back into another grinding day. I was grateful to have worn leggings under my jeans as my gathering speed blasted freezing air through the torn knee holes while I pedaled toward work.

Ten minutes before my shift started, I reached the motel, aptly named the Motel. Locking my bike at the rack, I shook the chill from my shoulders as I stepped into the warm office.

Bobby glanced up from his magazine for less than a second to mark my entrance. "There's a clogged toilet in number five," he informed me.

"All right"—I went to the ATM—"I'll get to that first."

After putting in my PIN, I deposited nearly all of the money I'd gotten from the pawn shop into the account I'd set up for Izzy; the remaining thirty I kept in my wallet. Then I gave Bobby a quick wave, though he didn't likely even notice, and started my shift.

It took me forty minutes to fix the disaster in number five's bathroom, but after that, it was smooth sailing. I didn't mind cleaning. It was a dirty business to be sure, and I didn't like to think about half of what I found, but it was a soothing, repetitive task. And I did get that nice jolt of pride when I left each room as pristine as the old fixtures and worn linens would allow.

A few hours later, I returned to the little office, unlocking the door that Bobby had bolted when he'd left without so much as a goodbye. And after tidying that space as well, I finally sat down on the stool behind the counter.

The place was quiet, only the soft hum of the fluorescent light overhead disturbing the silence. I grabbed the beige mouse of the ancient computer to check my email.

I didn't have a computer anymore; an orange juice "accident" involving my stepbrother had seen to the death of the laptop I'd taken to college, and I hadn't the extra cash to replace it. It would've been outdated by this point anyway though even an old computer was better than none.

Still, I hardly noticed the difference anymore. It had been years since I'd had a computer or cellphone. At first, I went through a lot of withdrawal; I'd been raised in a generation where technology had always been within my reach. But after a few months, I barely even noticed. I would go so far as to say I actually enjoyed the lack of tech. Sure, it was difficult to stay in touch with people, but it gave me a lot of solitude with my own thoughts.

Opening my email, I sent a quick message to Izzy.

Izzy,

The money for your spring crew club session has been deposited in your account. I'm sorry it was a little late. I know they wanted it by Monday, so I hope they won't punish you for it being a few days overdue.

Good luck this season! And don't forget to do your homework and get enough sleep.

Love,
Wren

I didn't tell my little sister that I had to pawn my camera to get the money she needed to continue crew. A sixteen-year-old shouldn't have to worry about that. And if she knew, I would have to explain how Sienna had moved in with her boyfriend and left me to cover all our rent, which is why I had to use the money I'd saved for her fees to cover the difference. She would have quit crew before letting me pawn my camera, and I didn't want her best shot at a scholarship to be lost for a few hundred dollars.

Hitting the send button, I logged out of my account and closed the browser.

I glanced at my watch. It was still a few hours before my night shift at the diner started. Raising my arms above my head, I stretched my back. This was the best part of working at the Motel—the quiet hours before the customers started to ask for things.

My eyes skipped toward the kettle in the corner, and I thought about whether to get up and make myself some tea. But as the overhead light flickered, the glossy pages of the magazine Bobby had been reading caught the light. Leaning my chin in my hand, I pulled the magazine toward me.

On the right page, there was an image of a mansion with text that read:

Apply today at Moonseed Manor
Now a hotel!

CHAPTER II.

I STARED DOWN at the help wanted ad. Beyond the naked winter trees, the grey stone of the Gothic revival mansion seemed almost cream against the dark clouds that menaced overhead. The pointed-arch windows gave no hint as to what might be inside, and the small patch of grass peeking above the boathouse was a distressed brown and yellow. The water in the foreground was black and disturbed, blurring the reflections of the manor and sky.

It was something out of Poe, something out of Brontë or Shelley. *What would it be like to work at a hotel like that?* A thrill ran through me.

Turning back to the computer, I reopened the browser and typed the listed website into the URL bar. The website was simple, clearly still under construction, with the same picture from the magazine ad and a homepage with only one button. I clicked "Apply Now" and was taken to another page, which had a list of job openings. The list was a set of hyperlinks, and I scanned the blue words for "housekeeping," hovering my pointer over each link as I read them.

Under the heading "Public Relations Office," there were two links. One was for a staff writer and the other for a photographer. The progress of my mouse pointer stalled on the latter of the two. If only I'd been able to finish college, if only my financial support hadn't dried up, I could've applied for this job.

With a morbid sense of curiosity, I clicked on the link despite knowing there was no way I was qualified on paper. But when I clicked on the tab where a PDF had opened, I found only one sentence. It instructed applicants to send cover letters, résumés, and portfolios to an email address. There was no list of required skills or qualifications; there wasn't even a job description or an expected salary.

It all felt pretty suspicious. This wasn't the old days when employers placed a help wanted ad in a newspaper and had to pay per word. Moonseed Manor had as much space as they needed to tell people about the job. I frowned at the nearly blank page, squinting against the grainy whiteness of the screen.

Well, what will it hurt to apply, right? I can ask any questions I have during an interview, not that I'm likely to get one.

I logged back into my email and sent my cover letter and a link to my résumé and portfolio to the email address indicated on the posting.

I had a variety of photographs in my portfolio, everything from landscapes and architecture to portraits and action shots. Most of them had been taken for college classes, but a few were from before, like pictures of Izzy and Dad in our little canoe on the calm lake we used to visit every summer. My very favorites were the few art pieces I'd taken just for myself—autumn leaves, brown and faded orange, resting on a grave, the stone marker worn and crumbling. I'd taken them at a small graveyard located in the woods near my university. I'd found it quite by accident, and it had never occurred to me to question why it was there. There were only a handful of graves, long forgotten.

I used to go there when I needed to be alone, away from the dorms, away from the flurry of university life. I did share this secret place with my college roommate, Cecily, though. It felt wrong to keep it to myself when I knew how much she'd love it. One time, she even put on all the wycche things she used for her rituals, and we had a photo shoot, but I didn't include any of those pictures in my portfolio.

After sending the email, I went back to the jobs listing page, frowning when I saw housekeeping and front desk were not among the available positions. *Oh well.*

Just as I was closing the browser, a guest came into the office with a decidedly displeased expression.

"My toilet is clogged again," number five informed me.

With a nod, I came out from behind the counter and followed the man to his room.

It was already dark by the time I handed control of the office over to Charles for the night. He was much friendlier than Bobby, always trying to delay me so we could chat.

I smiled at the man. "Sorry, Charles. I've got to run. I have a shift at the diner tonight."

Charles frowned but nodded. "It's nice to see young people working their hardest these days. But don't work yourself into an early grave, Wren. Your health is the most important, you hear me? Take it from an old man. You only notice how very important it is when your body stops acting the way it should."

"I'll keep that in mind," I told him, pulling my reflective vest over my coat and waving to him as I rode into the street.

It wasn't that I didn't agree with Charles. If I didn't have to work so much just to live, I would have loved free time. I would have loved to sleep more, to eat healthier, to go to the park once in a while. But minimum wage isn't enough to live on even with two full-time jobs. I often wondered if I should be grateful to my employers. Sure, I didn't have medical insurance. But even if I did, I couldn't afford to get sick or injured with the copays and deductibles anyway. Since they didn't want to pay me overtime, they only worked me forty hours each. But they were pretty flexible with my schedule, letting me schedule the two jobs around each other.

Parking my bike outside the diner, I calculated how much more I would have to work to pay the second half of the rent Sienna had saddled me with for the foreseeable future. *Will it be easier to find another job or a new roommate?* I knew it had to be one of those two choices because there was no possibility of finding a place with cheaper rent. I'd looked.

Pat smiled over at me as I entered the all-night diner.

"How's it been so far?" I asked her while I pinned my name tag to my faded black sweatshirt.

"Slow, but one of the truckers said there was a caravan coming up behind him, and I expect them to be getting hungry soon."

I nodded, ignoring her analyzing look as she regarded me.

"Why do you always wear the same old black sweatshirt?" she asked. "Don't you like color? And you know you get higher tips when you doll up a little."

It wasn't that I didn't like color although I did like black the best. And it wasn't as if I didn't care about my appearance or I didn't want to look pretty. It was that black hides stains, and makeup and new clothes cost money. My dark hair hadn't even been cut in two years, and the pastel pink that used to cover my whole head was now faded and only on the bottom half.

"What?" I said to Pat. "You don't like black? Black is classic."

CHAPTER III.

THE SUN WAS just starting to light the eastern horizon when I finished my shift at the diner though there was likely another hour before dawn broke, and I hoped to be asleep by then. I stifled a yawn, forcing my lips to stay closed even as my jaws stretched, while I unlocked my bicycle.

It was a half-hour ride back to my place. I was lucky, really, my two jobs were only fifteen minutes away from each other. The frosted air of a spring morning forced its way into my nose, tickling my nose hairs and cooling the wetness that welled to the surface of my eyes when I yawned again.

My apartment building was made of red brick and had windows that were staggered like Tetris tiles. There were empty lots on either side, too patchy to be called lawns and too littered with trash to be useful. The street it was on was lined with other buildings of the same character: red and square and unwashed. They may at one time have been connected into long row houses if their grey concrete sides were any indication. But if that was the case, something must have happened to the houses in between because there were only lonely lots and deserted alleys there now.

Braking as I reached the front door, I wondered if I would be able to stay here much longer. I only had a month left on my lease, and I couldn't afford to stay in even a studio by myself, at least not at my current wages. I'd moved in shortly after leaving the nearby university, when it was clear returning to my mother's house was a poor choice.

The thought of moving back in with my mom and her new family flashed into my mind again, and I promptly discarded the idea. Sure, I would get to see my sister more. But my mom and her husband would probably charge me more in rent than this place did.

Slipping my arm under the top tube of my bicycle, I lifted it onto my shoulder and entered the foyer of the building. After ascending a flight of stairs, I put the bike on the floor and shoved my hand into my pocket for my keys.

But just as I was sliding my key into the lock, my neighbor stuck her head out her door.

"Oh, Wren, it's only you," Mrs. Lewis murmured with her hand on her chest.

I smiled over at the elderly woman. "Yep, just me, Mrs. Lewis. How are you this morning?"

"I'm all right, honey. Thank you. Are you just getting in from work?"

I nodded, pushing my apartment door open. "Yeah."

Mrs. Lewis's all-seeing eyes softened with sympathy. "You work so hard." She shook her head. "When was the last time you ate? Did you lose weight?"

Mrs. Lewis was forever accusing me of losing weight. I didn't have a scale, but my clothes still fit as they always did. "I ate at the diner during my break," I assured her.

One grey eyebrow rose, her dark forehead crinkling as she regarded me. "If you say so."

Turning back to fully face her, I said, "Hey, I have some free time tomorrow afternoon if you'd like me to come over and help you move your couch."

Mrs. Lewis smiled brightly. "Thank you, honey. I'll see you then. Now, you go in and get some rest."

"Goodnight," I yawned.

Flicking the light switch near the door, I pushed my bike in and leaned it against the wall. The room seemed much bigger since Sienna had left though that was to be expected when she'd taken her bed and television. The only furniture that remained was my bed, a standing lamp, and the milk crate I used as a bookshelf and nightstand.

After locking the door behind me, I shuffled to the little kitchen. I took down my mug from the cupboard and filled it with water before downing the whole thing.

I eyed the bed as I turned back. My head seemed to get heavy just by looking at it. I wanted nothing more than to collapse onto its squeaky springs and sleep as long as I could. Instead, I entered the bathroom and took a shower.

The shampoo bottle sputtered, and I shook it to get every last drop. *I need to stop by the dollar store today for more shampoo.*

Finally, with the grime from the motel and the scent of grease from the diner washed off of me, I climbed into bed. It took all that remained of my energy to set my alarm clock to wake me up in six hours.

With the blaring buzz of my alarm, I gasped awake, squinting against the brightness of the midday sun that shone through the blinds of my window. My heart hammered in my chest, jolted out of some dream I already couldn't remember.

I breathed in slowly through my nose, closing my eyes to enjoy likely the only moment of peace I would have that day. Sighing it all out, I rose from my bed and went to my closet. The closet looked bare with Sienna's stuff gone. Her clothes had taken up her half plus part of mine. I skipped over the few pastel shirts I had—saved for those rare times I wasn't going to come into contact with dirt, grime, grease, and cleaning chemicals—and grabbed a black, long-sleeved T-shirt and a muted, plaid button-down. Picking up the jeans I'd worn the previous day, I examined them for stains and gave them a good sniff before pulling them on over a pair of black leggings.

After a quick stop in the bathroom, I filled the hot pot with water and plugged it in. And while I waited for it to boil, I made a peanut butter sandwich, which I wrapped up for lunch. The hot pot bubbled just as I was scooping quick oats into my bowl. I poured the water over the oats and added a few sugar packets—sugar packets I'd gathered every chance that presented itself.

I ate my breakfast standing in the kitchen, if I could even call the counter against one wall a kitchen when there wasn't even a stove, and washed it down with a mug of water. After brushing my teeth, I was out the door not twenty minutes from when my alarm had sounded.

The sun was a little warmer than it had been the previous day, and I thought about going back upstairs to leave my thicker jacket as I carried my bicycle outside. But I knew it would be cold once the sun went down on my ride home. Hesitating only for a second, I decided to keep it on. I congratulated myself on that choice as I rode toward the Motel, the wind freezing with my gathering speed.

I pulled into the Motel's parking lot early. Mr. McAllister would be angry if I clocked over my forty hours, so I couldn't punch in just yet. And as much as I wanted to keep this job, I wasn't going to work for free. Glancing at my watch, I decided to ride over to the dollar store half a block up and buy some shampoo. Maybe I would get really wild and buy conditioner as well.

CHAPTER IV.

———

WHEN I STARTED my shift, I was greeted to a complete mess in room eight. There were pizza boxes and beer cans strewn all over the room. I even found an empty can in the bathtub. The only place there wasn't trash was in the trashcan. But at least I didn't have to deal with another toilet issue in number five.

By the time I'd tidied the office, I needed that cup of tea I'd foregone the day before. I filled the kettle with water from the bathroom sink and put it in its base to boil. Then I crossed to the computer, the hard stool a welcome comfort just to rest my feet.

Opening my email, I saw that I had two unread messages. I clicked on the one sent the day before.

Wren,

Thanks for the fees. The club took it no problem.

I got an A on my history test from last week. I told Mom about it, but she just ignored me.

I know we've talked about it before, but do I really have to stay with her? Can't I come stay with you? I'm old enough to get a job now. I could quit crew and work after school. Your lease is up next month, right? We could take a different apartment, just me and you. I wouldn't be a burden. I promise.

I just miss you, and I know Mom and I would both be happier if I moved out. She doesn't even notice me unless she's yelling at me, and Paul cares even less. Did I tell you Steven is still living here, too? He's twenty, and they don't even make him pay rent!

Anyway…just think about it a little, please.

Love,
Izzy

I closed my eyes against the sting my sister's words elicited. Despite how much I knew our mother wanted to get rid of my sister and me—of any remnants of her previous family—I knew she would never let my sister leave, not while she was still in high school anyway. How could she? That would make her look like a bad mother, and she was all about appearing to be the perfect wife and mother. That's why my sister was still well-fed, why she still had decent clothes. But beyond the basics? Her cellphone? Her extracurriculars? Absolutely not. Those things were for Paul's children, for Steven and Brenden.

And as much as my stepbrothers got, my half-brother Dilan got even more. At only five, Dilan was already enrolled in every sport and lesson imaginable for a kid his age. In a lot of ways, I felt bad for my brother. He was so spoiled that he would have a lot of problems when he was eventually confronted with the real world, with not getting exactly what he wanted precisely when he wanted it. I wondered how long he would stick with his activities when he discovered he didn't have to do anything he didn't want to, when he discovered he could just laze around doing nothing like Steven.

While my tuition money had dried up after my father's death—or more accurately, the signature to co-sign my student loans—Steven didn't seem to have the same issue. He'd only been a freshman in high school when our parents had married, but once college-time came around, he was sent to the very university I'd had to drop out of. Despite every advantage, he was kicked out within a year for dealing drugs on campus. According to Izzy, he now spent most of his time playing video games in his rent-free room above the garage.

Brenden was the bright dandelion in the family of fungus-infested strangle ivy. He was sweet and kind and quiet. He knew when someone was hurting, and his gentle presence was a balm to any suffering soul. He must have taken after his mother because Paul was too much like Mom for Brenden to have gotten the traits from him.

I hit the reply button and typed out a message to my sister.

Izzy,

Congratulations on your history test! I know how hard you studied to get that A, and I'm really proud of you. I'm glad to hear the club took the fees without a fuss. I won't be late next time.

As to you coming to live with me, I don't know what to tell you. I wish you could. But you know you're still a minor, and there's no way I could get custody of you from Mom. Besides that, I don't want you to have to get a job so soon. Crew is your best chance at getting a scholarship. You deserve to go to college.

I know it sucks, I do. But please just stick it out for now, okay? Two more years and you'll be an adult. You will be out of that house and off starting your own adventure. Just hold on to those dreams.

Maybe we can meet up in a few weeks. Let me save enough money for a bus ticket, and you can come up for a visit. I'll let you know.

Hang in there, and give Brenden a hug for me.

I love you, and you could never be a burden to me.
Wren

I sighed as I hit the send button, rubbing my eyes with my thumb and forefinger. Izzy would not be pleased to read my response, but I didn't know what else I could do for her at the moment. The only thing I could think of was to give her emotional support and nurture her escape plan.

Going back to my inbox, I clicked the other email, which was sent earlier that morning.

Wren,
I had a weird dream about you last night. Are you okay?
Cecily

I stared at the words from my former college roommate, so straightforward, so innocuous. But I knew better. I hated when Cecily did that. I knew that she was only looking out for me, but her dreams seldom foreshadowed pleasant events. And I could never forget that the first dream she'd had of me happened the night before my dad died. I breathed out slowly, steadying the twinge of unease that fluttered in my stomach. *Her dreams aren't always indicative of something so dramatic as death. Maybe she was just picking up on this apartment situation with Sienna.*

But just as I hit the reply button to tell Cecily what was going on, the kettle beeped loudly, insistent that I give it my immediate attention. Getting up from my stool, I walked over to it, poured hot water into the office mug, and dropped an off-brand tea bag into it. I eyed the two allotted sugar packets I would normally have pocketed for my morning oatmeal and sprinkled them into my tea. *I could use the comfort after those two emails.*

By the time I'd settled back onto my stool, another email was waiting in my inbox. It was a reply to the application I'd sent the day before. *Well, that was the quickest rejection letter ever.*

Clicking on the email, I blinked at the response, my eyebrows crinkling as I read.

Dear Miss Mabry,

I have reviewed your résumé and portfolio in regard to the open photographer position here at Moonseed Manor, and I would like to set up a telephone interview with you. Are you available this Friday?

Please let me know at your earliest convenience.
William Courtland Bennings

CHAPTER V.

I REREAD THE email just to be sure I hadn't somehow misread a rejection letter. And then I read it again for good measure.

"Oh my God," I whispered, my voice barely audible above the whir of the ancient computer fan. "I got an interview…"

But just as excitement started to hum through my veins, I remembered that I didn't have a phone to even talk to this William Courtland Bennings. My mind raced, trying to land on a solution. The payphone on West Montgomery at the gas station where I usually pumped air into my bike tires was broken; someone had ripped the handset out. *Mrs. Lewis may let me use her phone if she can find it. Too bad Izzy doesn't live closer.* I paid my sister's cellphone bill after all; she could've spared it for however long it took to do the interview.

I frowned, disappointment creeping in. *No, I can't fail so easily, not when I've been given such an unexpected opportunity.* Sitting up straighter on my stool, I clicked back to Cecily's email and hit reply.

Cecily,

I'm fine. Thanks for asking. Actually, I have an interview
tomorrow, but I don't have a phone… Do you think I could
borrow yours? You can come over and tell me about your
dream, and we can catch up, too. I don't have to work
until five.

Let me know as soon as you can.
Wren

I hit send and took a sip of tea, the warm brew pooling in
my belly in the most pleasant sensation, despite the stuffiness
of the small office. Cecily's response came before I even put my
mug back on the counter.

Of course you can use my phone for your interview!
That's so exciting. Congratulations. The stars must be
aligning for you. This is my first weekday off in months. I'll
bring lunch, yeah? See you tomorrow.
C

I wasn't about to tell Cecily to come later than lunchtime,
that tomorrow was one of the few days I was able to sleep in. If
she was going to let me use her phone, and even bring me food,
I didn't care how many hours I would be running on when she
arrived. I sent her a quick note of thanks before pulling up the
email from Moonseed Manor.

Dear Mr. Bennings,

Thank you for reaching out to me about the photographer
job I applied for. I would be happy to do a telephone

interview with you tomorrow (Friday). I am free any time before 4:30 p.m. Please let me know what time works for you, and what number you would like me to call.

I look forward to speaking with you.

Sincerely,
Katherine Mabry

I reread my email to make sure there weren't any typos. The air whistled through my nostrils and my chest expanded as I took a deep breath. Then I hit the send button.

A real photography job… I wished I hadn't already cleaned the motel rooms—so difficult was it to sit still while my mind whirled with possible outcomes.

I'd almost forgotten what hope felt like; I'd almost forgotten what a crushed hope felt like. That isn't to say I'd been depressed. It was more that I could see the path in front of me, and there had been no surprises, no unexpected chances. Work as much as I could, pay my bills, help support Izzy. There was no room for dreams in that space. There was barely room to take a breath.

I tried to temper my emotions, my natural tendency to long for more. *An interview isn't a job offer. And besides, the terms of the job could be bad. They didn't give an explanation as to the job duties online. I might not even want it once I know more about it. And why would a place like this want an underqualified candidate like me anyway? Is there something wrong with them, or are they that desperate?*

Appropriately sobered, I pulled a motel notepad and pen, which sat beside the keyboard, toward me and began writing questions for my interview. Moonseed Manor wasn't anywhere near here. If I was going to even think about taking this job—if it was offered to me—then I needed to be very sure it was worth moving for. It needed to be worth taking the risk of leaving my apartment and two jobs. Because once those threads were cut, they would be difficult—or impossible—to join back together.

I tapped my pen against the notepad, staring down at the few questions I'd written. I pursed my lips. *Is this enough?* Dropping the pen on the pad, I turned back to the computer and typed "Moonseed Manor" into the search engine. If I was going to have informed questions for Mr. Bennings, I needed to do more research about the place.

The top results were the hotel's sparse website and a few job-hunting networks, nothing that really told me anything more than what I already knew.

I was on the third page of search results before I found something different. The blue hyperlink promised "The Most Haunted Mansions in the United States" from a site called Ghosties and Ghoulies.

Tilting my head, I clicked on the link and was directed to a blog post. The website's background was black, and the gentle sound of rain trickled through the computer's crackling speakers.

Welcome back, my long-legged beasties. As promised, I've compiled a list of all of the creepiest, crawliest, spine-tingling-est haunted mansions in the United States. You know me, I'm always up for a scream, so most of these are places I've actually visited (and of course I've included some of my most intriguing photos). But I also included a few honorable mentions that are on my to-visit list.

I scrolled down the list. Helpfully, the name of each mansion was formatted as a bold heading, so I was able to skim fairly quickly. I didn't pay any mind to the grainy pictures of supposed ghosts caught on camera but kept scrolling. Just when I was thinking of using the find function, my eyes landed on the heading "Moonseed Manor." I yelped aloud when a clap of thunder erupted from the speakers as lightning flashed across the screen.

But my alarm was only momentary, and I rolled my eyes at the foolishness of being startled by a website's background. Refocusing on the blog post, I read the entry for Moonseed Manor.

And finally, I would lose all respect for myself if I didn't mention the elusive Moonseed Manor. You read that right. I said elusive. Even among ghost hunters, this place is a myth. Oh, it's real enough. The mansion is on Nightfall Island in Lake Ontario. But details on its history are hard to come by. The Bennings family has never allowed visitors on their island—at least not in my lifetime. (Believe me, I've tried.) If that wasn't suspicious enough, some strange whispers have sometimes reached the mainland in the form of ferrymen who bring supplies to the island. Are they all just seamen's tales? Who knows?

UPDATE: It has recently come to my attention that Moonseed Manor is being turned into a hotel. It is not yet clear when it will be open to guests, but you can believe this hunter will be the first to check in.

A shiver ran over my skin and goose bumps raised the hair on my arms. I clicked my tongue and sighed. "Oh, come on," I chided myself, closing the browser. I didn't believe in ghosts, not that I hadn't been open to the idea. After my father had died, Cecily and I had broken out her spirit board a few times. No matter how much I'd hoped, how much I'd pleaded, my father had never established contact with us. And if he hadn't come back to reassure me, then there was no possible way ghosts were real.

But as my momentary fear subsided, the normal anxiety that comes from having an impending interview took its place. The closer I got to the end of my shift, the more nervous I became about whether I would get Mr. Bennings's response while I still had access to a computer.

But I needn't have worried. An email from Mr. Bennings confirming the time and telephone number of my interview came through with plenty of time to spare before my shift was over. I wrote the number atop the paper on which I'd written my questions.

I was grateful that I had a shift at the diner that night. The ride let me blow off some of my nervous energy, and the busy flow of late-night customers gave my mind something to focus on. The cherry on top was that I was so tired by the time I reached my apartment the next morning that I couldn't be bothered to worry about my interview that afternoon. I just showered and collapsed onto my bed, asleep not a minute after my head hit the pillow.

CHAPTER VI.

A LOUD POUNDING on my door woke me from a dead sleep. I gasped, my eyes flying open and darting around the room. I sighed out my surprise, the lump in my throat settling into my stomach when I realized that Cecily must have arrived. A quick glance at my alarm clock told me I'd gotten just over four hours of sleep.

"Coming," I croaked, not sure it was even loud enough for her to hear.

My bare feet thumped on the floor as I hurried to answer, and I hoped my downstairs neighbor was at work so I wouldn't receive a passive-aggressive letter shoved under my door later.

When I opened the door, Cecily stood in the hallway, the swept bangs of her smooth, nut-brown hair falling over half her face as she looked down at the goodies she juggled in her hands.

I reached out and grabbed the cup carrier when it wobbled. Glancing up, her green eyes sparkled as she smiled brightly at me.

"Thanks," she said.

I tilted my head at the bakery box, which she secured between her hands now that one was free. "Is that what I think it is?" I asked.

Her grin widened. "I thought we could celebrate with some mini éclairs since we haven't seen each other in a while."

"But Weinrich's is like forty minutes from here. You didn't have to go to all that trouble."

Cecily shrugged, rolling her eyes upward. "Well…if you don't want them, I can always—"

"Now you're just talking nonsense. Come in, and let's see how many we can eat until we burst."

Cecily chuckled. "That's the Wren I know and love."

I stepped aside for her to enter, and she did so without hesitation, walking with that same sure-footed confidence she'd always had as if she understood everything about the world and how she fit into it.

While I placed the drink carrier on the kitchen counter, she settled cross-legged in the center of the floor.

"Oh, the one with the drink stirrer in the lid is yours. I got you a chai latte," she informed me.

I removed the two cups from the holder and carried them to where she sat, then I joined her on the floor, offering her the cup she hadn't described. "Thanks," I said, not at all surprised that she remembered what I'd always ordered at the university's café.

She looked around me to the blank wall where Sienna's stuff used to be. "Uh, what's going on here? Did Sienna move out?"

I nodded. "Yeah, she moved in with her boyfriend, leaving me with all the bills."

Cecily's green eyes flashed, and she clicked her tongue in disgust. "Do you want me to put a hex on her?"

I chuckled. "I don't think that will be necessary."

"If you say so," she muttered, taking a sip of her coffee.

"So how's work? You said you haven't had a real day off in a while?" I asked, trying to dispel her irritation.

She took the bait with gusto. "Oh my gods! It's insane. One of the vet techs is on maternity leave, and another is taking a round-the-world honeymoon vacation or something. I seriously think he was in Nepal last week. Yeah, it was Nepal. I saw the pictures online. And then another one just quit without notice. So, needless to say, we're completely overrun with work."

I frowned, nodding in sympathy to Cecily's situation. "That doesn't sound great."

"Yeah, but at least the other vets are stepping up, so I'm not the only one helping the techs out. And we're interviewing another one next week, so that should help."

I took a sip of latte before asking, "And what about that guy you were seeing? Are you still a thing?"

Cecily tilted her head. "Which guy?"

I shrugged. "I don't know. How many are there? The one with the fluffy dog."

"Hot Pomeranian Dad? Oh, that was over weeks ago."

"Aww, you seemed to like him. What happened?"

Cecily blew out a sigh, her hair fluttering as she did so. "He kept bugging me to go to church. I told him that I didn't care if he was Christian or whatever, that his religion was his own personal thing. But he didn't give me the same courtesy. I think his exact words were: 'I couldn't handle the idea of someone I love burning in Hell.' So yeah…that ended. At least it happened before things got too serious."

"That sucks."

She shrugged noncommittally. "Well, I have been exchanging smiles with this dude at the bookstore near my house. He's got a chill sort of aura. I wonder if he plays the bass."

I laughed. "What makes you think he plays bass?"

But she didn't answer that all-important question, she just

stared at me for a timeless moment, her green eyes serious and absorbent. "It's good to hear you laugh again," she said.

My laughter petered out, but my smile remained, the muscles stretched and stiff from lack of use. "I suppose it has been a while."

"You're doing great. I'm proud of you," she said encouragingly. She didn't ask me what I'd been dealing with. She gave me room to talk if I wanted to, but she didn't push me to do so. And, as always, she said the one thing I needed to hear.

I could feel the emotion climbing up my throat, and I washed it down with a drink of chai latte.

"So you have an interview today? Anything good?" she asked, offering me the pastry box of éclairs.

I took one of the delicacies, the chocolate icing smearing onto my fingertips as I shoved the entire mini éclair into my mouth. I groaned when the sweet cream filling hit my tongue. "Fo fweagin' goo," I said, my mouth still full.

Cecily burst into laughter, her giggles loud in the small space of my apartment. "What was that?"

I swallowed with effort. "I said, 'so freaking good.'" I reached for another one. It had been a long time since I'd had a treat, and likely four times as long since I'd eaten an éclair from Weinrich's.

"So…the job?" Cecily prompted again before I could shove a third éclair into my mouth.

I took the pastry between my fingers but delayed eating it to answer her question. "It's a photography job actually. I'm kind of shocked I even got an interview, what with me not having finished my degree and everything."

Cecily's face lit up. "Yeah? That's great! Does it pay well? Will you be able to quit some of your other jobs? Where is it?"

I pressed the frosting on the éclair I held, watching the sweet goop gather on my fingertip. "It's at Moonseed Manor. I don't know what the pay is yet."

Cecily squinted in thought. "I don't think I know it."

"I didn't either. I had to look it up. It's a hotel, I guess. Looks like it's on an island in Lake Ontario."

She nodded while reaching for an éclair. "Ah, way up there, huh? And it's a manor? That would be cool. What do they have you doing though? Weddings and stuff? Do hotels normally have on-site photographers?"

I shrugged, biting the mini éclair in half. "I didn't think so. Maybe it's only temporary?"

Cecily frowned, her gaze fixed on the half-eaten éclair in my fingers—the cream filling oozing from the middle onto my palm. Her brow crinkled, and she tilted her head. "I just got a weird feeling all of a sudden," she murmured, her voice soft and confused.

I regretted eating so much sugar right after waking up as my stomach churned. "Something bad?"

The lines between her eyebrows deepened when she squinted. "I'm not sure. It's on an island, you said? There was an island in my dream..."

I froze, waiting for her to continue.

Her eyes seemed to lose focus though they were still directed at the éclair in my hand. "In my dream, there was a coal black crow. It was flying over dark water. It was one of those red sunrises, you know where everything is dyed either red or black. I could still see the moon. The crow had a streamer—cloth or ribbon—tied to each foot, and it was flying real low, so the cloth was dragging in the water. It approached land, and you were standing on the shore. As it flew over you, water droplets from the streamers sprinkled onto your head. And there was someone with you, too. A man. I can't tell you what he looked like. He was shadowed by the silhouette of a large house. The water dripped on him as well. Then the crow landed on the roof."

 D. LIEBER

A chill ran down my spine, and her eyes snapped to my face.

"That's it." She shrugged, her voice light and clear as I tried to remember how to swallow.

She didn't say what she thought it meant; she didn't even tell me how it made her feel. She just took a bite of the pastry in her hand.

CHAPTER VII.

AS PROMISED, Cecily and I went over to Mrs. Lewis's apartment and helped her move her couch after we were done eating. Then we sat and chatted with her for a while. It wasn't long before she was showing us pictures of her son, who was serving in the Army overseas, and her grandkids.

Not two hours later, Mrs. Lewis insisted on making us grilled turkey and cheese sandwiches as thanks for helping her out. I told her that it wasn't necessary, but the lady wouldn't take no for an answer. Maybe I didn't push back hard enough, but I wasn't normally one to turn down free food.

Satisfied by the meal, Cecily asked Mrs. Lewis if there was anything else we could do for her. The elder reluctantly let slip that her wireless router had been out for a while, and she didn't know how to get it back up. I looked at the overly large clock above the television. It was getting close to the time of my interview, and I didn't know how long Mrs. Lewis's internet issues would take to resolve.

But Cecily dug into her pocket and held out her phone to me. "I've got this. Good luck."

I nodded. "Thanks. I'll be back in a bit."

"No rush," she assured me.

Upon returning to my apartment, I pulled out my list of questions and sat on my bed. The seconds slowly marched on, and I could almost hear the tick of a clock in my mind, despite the fact that my alarm clock was digital.

I typed in the number and hit the call button the moment 12:59 flipped over to 1:00 at the top of the screen. *Riiiiing. Riiiiing. Riiiiing. Riiiiing.* The sound of the call trying to connect seemed drawn out. *Should I leave a message or just hang up?*

"Hello," a man's voice answered.

He picked up so suddenly that I stumbled over my response. "O-oh. Good afternoon. This is Katherine Mabry. I have an interview with Mr. Bennings…?"

Silence answered me, and I bit my lip. *I wrote down the number wrong. Damn it. Now, I'm going to have to look it up, and I'll be late for my interview.*

"Yes, good afternoon, Miss Mabry. This is William Courtland Bennings. Give me a moment to pull up your files." Mr. Bennings's voice, even when saying something polite and pleasant, was cool and professional. This was not a man who would be friendly and easy to interview with.

"No problem," I said. *At least I got the right number.*

After a minute, he jumped back in without so much as a transition. "Let me tell you a little about Moonseed Manor and what we're trying to do here before we start since there isn't a lot of information online at the moment."

He's not wrong about that. I nodded. "All right."

"Moonseed Manor, and Nightfall Island, have been my family's home for more than a century. It has only been in the last few years that I've begun turning it into a hotel. After much renovation, we're close to opening our doors to guests. You indicated in your cover letter that you heard of our opening through my magazine advertisement and went to our website. As you no doubt noticed, our website is still being built. We do have a web designer working on it. And I've hired a staff writer to work with him and on other public relations needs. But I also need a photographer."

He paused, and I used the opportunity to ask one of my questions. "So you need someone to take pictures for future advertisements and your website? Is this a temporary position then?"

"No, it is a full-time, permanent position. I do need a photographer for those things. But I would also like someone for events, and I'd like to offer guests the option of having their pictures taken professionally on the grounds. Tell me, do you have any graphic design experience? That wasn't included in your portfolio."

I frowned. "I have a little. I know how to use Photoshop, Illustrator, and InDesign though it has been a while if I'm being honest. I'm sorry. I didn't think to include any graphic design stuff. I could send some projects to you if you'd like."

"That would be fine. One important point I must emphasize is that we are trying to create an atmosphere here. We require all of our employees to wear a uniform, which is designed to reflect when the manor was built in 1886. You can wear either the male or female uniform, your choice, but modern clothes will not be permitted in public areas. Will this be an issue for you?"

I thought about what tasks would be required of me based on what he'd said so far. "I don't think so. I may need both a male and female uniform though. Photographers do need a certain amount of mobility, so access to pants would be good depending on what I'm doing."

"Understood. Perhaps more important than that is the technology. Cellphones and computers are not permitted where guests can see them. They will be allowed in your room, and we do have an office where we have computers and things guests can't see. The only obvious exception to this will be your camera. We have an in-house camera, or you can bring your own."

"I don't mind using the one you have," I affirmed. *Until I can get mine out of the pawn shop at least.*

"Very well. Do you have any questions for me?"

My eyebrows drew together. *Are interviews usually this short?* "Yes, I have a few. As you saw from my résumé, I live in Philadelphia. Nightfall Island isn't close to here. Will Moonseed Manor be covering relocation costs?"

"Yes, relocation costs are covered by the hotel. And a furnished room on the island is provided as part of your benefits, though if you'd like to commute from the mainland, you can if you wish."

"No, no. I'm fine with living on the island. When are you looking for this position to start?"

"As soon as possible. I understand if two weeks' notice is required of your current employers."

I hummed my acknowledgment of his answer. "There is… one more thing I'd like to ask. It's a little unusual. But you haven't asked anything about my experience or how I work with others or anything like that. I may be shooting myself in the foot here, but you can see for yourself that I'm not that qualified for a professional job of this level. Why did you decide to interview me?"

There was only a short pause before Mr. Bennings answered in that same self-assured, matter-of-fact tone. "I saw your portfolio. You have just the eye I need. I can see from the fact that you are working two full-time jobs that you're a hard worker. And you've been at those jobs for a long while now, so you aren't likely to quit if things are tough."

I lowered my head at the praise he heaped on me in that cold, professional voice.

"Is there anything else?" he asked.

Should I ask about salary, or is it too presumptuous in a first interview? I bit my lip in thought. *I'll wait.* "No. I'll send you those graphic design projects today so you can make a determination."

I could practically hear him waving away my statement. "That is a mere formality. If you'd like the job, it's yours. When I receive your email, I will attach a document with the offer letter, which will detail your salary and benefits package. I'd very much appreciate an answer by Monday if you would."

I froze, blinking stupidly as I sat cross-legged on my bed.

"Miss Mabry?"

"Y-yes, Mr. Bennings. I'll be sure to get back to you by Monday. Thank you."

"Good. I'll expect your answer by then. Goodbye."

"Goodbye, Mr. Bennings. Have a good day."

CHAPTER VIII.

THE PHONE beeped in my ear when the line disconnected, and my hand fell into my lap. I squinted at the blank wall across the room where Sienna's things used to be and tilted my head as if the motion would knock loose some thoughts. The gesture seemed to work as thoughts, possibilities, hopes flooded into me.

Did I just get a full-time, with-benefits job as a photographer? How? Mr. Bennings liked my work. I hope Izzy takes it well. I need to tell my bosses. I need to tell my landlord. What can I bring? What should I do with the things I can't take with me?

My heart raced with anxiety and excitement. This sudden path before me was untrodden. I didn't know what to expect, and the thought of leaving my current, familiar situation—however dire and exhausting—filled me with apprehension. But this was my chance. I was finally getting a break. My hard work had paid off.

A little flicker of hope sparked inside me. "I haven't even seen the offer letter yet," I told myself. "Let's just send those graphics projects and wait for the final details before I get all excited." Despite my words, I cupped my hands around the little flame, sheltering it from the harsh world.

Using Cecily's phone, I logged into my email and attached a few graphics files from my cloud drive before sending them off to Mr. Bennings with a note of thanks.

I took a deep breath, then sighed heavily. By the time I knocked at Mrs. Lewis's door, the weight of my present situation—the situation I'd been in since my father died—had settled back into me. The little ripple, the slight disturbance, that the hope had created on the calm surface of my mind had stilled. Far off in the distance, the little hope flickered, its light reflected on the smooth surface, beckoning but still out of reach.

Mrs. Lewis opened the door, an apron tied around her neck and waist and an oven mitt still on one hand. The sweet scent of chocolate chip cookies filled the air, and I breathed deep in appreciation. Cecily sat cross-legged on Mrs. Lewis's couch, tapping the keys of the laptop on her lap.

"Something smells good," I complimented as Mrs. Lewis motioned me inside.

She smiled warmly. "Your friend was working so hard to fix my internet, and I couldn't help at all. So I wanted to do something useful. And I do love to see people enjoy my cooking."

"Based off how it smells, I think I'm definitely going to enjoy it," I said.

"That's the key." Mrs. Lewis tapped her nose. "The scent gives you that feeling of anticipation, makes your mouth water. It makes them taste so much better."

"I believe that," Cecily chimed in. "I've been Pavlov's dog over here for the last ten minutes."

Mrs. Lewis chuckled before turning toward her kitchen counter.

I held Cecily's phone out to her and thanked her.

"That was quick. How did it go?" she asked, taking the device from my hand.

I nodded slightly. "It went well. I'm waiting on an offer letter."

Cecily sat up straighter, her eyes widening as they lit up. "Wow, that's amazing! So you definitely got it then?"

I shrugged a little. "I mean…he said I got it. But he also wants me to do some graphic design, and he hasn't seen my stuff yet. Plus, we didn't discuss salary. It might not be enough to cover everything."

Cecily scowled at me. "You're allowed to celebrate little victories, Wren. Even if the salary isn't enough, it's still amazing you were offered the job. Besides, if it's making only what you're making right now, it will be one job instead of two. You'd be working less hours overall, and you'd be doing something you love. They have to offer you more hourly than what you're at now. And if it's the exact same, it's a way into the professional photography field."

"That's true." I frowned. "But I'm already farther from Izzy than I'd like, and this is way up in Lake Ontario. How am I supposed to get to her if she needs me? I'll be out there in the middle of a lake."

Cecily sighed, then reached out and took my hand. She tugged, pulling me down to sit next to her and forcing her green eyes on me. "Look, I know your sister is the most important person to you, and she's in a rough situation. But you need to think about yourself a little, too. This job could be everything you've hoped for. You're allowed to take a piece for yourself. Plus, look at it this way: if it pays enough, you could even put money away for Izzy's college fund, right? Especially if you continue to be as frugal as you are now."

As usual, Cecily's words rang true. I nodded. But still, something inside me was reluctant, tethered like a boat moored.

"I hear what you're saying. But let's just see what I'm offered before I think about uprooting."

Cecily squeezed my hand. "Just be open to it. I know you'll do what's best for everyone when you have all the information."

I gave her a tentative smile.

"Here you are, girls," Mrs. Lewis said, holding out a plate of cookies to us.

We each took a soft, golden-brown cookie from the plate. How she'd managed to make them so perfect in a toaster oven of all things I couldn't imagine. I wondered if it was difficult for someone who loved to cook not to have a proper kitchen. But when you had as little as we did, you made do.

"Your internet is all set, Mrs. L," Cecily announced.

I took a bite of the cookie. It was warm and sweet and everything that day promised for the future.

CHAPTER IX.

THE OFFER letter from Moonseed Manor was waiting in my inbox when I finally logged into my email Saturday evening at the Motel. My heart squeezed, and my pulse pounded in my fingertips as I moved the mouse to click on the bold text of the unread email.

The offer was more than I ever would have hoped for, nearly twice as much as what I was making now. It was too good to be true, so good that I almost wrote an email rejecting it. *Who would offer that salary to an unqualified person like me? Is this a scam?*

But Mr. Bennings's cool voice hadn't struck me as suspicious. *If this is all a scam, wouldn't it have served him better to be friendlier?* My apprehension was put to rest when I searched the internet for the average salary for a professional photographer in the state of New York. Moonseed Manor's offer was a little lower than the average. Though with a room provided on-site, he wouldn't hear me complain.

With all the information in, there was really nothing else to think about. Cecily was right. This was fewer hours and more pay. This was my chance to get into the photography field as a professional. I would be able to pay my bills and put a little money away. Though I normally would have taken the time to think this situation through from every angle, I sent a reply to Mr. Bennings on the spot, accepting his offer. It felt downright impulsive; I'd gotten used to taking each step carefully as if one false move could spell disaster. Following my heart with abandon used to be so much a part of my personality, but now it felt a little strange.

The moment I hit the send button, my mind spun with all the things I needed to do. I pulled a motel notepad toward me and made a list, which gave me focus.

After finishing my list, I wrote Mr. McAllister and Ms. Albright each a letter of resignation, giving them the two weeks that was a professional courtesy. I put Mr. McAllister's letter in his wire inbox basket and put Ms. Albright's in my bag to give to her at the diner later that night. I then wrote a quick email to Cecily to catch her up.

I opened another blank email and stared at the cursor as it blinked impatiently. There was no easy way to have this conversation; there was definitely no getting around it. And when I started to type, my keystrokes were slow and deliberate as if I were still learning the layout of the keyboard.

Izzy,

You'll never believe this, but I got a new job! It's a full-time, professional photographer job working for Moonseed Manor. So I'll be making twice the pay with half the hours. And it's hourly, so I'll even get overtime. Isn't that great?

The downside is that it's in upstate New York, on Nightfall

Island in Lake Ontario to be exact. But don't worry. With all the extra money I'll be making, it will be easier for me to get to you if I need to, despite the fact that it's farther away. And the first thing I'm going to ask when I get there is about employees having visitors so you can come see me.

I won't be leaving for another two weeks, and I'll let you know the particulars of my itinerary.

Love,
Wren

The knot in my stomach eased as I hit the send button on my email to Izzy. It was done now. I could only hope my faux enthusiasm would convince her. I wasn't really lying exactly. I was excited, and nervous, and a little overwhelmed. I just wasn't excited about telling Izzy. I didn't know how she would react to me moving farther away. But it was too late to worry about that now. The messages were sent, and I had a lot to do.

The next two weeks flew by. I didn't have much to pack. All of the things I was taking—my clothes, my bedding, my alarm clock, my bag of toiletries, and my very small collection of books—fit in one large roller suitcase and an old backpack. I managed to find someone, a friend of Pat's, to purchase my bed and few dishes from me. And though I didn't get much, I was feeling comfortable with my bank account in the three digits.

My biggest concern was my bicycle; it was the most valuable thing I owned next to the camera, which was still in the pawn shop. But again, Cecily came to the rescue, saying she would store it in her garage for me until I returned or could retrieve it.

Unfortunately, I couldn't convince my landlord to let me off the hook for my last month of rent, during which I would not even be occupying the apartment. So I had to pay the full rent for that month, which drained the bit I got from selling my things.

Pat was pretty emotional during my final shift at the diner, and I had to admit I would miss working with her too. She was the perfect coworker. She was kind and friendly, and she was always ready to lend a hand or offer words of encouragement.

It was almost warm as I rode back to my apartment from the diner for the final time. The day before hadn't broken sixty-five, and it hadn't warmed up once the sun had gone down. With winter behind us, the days were getting longer. Still, I reached my apartment before dawn broke.

After taking a shower, I packed away my toiletries. The only things left out were the clothes I was going to change into before leaving and the pillow and blanket I'd laid out on the floor.

My train didn't leave until later that afternoon, and I knew I would need sleep for the trip ahead. But as I lay on the floor, staring out the window at the rising sun, my stomach wouldn't unclench enough to let me rest. Anxiety and excitement again danced together in my mind, twirling and twisting at a speed I could hardly keep up with. And though my thoughts couldn't gain traction, the feelings they elicited were still clearly felt.

"It's too late to turn back now," I whispered into the empty room. Then I forced my eyes closed, resting them, even though I did not sleep.

———

CHAPTER X

I DIDN'T SLEEP at all in the hours I lay on my apartment floor with my eyes closed. All I could think about was Izzy's response to my initial email and the unknown I was flinging myself into.

My sister hadn't said anything discouraging or overtly worrisome. It was more the clipped nature of her correspondence that concerned me.

That's great. Congratulations.

And that was the extent of her reply.

To me, this said one of three things: Either she was too busy to respond properly, she was unhappy with my news, or she just needed time to adjust to the idea. The first seemed unlikely. Even if she wanted to respond quickly and was too busy at the moment, she would have followed it up later with a more robust answer. The second was a real possibility, but I thought the third the most likely.

Izzy didn't deal well with change, and I could understand why. She had experienced a lot of life-changing events in a very short amount of time. She'd never been given time to properly adjust. I went away when she was only eight. Two years later, our father died. And not a year after that, our mother was remarried and had given birth to Dilan.

Izzy hadn't responded to my second email, the one with my travel itinerary. I debated with myself as I waited on the stoop for Cecily to take me to the train station. *Should I use Cecily's phone to call Izzy on the ride there? But it's not that long of a drive, and Izzy may just need time to work through it on her own.*

Cecily pulled up in her silver SUV before I could really work through the problem. She parked at the curb and got out, smiling with a little wave.

"You ready?" she asked, tilting her head at the things on the sidewalk beside me—the extent of my worldly possessions. "Did you give your landlord the keys?"

"I left them on the counter like he told me to," I answered.

Cecily nodded. "We should probably get the bike in first, yeah?"

"Right."

It took us a couple of tries, but we eventually got the bicycle in, though at a strange angle to be sure. And after shoving my suitcase and backpack on top of it, we were buckled in and driving away from my apartment in no time.

I stared out the window from the passenger seat, mentally checking off everything to make sure I hadn't forgotten anything.

"Are you nervous?" Cecily asked.

I didn't look over at her. "Yeah."

"Excited?" she prodded gently.

I dipped my head, and she must've seen it because she didn't ask again.

Not long after, we pulled into a parking space near the train station.

"I got you something. Right behind my seat." Cecily thrust her thumb over her right shoulder for emphasis.

I glanced over at my friend. "You didn't have to do that."

She waved away my concern. "I wanted to. Take a look."

Leaning over, I reached behind her seat and pulled out a cream tote bag.

"What is it?" I asked.

Cecily chuckled. "Well, you have to open it to find out, silly."

Inside the bag was a large, white paper bag. I opened it, and the savory scent of a Philly cheesesteak wafted out. My mouth watered.

Cecily grinned when I met her eyes. "I figured you'd be hungry and thought you'd like to take a little piece of Philly with you."

I smiled at my friend. "You know me so well."

"Come on." Cecily opened her car door. "Let's get your bag checked and find your gate."

I put the cheesesteak bag back into the tote and pulled the straps onto my shoulder as I climbed out of the car.

It didn't take us too long to get my ticket and check my bag. And I was soon standing beside a pew-style bench at my assigned gate. I clutched the straps of my backpack as I looked around at the space. The tall hanging lights above us didn't provide nearly as much light as the many paned windows on every side of the terminal.

"Hey," Cecily murmured, resting her hand on my shoulder.

I flinched at the sudden contact, even though it was meant to comfort. I looked back at Cecily, her green eyes warm as a well-watered lawn on a summer's day.

"You're going to do great," she encouraged with a smile.

I sighed out a steadying breath, though it did little to relieve the pressure in my chest. I nodded at her words, trying to internalize her calm reassurance.

The apprehension on my face must've eased because Cecily said, "Good. Now let me know when you get there, all right? Send me an email, or give me a call."

"I will," I promised. "And thanks for everything—the ride, the sandwich…just everything."

Cecily pulled me into an embrace. I stiffened. Cecily and I didn't really have a hug relationship. Then again, I wasn't really a hugger with pretty much anyone other than my immediate family. But after a tense moment, I relaxed into the exchange, lifting my hands and resting my fingertips gently on her back.

"You be careful, yeah?" she said, her chin on my shoulder.

I nodded.

After a few more seconds, she gave me an extra squeeze and pulled away. "All right." She cleared her throat when the words came out a bit thick. "Good luck."

I gave her a little smile. "Thank you, Cecily. You're a great friend, and I feel blessed to have you in my life."

The green in her eyes wavered as they filled with tears. "Now, don't get all sentimental on me. I don't know how to handle it."

My smile widened. "You better go. The meter is running. Thanks again."

Cecily sniffed hard, her tears unspilled, and nodded. "Right. Well, stay in touch."

"I will."

And with one last look, my friend—the only friend who had stuck with me through everything I'd been through over the last few years—turned and left.

CHAPTER XI.

I TOOK THE train to New York City, then got on a bus heading to Syracuse. The trip was exhausting in light of the little sleep I'd gotten the night before, and I was glad to settle into a six-hour bus ride. After eating half the Philly cheesesteak Cecily had given me—saving the second half for a late snack on the road—I slumped in my chair, my knees hitting the seat in front of me, and drifted into a fitful sleep.

When I finally arrived in Syracuse, I was so tired that I took a taxi to the hotel Moonseed Manor had arranged for me rather than waiting an hour and a half for a bus, though the extra cost did make me cringe. I thought about whether I wanted to take a quick shower before I went to bed and decided against it. I was way too tired from travel, and worry, and lack of proper sleep. I had only enough energy to check the sheets for bedbugs and set the alarm for five the next morning. I fell asleep without even turning off the light.

It was still dark outside when the alarm went off, and a cursory glance out the window told me it was also raining, though not hard, judging by the little beads of mist on the glass.

I stretched my back while lying in bed. The soreness subsided into a dull ache before going away as my vertebrae settled.

Then I just lay there, enjoying the stillness, enjoying the solitude and the melancholy atmosphere that came from leaving something known behind. I watched the rain flick the window for a good ten minutes before I forced myself to get up. I had an hour and a half before my bus left, and I would be arriving at my new job that day.

I took a shower and dressed in my best clothes—a black skirt with a black collared shirt and a pastel pink sweater. I frowned at my reflection as I brushed my teeth. I'd liked the pastel tips of my long hair, but I'd dyed my whole head a color close to my natural dark brown a week before with the cheapest boxed dye I could find. Mr. Bennings had said that the hotel was trying to create an atmosphere, and I didn't think pink hair was part of that vision. But it still felt strange to see a plain color where there had been such vibrance not long before. It felt a little like covering up the last bit of whom I used to be.

With some time to spare, I decided to head down to the complimentary breakfast the hotel offered to guests. I knew it wouldn't be great. But something was better than nothing, and free food was free food.

The breakfast offered was better than I'd expected. I couldn't remember the last time I'd had waffles. With a plate full of buttery, syrupy goodness—and a banana for the extra vitamins—I turned toward the dining tables.

The few tables set out in the breakfast area were full of travelers hurriedly eating with their baggage pulled up beside them.

I'll just eat in my room.

But when I turned to leave, one woman raised her hand, waving me toward her.

"You can sit with me if you want," she offered in a cheerful tone.

I hesitated only for a second. But unable to deny her friendly smile, I sat down and started to eat.

The woman's blue eyes looked over her plastic, cat-eye glasses at me from across the small table. She smiled, and a dimple appeared in her cheek while I shoved a magnificent bite of waffle into my mouth. If she'd had breakfast, she'd already finished it and cleared it away. She had only a paper cup of what smelled to be coffee clasped between her perfectly painted pink fingernails. In true 1950s fashion, her lipstick matched her nail color. In fact, her whole look was reminiscent of the 1950s—the precise makeup, the side-part blonde bob, even her cute little pearl-buttoned cardigan.

Just when I swallowed to compliment her whole everything, she asked, "So what brings you to Syracuse?"

I wasn't great at small talk. I always felt that if there were only so many things we could say in this life, we might as well have them be worth saying. I didn't know if it was the woman's keen eyes and rapt attention—as if she was truly interested in what I had to say—or if it was her cheeriness so early in the morning, but I found myself answering her and not feeling uncomfortable about it.

"I'm just passing through. I'm taking a bus to Oswego this morning. I'm starting a new job today."

"No way! Me too," she exclaimed. "Are you taking the 6:37?"

I nodded.

"And a new job too, just like me. Isn't that funny? Where's your new job?"

I took a sip of apple juice before glancing back up at her. "You probably haven't heard of it. It seems like they're just opening up. Moonseed Manor?"

My companion laughed a happy little giggle. "A month ago,

I would've agreed with you. But I'm also heading to Moonseed Manor."

My eyes widened. "Really? That is funny. Mr. Bennings must've packaged our travel together."

She tilted her head. "Must have," she said brightly. "Speaking of which"—she glanced down at the delicate, rectangular watch on her wrist—"it's nearly six. Have you checked out yet?"

"I haven't, no," I answered.

"Neither have I. Since we're on the same bus, why don't we split up, check out, and we can share a cab? Okay?" She rose from her chair, downing the rest of her coffee.

Once she was standing, I realized she was quite tall. I looked down at her stiletto heels. Even without the added inches, she still had to be at least six feet.

I nodded. "I'll just finish this banana first."

"Great. See you in a bit."

Having packed while I was getting ready, it didn't take me long to grab my things from my room. And I met my new coworker in the hotel lobby some fifteen minutes later, where we both checked out. It turned out she was quite organized; she'd already ordered a taxi the night before, which was something I hadn't even thought of.

Ten minutes after leaving the hotel, we were standing at the bus pass machine at the transportation center I'd arrived at the night before, buying our tickets for the bus to Oswego. My companion had no trouble. But I hadn't used one for a while, so it took me a bit to figure it out. We found the correct bus stop without incident. It was cold and windy that misty morning, and I was glad I'd decided to wear black tights under my skirt.

"Oh," my new colleague said. "Silly me, I didn't even introduce myself. I'm Alia."

Alia held out her hand to me, and I shook it.

"Nice to meet you, Alia. I'm Wren."

Alia dipped her head in polite acknowledgment. "So what do you do, Wren? What did you get hired for at the hotel?"

"I-I'm a photographer." I stumbled over my words, the title sounding too heavy for me still. My uncertainty made my answer soft, and I wondered if she'd heard me over the wind.

"We must work in the same office then, you think? I was hired as the staff writer." Alia looked down at me.

I nodded. "I think you're right. I remember from the job posting that writer and photographer were both listed under the public relations office, and Mr. Bennings mentioned a staff writer and web designer to me during my interview."

Alia's dimple reappeared. "I'm so excited for this fresh start."

Her enthusiasm seemed to make the entire atmosphere sparkle as if all the little specks of rain had turned into glitter. She was the type of person who shared her joy, the type of person one couldn't be sad around if she was happy.

"Okay," she said like a punctuation mark. "I don't know anyone at all where we're headed, and I like to make friends. Let's tell each other about ourselves. I'll start. As I said, my name is Alia, and I'm a writer. I'm a Leo. I like to do crafts, particularly crocheting. I'll try anything once, and I will date any man who doesn't mind that I'm taller than him. Well... maybe not any man."

She pursed her perfect lips.

"Let's see...What else? My last job was working for the government. I can't tell you how glad I am to get out of D.C. This opportunity at Moonseed Manor really came out of nowhere to tell you the truth. I'm sure I'm leaving something out. Now you go."

I jumped, pressure building as she turned her solicitous eyes on me. "Oh, um. I'm Wren, short for Katherine. And this is my first job as a professional photographer. I used to do some embroidery, but I don't really have the supplies anymore. I, uh,

I'm pretty boring, I guess. I prefer a book and a cup of tea or a quiet walk in the woods to anything adventurous. And I've not dated anyone in…a long time. I haven't really had the time for dating."

Alia didn't respond. I peeked over at her, and she broke into another bright smile.

"I'm great at reading people, and I can already tell I like you, Wren," Alia declared.

CHAPTER XII.

I GAVE ALIA a small smile. It was nice to be told that I was liked, though I didn't know how she could tell she liked me with our very short acquaintance.

Still, I also had a favorable impression of her out the gate. I usually got along with outgoing people as long as they gave me space alone when I needed it, and I was pleased to be on friendly terms with a colleague before even reaching my new workplace.

"Thank you," I told Alia. "And, since we're exchanging compliments, I want to say that I love your whole aesthetic. It's so classic, and you really pull it off."

Alia lowered the frames of her glasses down to look at me over the top. "You just made a friend for life, Wren," she proclaimed with a grin.

I huffed a laugh. "That was easy." The heaviness in my chest, the heaviness that had been there for so long, eased a little. My future suddenly looked much brighter than it had even just the day before. I couldn't remember the last time I'd joked around like this. That thought made me a little sad, halting my upward shift in mood.

"What can I say?" Alia said lightly. "I guess I'm just a simple girl at heart. Oh! We should take a picture. Do you have social media? I can add you."

I shook my head. "I used to, but I don't have a phone or a computer anymore, so I closed my accounts."

Alia gasped in horror. "I think I would actually die."

"It was hard at first," I admitted. "But after a while, I sort of liked it. I never realized how much time it wasted. It was probably one of the healthier decisions I've made in my life."

Alia waved her hand. "You're probably right. It's addictive for sure. But I don't have the mental fortitude to deny myself."

I understood exactly what she meant. "I didn't have a lot of choice in the matter, so that helped."

She took her phone from her handbag. "Do you mind if I take a picture of us and post it though?"

"That's fine," I told her.

Alia leaned down so we could both be in the frame while she held up her phone to take a selfie of us.

"Oh, that's a cute one. I'm going to post it right now." She gave her attention to her phone, her nails tapping on the touchscreen while she typed.

I looked down the road, leaning past the gathered crowd to see. A white bus with three stripes—green, light blue, and dark blue—with an electronic marquee reading 246x was headed right for our stop.

"Our bus is coming," I told Alia.

She looked up from her phone, then quickly shoved it into her bag.

It was a real pain hauling our things onto the bus. But with a little maneuvering and a lot of grunting, Alia and I were soon settled in aisle-facing seats, our large bags pulled up against our knees.

Alia took out her phone again and continued to tap. "Done,"

she said finally, putting her phone back into her bag.

I thought about her earlier words and wondered how she would cope with keeping her tech time limited while on the island. "Are you going to be okay with not having access to your phone most of the time?" I asked.

Alia tilted her head. "What?"

"Didn't Mr. Bennings tell you that we can only use personal devices in our rooms?" I elaborated.

"Oh, that. Yeah, he told me. Sorry, that conversation was like ten minutes ago, so my brain already moved on. I was surprised, but I understand what he's going for. I'm super excited about wearing period clothing. Besides, it's not like they're taking away our phones completely. I never would have accepted a job like that." She shrugged. "But who knows? I might be looking for another job by next weekend. Maybe you could give me some tips on how to cope?"

Her blue eyes prodded me as if I had some arcane wisdom to impart.

"Uh…think about all the drama you're avoiding?" I suggested.

Alia groaned. "Now you're just torturing me. How can I get satisfaction from my day unless I can troll someone?"

I chuckled and looked over my shoulder at the rain-speckled window, my reflection smiling back at me. The eastern horizon was lightening slowly due to the grey clouds, and I didn't think I would see the sun that day. Not that it bothered me. I preferred cool and rainy to warm and sunny any day.

"What did you think of Mr. Bennings?" I asked quietly, my voice barely audible over the rattling and hissing of the bus.

I glanced over at Alia. Her pink lips were turned down into a frown, and her expression was serious and thoughtful. It was such a transformation from her earlier bubbliness that she seemed an entirely different person. Like Marilyn Monroe in

Niagara rather than *Some Like It Hot.*

I waited patiently for her response.

"I think…" she said some thirty seconds later, "he seemed very professional to me. He wants this hotel to be a success. He has a clear vision, and I think he'll make a good and fair boss. But…there is something about him that just strikes me as… odd. He didn't really say anything off." She shrugged again, a subdued smile returning to her face. "I said I'm good at reading people, right?"

I nodded.

"Well, I couldn't get a good read on Mr. Bennings. It was like trying to look through a boarded-up window. Maybe there just wasn't anything to see. Or maybe…he has something to hide."

Her words seemed dark and foreboding when she said them in that hushed, low tone. Beneath my button-down shirt and sweater, goose bumps rose on my arms. I thought about putting my coat, which was draped over my suitcase, back on. Instead, I turned my attention to the grey morning, replaying my interview with Mr. Bennings in my head.

CHAPTER XIII.

WE REACHED our stop in Oswego a little over an hour later. As we stood on the corner of West Bridge Street and West 2nd, I looked up at the grey clouds overhead. It wasn't raining at the moment, but a cold blast of wind made me wonder how chilly it would be once we were on the water.

"The marina where we're supposed to catch the boat is a fifteen-minute walk, and that's just about when we're expected to meet them," Alia said, staring down at her phone. She glanced over at me. "Are you ready? I got the walking directions pulled up."

I nodded, extending the handle of my roller suitcase.

The street we started down was a nice little area with cute storefronts, local restaurants, and a few bars. I imagined it would be quite crowded on a Friday or Saturday night.

Alia's phone directed us to turn, and I was reminded just how much more convenient GPS was compared to following the map neatly folded in my coat pocket.

As we walked over a bridge, the icy wind blew off the water, making me clench my teeth. It really wasn't a long walk, but the cold made it feel longer. I was relieved when the little marina finally came into view.

The marina was pretty deserted, sleek speeders—some with little cabins and some without—bobbed gently at their simple moors.

"Did they tell you the name of the boat we should be looking for?" Alia's head swiveled well above mine in an attempt to locate our transport.

"No, they didn't." I scanned the area for human life. "What about over there?" I pointed to the very end of the dock where a tall blue and white boat with a large cabin was tethered. It looked like there was some kind of movement though I couldn't see anything in detail.

Alia squinted in that direction. "Yeah, I think you're right. In any case, we should be able to ask them."

As we approached the boat, I could see three men loading crates into the cabin behind rows of benches as a woman watched, her silvery-white hair blowing and her shoulders hunched against the wind.

"Excuse me," Alia called as we neared the woman.

She turned to us, and I was a little surprised to see that her face didn't look nearly as old as her hair suggested. She was probably the same age as my mother, perhaps a few years younger. She frowned, and it was clear that the expression was a common one for her as well-worn lines deepened on her face.

"Is this the boat to Nightfall Island?" Alia asked.

The woman dipped her head gently. "You two must be Alia and Katherine." Her tone was neither friendly nor guarded. I couldn't quite place the emotion in her vibe, in her voice.

Alia smiled. "Yes, I'm Alia." She offered the woman her hand.

After shaking Alia's hand, she turned to me.

"You can call me Wren."

Her hand was dry and calloused in mine, and her hazel eyes seemed flat despite their beautiful color. "Nora. I'm the cook at the manor."

Alia and I both nodded in acknowledgment.

"You'll be taking your orders directly from Mr. Bennings. I had to come into town for supplies, so he asked me to bring you back."

One of the men loading boxes approached Nora. "All set when you're ready, Miss."

"Yes, thank you, Phil. These are the two young ladies we're bringing with us today." Nora gestured to us before climbing into the boat.

The man turned toward us, his knit cap folded to cover just the tips of his ears. His nose was red from the chill, and he wore black overalls over a grey plaid button-down. "Do you need any help with your bags?"

Alia smiled warmly, her blue eyes taking in the beefy man with appreciation. "I'd love some help, Phil," she purred.

Alia giggled as that full-grown, hulk of a man had the gall to blush at her flirtatious attention.

He cleared his throat. "Of course, Miss." He reached for the handle of her suitcase.

She gently rested her fingertips on his hand. "Oh, you don't have to be so formal with me, Phil. I want us to be friends. Call me Alia."

Phil froze and met her eyes.

"Don't you want to be my friend, Phil?" Alia simpered.

His blush deepened, but he nodded his head once. Then he turned to load our bags onto the boat.

Alia never took her eyes off him. "I knew this was a good idea," she murmured to me.

I watched the whole exchange with a degree of awe. I'd never been so blatant with a man before. I wouldn't say I was sheltered or shy on that front, but this was next level for me. My astonishment must have shown on my face because when Alia glanced over at me, she grinned.

"Oh, great. Now, I've shocked your delicate sensibilities."

I shook my head. "Not at all, I really admire how confident you are."

"You are too adorable, Wren. I just want to squeeze you until your head pops off."

I snorted. "Please don't. I like my head where it is."

She sighed exaggeratedly. "Fine…if you insist."

After Phil had loaded our bags, he offered us a helping hand into the boat. And I didn't miss how Alia's fingers lingered in his.

I looked around the deck and cursed internally. I was prone to seasickness, and I hadn't brought any medicine with me. Normally, when I absolutely had to be on a boat, I would just stay on the deck—the fresh air was enough to keep my stomach mostly in check. But as fat drops of rain began to sprinkle down overhead, and the cold wind made my teeth chatter, I thought it would be better to face an upset stomach rather than hypothermia.

Entering the cabin, I leaned my face against the cool glass window. It was probably dirty, but better to get dirt on my face than vomit on my new coworkers' shoes.

Alia settled onto the bench beside me. "You know, Wren. I wasn't really joking before."

I glanced over at her.

"Well, I was about popping your head off. Obviously, I wouldn't want to do that. I know outwardly I come off as all confident and self-assured. But even Leos are self-conscious sometimes."

My chest tightened. *Did I offended her?* "I didn't mean to suggest—"

She smiled and shook her head. "That's not what I'm trying to say. What I mean is that this approach works for me. The type of men I prefer… Well, let's just say I like to do the chasing. But it's okay if you aren't like that. You don't have to try to be like me. You're pretty and funny, and I can already tell how kind you are. Plus, I'm sure you have a whole bunch of great qualities I don't know about yet. What I'm saying is that someone is going to notice all that about you, and you won't have to chase them. You can just be yourself, and the right person will find you. That is, if you're looking for someone. There's nothing saying you need a lover if you don't want one."

My chest warmed at her words. *What a kind person.* She had completely misunderstood, but that hadn't stopped her words from moving me. It wasn't that I didn't like a little chase. My romantic experiences always seemed to unfold like a game of hide and seek, or—more accurately—like a sailor lured to her own demise by a siren's song. I had a type and a bad habit of conflating certain emotions. I may not be as blatant as Alia, but that had more to do with how I normally connected with people. My relationships hadn't started with simple physical attraction, at least not on my end.

"Thanks, Alia. I'll keep that in mind. I hope you find what you're looking for, too."

Alia's eyes followed Phil when he walked by the window, going about whatever work he was tasked with as the boat's engine rumbled to life.

"'Once more unto the breach…' In any case"—she held up her phone—"I already got his number."

CHAPTER XIV.

AS SOON AS we pulled out of the dock, my stomach started to sway. I tried to concentrate on my slow breathing and ignore the unsteady water under my feet. I stared at the floor of the cabin, too much of a coward to look out the window and too smart to close my eyes.

"This will help." Nora's hand appeared in my line of sight, offering me a small candy with a green and purple wrapper. "It's a ginger chew. It will help with motion sickness."

I looked up at the woman. Her hazel eyes were still flat, but her frown lines were gone. I thanked her and went about peeling the wrapper from the sticky remedy.

The sweetness of sugar and the spice of ginger momentarily distracted me, and it wasn't long before I was feeling steadier.

"So how long have you worked at Moonseed Manor?" Alia asked Nora, who sat across from us in the small cabin.

Again, I admired Alia. Nora didn't give off an overly welcoming demeanor, but that hadn't deterred Alia in the least.

Nora answered without hesitation. "I've worked for the

Benningses for over thirty years now. They hired me for my first job as a kitchen maid."

"Wow, that's a long time. You must really like it there," Alia said.

Nora didn't respond but looked out the window.

"Do you live on the island then?" Alia continued.

Nora dipped her head.

"Does everyone who works there live on the island? I haven't decided whether I want to try to find a place on the mainland or not."

"Most live on the mainland. Mr. Bennings and Watt—the caretaker—live on Nightfall Island full-time. But Dominick, Lucero, Emmaline, and Gwynn live off-island. I believe they all meet up at the marina and take a boat together. You can ask them about it when you meet them. Dominick is on your team; he's the web designer."

Alia nodded thoughtfully.

Now that my stomach had calmed down, I was feeling brave and looked out the window. The marina was well behind us, and I couldn't see much out the fogged and rain-speckled glass. I raised my arm and used the sleeve of my coat to wipe some of the condensation away. But as I peered past the raindrops into the misty morning, all I could see was grey water and grey clouds.

"How long of a ride is it?" I asked, not taking my eyes off the lake that surrounded us.

"Three-quarters of an hour," Nora replied.

I suppressed a sigh. *I definitely won't be moving to the mainland. I wouldn't want to face this commute twice a day, and that's not even considering I'd be sacrificing free room and board.*

The conversation between us lulled, and Alia pulled out her phone. I just stared into the rain, searching for any sign of land.

After a long while, Nora glanced down at her watch. "You

should be able to see the island pretty soon."

I sat up straighter and swiveled my head at the surrounding windows. "Where?"

"Over there." Nora pointed over her shoulder.

I rose from my seat and took careful steps to the door facing the bow. Its little window, like all the others, was fogged and flecked with rain. I rubbed at the fog, but I still couldn't see well. Turning the handle, I pushed open the door and slipped outside onto the deck at the front of the boat.

The rain sprayed me with a fine mist, punctuated by occasional fat drops. The engine, so loud in the enclosed cabin, was overshadowed by the sound of the boat cutting through the waves. I gripped the railing, squinting into the distance for any sign of Nightfall Island as the freezing metal burned my hands.

Finally, a dark shape appeared ahead, seeming to pop into existence much closer than expected. I saw the boathouse first, the grey tiles of the roof appearing almost blue in the struggling light. I peered at the surrounding trees and only managed to see the very top of a tower—flat with spires on the corners.

The boat's engine quieted while the vessel slowed, and I could hear the thumps of boots on the deck as the boatmen prepared to moor.

My heart swelled and my skin tingled in giddy excitement. I began to feel light as though I could simply float away. This was it. This was real. I was finally getting a chance to turn my life around, to step into a space where dreams were not only allowed but could be realized.

The captain skillfully drove the boat nearer a long dock beside the boathouse, and as we got closer, I saw a man standing on the boards. He seemed to have stepped right off the pages of my favorite novels.

He was pale and lean in his Victorian dress. He wore a black frock coat and waistcoat over his high-collared white shirt, an expertly tied knot at his neck. His black hair swirled in curl-tipped waves under his top hat. He had a square jaw and full lips. And when his dark eyes met mine under the brim of his hat, I froze as my chest tightened at their intensity.

He inclined his head in a polite gesture. I don't know what else I'd expected. Due to the forcefulness of his gaze, perhaps I thought a scowl would look more natural on him. Still, he didn't exactly smile either. His expression was simply cool and courteous.

This must be Mr. Bennings. The man's demeanor perfectly matched what I'd expected from the professional voice I'd heard during my interview, though he was younger than I'd supposed him to be. He seemed around my age, perhaps a few years older.

The boat's engine silenced as we pulled up to the dock. Phil jumped out and tethered it before unloading our suitcases first.

I went back inside the cabin to retrieve my backpack and followed Nora and Alia to where we could disembark.

Nora immediately went about supervising the unloading of her supplies while Phil took a brief moment to assist Alia onto the dock.

I didn't want to interrupt their exchange, so I attempted to climb out of the boat on my own. I must have looked like I was struggling because the man who'd been waiting for us on the dock offered me his hand.

His skin was smooth but cold, and he pulled away the moment I had my footing. I looked up into his face at his simply courteous expression. He was as tall as Alia with her heels on.

With Phil going about his other duties, Alia turned her attention to the man, who dipped his head at her.

"Welcome to Moonseed Manor," he said. "I'm William Courtland Bennings."

CHAPTER XV.

"THANKS SO much," Alia stuck out her hand toward Mr. Bennings with a broad smile. "I'm glad to be here. I'm Alia Geller."

Mr. Bennings shook Alia's hand, his expression unchanged in the face of her friendliness, then turned his black eyes on me.

"Then you must be Miss Mabry."

I stared down at his outstretched hand almost as if I didn't know what to do with it. With his intense gaze on me, I felt just how imposing his presence was. I dropped my head in a nod. It took all my self-discipline to place my hand in his. "Yes." My voice came out far too quiet. I cleared my throat. "Yes, thank you. I look forward to working with you."

I scolded myself as he released my hand. *What the heck is wrong with me? Why am I feeling so shy all of a sudden? Not everyone is outwardly friendly. This man gave me the opportunity of a lifetime on a silver platter, and I can barely make eye contact? Get a grip!* Gathering my nerve, I dared to meet Mr. Bennings's gaze. I even managed to offer him a small smile.

My effort was not rewarded. He just blinked coolly at me,

offering no warmth in return.

Luckily, he turned his attention to Nora. "Thank you, Nora, for going to the mainland for supplies and for escorting these ladies here."

To my surprise, Nora gave him a genuine smile, no trace of the dullness that had been in her eyes. "Of course, Mr. Bennings. Getting supplies is my job after all, but I appreciate your gratitude just the same."

Even with his long-time employee, Mr. Bennings was distant and professional in his response, though he had called her by her first name. "I will send Mr. Fitz down here to help you bring everything to the kitchen."

Nora nodded, her smile undeterred. "Thank you. Will we be having supper in the dining room tonight?"

"Yes, as we usually do when we welcome new employees." He looked over at Alia and me. "If you'll just follow me, I'll show you to your rooms and start the onboarding process."

With that, he turned and began walking up the dock toward shore. I quickly grabbed the handle of my suitcase to follow him. Alia gave Phil a little wave and did the same.

The wheels of my case thumped as they bumped over the grooves between the boards of the dock. I scanned the path ahead, my anticipation growing with every step, in search of my first full glimpse of Moonseed Manor. But all I could see was the boathouse and treetops.

The dock ended and a brick path began, rising as it sloped. Now on the far side of the boathouse, the top of the manor was visible. Every step up the hill showed another element as we neared it.

On this grey May morning, the stones held no warmth of color. It was as if the sky's mood was reflected in the very walls of the manor. Or perhaps it was the other way around. The façade was everything a Gothic revival should be, with pointed-arch windows and doors and gables with round windows. The majority of the house, judging by the windows, was at least four stories tall. There was a glass vestibule near the center, with an arched, stained-glass window above it. The tower, to the immediate left of the vestibule, was six stories.

It seemed unusually quiet. Even the calls of the seagulls were muffled, and the wheels on my suitcase sounded farther away with each step I took toward the hotel.

Looking up at his ancestral home, Mr. Bennings froze. I pulled up short to avoid bumping into him, and Alia stumbled a little on her heels at the abrupt halt. I stared up into his face, his black eyes widening as his nostrils flared. I followed his gaze to a window on the second floor. I couldn't see anything that would have caused him to stop. But when I looked back at him, the expression was gone.

He turned to us. "The employee dormitories are this way."

He took a path that split off to the left, heading around to the south side of the manor. He paused when we hit a perpendicular path and pointed to the main house.

"This will lead into the kitchens." Then he pointed in the opposite direction. "This leads to the greenhouse and dormitories." He started in the latter direction. "There's a tunnel directly from the dormitories to the kitchen cellars, which runs under the greenhouse as well."

"That will be convenient on rainy days," Alia said.

Mr. Bennings opened the greenhouse door for us.

Warm, humid air caressed my face and hands, soothing the chill that had seeped into my muscles, which had tightened since I'd stepped out of the boat's cabin. The greenhouse sprawled out on either side of us, with carefully laid brick paths meandering through thick walls of green leaves.

I sniffed deeply at the heavily perfumed air, sighing with pleasure.

"Beautiful," I murmured.

I knew the instant Mr. Bennings's eyes were on me, pressing in on me like the heavy air filling my lungs.

"You've got quite the variety here," Alia pointed out.

Mr. Bennings nodded at her comment. "Yes, we also have a few rare species. Most of the inner part of the greenhouse we keep lush for the guests, but we have some vegetables and an herb garden for the kitchen as well."

"Oh!" A young woman with dark eyes and an olive complexion gasped as she pulled up short on the greenhouse path. Her pin-striped pink dress was down to her ankles and up to her neck; she'd rolled the long sleeves to her elbows, a basket of fresh herbs hanging on one arm. Over the lower half of her dress, she wore a white apron, and her dark curls tumbled from the slightly crooked white cap atop her head. "Good morning, Mr. Bennings." Her chest heaved as if she were more out of breath than surprised.

"Good morning, Miss Martín. I apologize if we startled you."

"Only a little," she admitted with a strained smile.

"I'd like to introduce you to the newest members of our team." Mr. Bennings gestured toward us. "This is Miss Alia Geller, our new staff writer, and Miss Katherine Mabry, our photographer. Ladies, this is Nora's assistant, Miss Lucero Martín."

We shook hands with the woman, who smiled politely at us.

"Miss Martín," Mr. Bennings continued. "Nora has returned and could no doubt use your help with putting things away in the kitchen."

As I watched Mr. Bennings interact with Lucero in the same formal way he had with Nora, Alia, and me, I marked the incongruity of his age and his manner of speaking yet again. I would've been surprised if he was even thirty years old, yet he carried himself as though he were from another century. Was it because he was so young? Was he overcompensating in order to be taken seriously? Or did he just have a cold personality?

"Of course." Lucero took a step to move past us on the path.

Lucero, and Nora too, seem to be used to his formality.

"Have you seen Mr. Fitz this morning?" Mr. Bennings asked.

Lucero froze, her smile faltering. "What do you mean?"

He tilted his head. "I'd like to ask him to help move the boxes into the kitchen."

Her expression relaxed. "Oh, yes. I saw him when he passed through here earlier. I think he was on his way to the dormitory."

Mr. Bennings nodded slightly. "Thank you." His tone was a clear dismissal.

As Lucero scurried along her way, I glanced over my shoulder at her retreating form. Bits of rosemary fell from her basket onto the path as she lifted her hands to stuff her hair back into her cap.

CHAPTER XVI.

AFTER PASSING through the greenhouse, we found another neatly bricked path, which led to a long building of grey stones with a blue door.

Mr. Bennings held the door open for us, and Alia and I dragged our suitcases in.

The room we entered seemed to be a common room with couches and plush chairs and a fireplace with a large television hanging on the mantle. There was an oblong table farther in near a small kitchenette. A hallway branched off on either side of the shared space.

Mr. Bennings gestured to the left. "This hall is for female employees."

Alia headed in that direction, and I followed.

"You can choose any of the free rooms you like," Mr. Bennings said from behind us, waiting in the common room.

We entered the long hall, where all of the doors but one were open. I assumed that must be Nora's room. The first room we looked into was very plain but functional. There was a single bed with a nightstand beside it. There was also a dresser, a small space heater, a wooden chair, and a round mirror over a sink built into the wall. Beside the sink was a door.

Alia entered the room, leaving her case in the hall, and opened the door. "It's a bathroom. Looks like it's shared with the room on the other side."

The small window in the bedroom faced the lake.

Alia returned to the hall. "I'd like to look at them all to see which one I like best."

I agreed with her, and we continued on. Each room in the hall was pretty much the same. The ones on the north side faced the greenhouse and the nearby trees. The ones on the south side faced the lake.

At the threshold of the last room on the left, Alia gasped. "Jesus, man! You scared me to death."

I peeked around the corner and found a man standing on a stepladder, his arms above his head. His broad back was to us as he tinkered with the overhead light. His thighs filled out his brown pants, and he had a news cap shoved into his back pocket. His white shirt sleeves were rolled up under his brown waistcoat, and his jacket was draped over the wooden chair in the corner. He had a mess of bronzy red hair, and I couldn't tell whether it was curly or just mussed.

He lowered his arms and glanced back at us. "Flip that switch for me, will ya?"

Alia toggled the switch near the door, and the light came on.

The man smiled in satisfaction and descended the stepladder. He glanced at Alia only momentarily before his eyes fell on me. His face was well-balanced with a straight nose and a short scruff of facial hair. He quirked one eyebrow, then broke into a grin. My heart skipped a beat as his amber eyes warmed.

"You must be the new recruits." His tone was friendly and his deep voice welcoming. "I'm the caretaker, Walter Fitz, but you can just call me Watt."

He didn't hold out his hand but pulled his hat from his back pocket and fixed it atop his head.

"I'm Wren, the photographer, and this is Alia. She's a writer."

I gestured toward Alia, but he didn't so much as glance at her. I could feel my face starting to heat under the attention of his steady gaze. But though I was feeling a little embarrassed, it wasn't unpleasant. His face was just too open and amicable to make me feel self-conscious.

"Nice to meet you. I'll get out of your hair now. I was just fixing the light. Don't want you to have to sit in the dark all by yourself." He chuckled, and the sound was caramel drizzled over a freshly baked brownie.

He grabbed his jacket and stepladder and headed for the door, but he stopped at the threshold and looked over his shoulder at me. "Welcome to Moonseed Manor. I look forward to working with you." He gave me another smile, then started down the hall.

Once he was gone, I felt like I'd just stepped out of the greenhouse into the chilly misty morning, his presence warm and relaxing like the humid air that made the plants thrive. I turned my attention back to Alia.

A frown marred her flawless face as she stared at the now-empty threshold.

"Are you all right?" I asked.

Her blue eyes flicked to mine, and her expression eased. "Yeah. I think I prefer a lake-facing room. Don't you?"

I glanced out the window. This room was the farthest from the common room. All I could see from the window was trees; I couldn't even see the greenhouse or the path that led to it. It felt secluded and quiet.

"Actually, I think I like this one best."

Alia shrugged. "All right. I'm going to take the one across from Nora. I can see the lake from the window, and it's close to the common room and front door." Alia grabbed the handle of her suitcase and left my new bedroom.

I relaxed a little, sighing in the quiet space. I liked Alia, and I was excited about this new job, but nothing felt so blissful as existing in my own space. The wind whished around outside, and I imagined that I'd be able to hear it rustling the leaves of the trees once they got bigger. I closed my eyes, listening hard for the waves of the lake. Either the dorms weren't close enough or the waves weren't wild enough that day because I couldn't hear them.

I wouldn't say I was more centered, but the wood floor felt a little steadier beneath my feet when I opened my eyes and looked about the room. After taking off my backpack, I placed it on the chair where Watt's jacket had so recently been. Then I rolled my suitcase to the foot of the bed and closed the door as I left to meet the others in the common room.

CHAPTER XVII.

I JOINED MR. Bennings back in the common room just as he was sending Watt to go help Nora and Lucero.

He turned to me. "Everything to your satisfaction?"

"Yes, thank you."

Silence fell between us.

I took a deep breath and straightened my spine. "Mr. Bennings, I want—"

"Sorry to keep you waiting," Alia said as she joined us, the smile back on her face.

Mr. Bennings acknowledged her words and turned his attention back to me, raising an eyebrow to ask me to continue.

With his eyes keenly watching, and Alia inclining her head in curiosity, I felt like my words of gratitude and appreciation were too childish and desperate to speak aloud. I shook my head to indicate that I had nothing else to say.

"If you're both ready, I'll take you up to the main house." He glanced at each of us before heading out the door.

I would have thought that, given the cold and rain, we would have taken the tunnel he'd mentioned. But as we walked around to the front door, I appreciated that we took this route instead. This was how the guests would see Moonseed Manor for the first time, and it was beneficial to get similar first impressions.

We entered the vestibule, the lower half of which was enclosed in paned glass. I looked up at the ribbed, vaulted ceiling and the arched, stained-glass window that would paint the space with color should the sun ever hit it. A short bench sat on either side of the beveled-glass, double front doors, one of which was already open.

We followed Mr. Bennings into the entrance hall, Alia's heels clacking on the black and teal ceramic tiles—swirling and swooping in geometric patterns beneath our feet. A lantern-style light hung from the ribbed ceiling, and the walls were the same grey stone as the exterior. An ornate mirror reflected a splendid tapestry hanging on the opposite wall. The tapestry depicted Dionysus celebrating with his followers and was bordered with vines fat with grapes.

While we passed, the fabric of the tapestry rippled in the reflection of the mirror as if the wind made it move away from the wall. Something about the movement caught in my mind and made my heart stumble. I abruptly halted my steps, the others moving forward without me, as I looked back where the artwork hung.

Though I had felt no breeze, goose bumps raised on my arms. The tapestry showed no signs of movement. I frowned, blinking, before shaking the little curiosity from my mind. *Perhaps I didn't see what I thought I saw, or maybe our passing by created a breeze.* I glanced at the mirror again before moving forward to catch up with the others.

Straight ahead was the hotel's front desk, heavy in polished mahogany. Behind the desk was a door, and as we approached it, the left wall opened up into a staircase. A set of open double doors on the right led to what looked like a parlor.

Mr. Bennings escorted us around the desk and ushered us through the door. I didn't know what the room used to be, but it was an office now. Despite the modern desks and flat-screen computers, there was no covering the opulence of the original room. At the far end were three windows, angled as to make the room look rounded. Each was a delicate mixture of clear and stained glass. In front of the windows were seats, cushioned in red velvet with gold trim. The cream wallpaper featured a damask-style pattern in off-white, which I could only make out when I moved. There were three desks—barely fitting in the small room—equipped with everything a modern hotel office might need.

As we entered, a man stood from the desk nearest a marble fireplace. He was neither tall nor short, and his black suit complemented his dark skin. He looked sleek and cool with his close-cropped hair and full beard. And when he smiled, I knew he was happy to see us.

"This is our web developer, Mr. Dominick Wright. You will be working closely with him. Mr. Wright, this is Miss Alia Geller, our staff writer, and Miss Katherine Mabry, our photographer."

Dominick's hand was warm as he shook ours. "Glad you're here. Now we can get some real work done."

"I need to start filling out the official employment paperwork," Mr. Bennings said. "If one of you would like to come with me, the other can stay with Mr. Wright and get up-to-date on what he's been working on."

"I'd like to get a feel for what's in store." Alia turned to me. "If you don't mind doing paperwork first."

"Sure," I agreed.

Mr. Bennings nodded and gestured for me to follow him back the way we'd come. Upon returning to the reception desk, we headed toward the stairs.

I was getting the impression that no detail had been

neglected when designing this house. Each baluster of the stairs was elaborately carved with delicate precision. The rug, which muffled the sound of our footfalls, was a cobalt blue with gold and red designs. I looked up, but the flights above obscured what was on the upper floors.

On the landing of the second floor, a long hallway stretched out before us, with pointed-arch windows on one side and paintings on the wall opposite. There was a door immediately to the left, another farther down, and one at the end of the hall.

"This way, please," Mr. Bennings beckoned me to the nearest door.

We passed through what I guessed was a massive drawing room. A giant candelabra chandelier in twisted iron hung overhead, illuminating the comparatively simple decor. Leather couches and chairs gathered around low coffee tables, and wooden chairs were tucked under round tables near tall windows—their dark velvet curtains pulled aside to let the weak light in. The walls and ribbing of the ceiling were dark wood, appearing even darker against the cream in between. There was a heavy, carved fireplace in one corner, a moose's severed head hanging above the mantle.

I averted my eyes from the corpse, shot down in his prime for someone's sick enjoyment, and followed Mr. Bennings through a door.

The room we entered was much wider than it was long. An antique desk sat in the center, with bookshelves and filing cabinets lining most of the walls. There was a huge rug of muted grey and black over the wood floor. His desk held a computer and printer, so out of place among the lavish Gothic revival designs.

Mr. Bennings gestured to two leather chairs in front of his desk as he sat behind it. "Please, have a seat."

CHAPTER XVIII.

"WOULD YOU fill this out for me, please?" Mr. Bennings held out a sheet of paper to me.

Taking it from him, I saw that it was a standard employee information form. I picked up a pen and leaned forward to fill it out on the desk.

"Could I see your driver's license and Social Security card, please?" Mr. Bennings asked.

I stopped writing in the middle of my name and pulled my wallet out of my coat pocket, putting it on the desk. After sliding my cards from their slots, I offered them to Mr. Bennings. He took them from me and opened the scanner bed of his printer to make copies. I gave my attention back to the employee form.

The paperwork didn't take long to fill out; it was all basic information. The only thing I didn't know off the top of my head was my bank account numbers for my paycheck, but a quick look in my wallet provided those.

For a good ten minutes, the only sounds in the room were my pen on the paper, Mr. Bennings's keystrokes, and an occasional, over-enthusiastic speck of rain pelting the windows. It was quiet—intimate—and my unfamiliarity with this man made the atmosphere heavy.

When I finished, I passed the paper back across the desk. Mr. Bennings set it before him without glancing at it.

His dark eyes met mine, and I froze, unable to look away. *What is he thinking with such a deep look in his eyes?*

"As you no doubt noticed from our website, we have hardly any pictures of Moonseed Manor. I'd like your first task to be taking photos of the rooms of the manor so Mr. Wright can begin creating guest room pages and photo galleries. You can move on to outdoor spaces when the weather warms up. Your camera is on your desk. I've tried to think of everything you might need, but if you need additional lighting or other accessories, let me know. Feel free to move about the house and start wherever you like. Coordinate with Mr. Fitz on which rooms he may be working on, and let the maids know so they can work around you. The only rooms I don't want photographed are this office and my bedroom, which I will point out to you." He handed me a notecard with neat handwriting on it. "Here is your work email and password. Please change your password your first time logging in."

He stood from his desk, but I stayed seated.

"Mr. Bennings." I ran my thumb along the edge of the notecard, building up my courage to say what I needed to.

"Yes?"

Standing from my chair, I stared up at him. He'd raised one eyebrow in expectation.

"I want to thank you for this opportunity. You don't know what it means to me to be given this chance. I don't want to sound dramatic, but you saved my career, possibly my whole future. I'm so grateful that you took a chance on me, and I just had to tell you."

His lips turned up in the smallest of smiles, and the intensity of his gaze softened a little.

"Miss Mabry." His cool tone held the warm hint of spring. "I appreciate your feelings, but I don't see hiring you as taking a chance. I admire your art, and I'm glad that you decided to join us. I did not save your career or your future. You did that."

My heart leapt at his kind words, and I felt like I was going to burst into tears. I lowered my head, trying to get a hold of the sudden emotion. "Thank you," I whispered, the words wavering with my unsteady breath.

After a brief moment of silence, he said, "I will lead you to the closet where we keep the uniforms."

I looked up as his professionally distant tone returned. Whatever warmth we had just shared was gone so fast that I wondered if I'd imagined it. Still, despite his cool demeanor, I couldn't think badly of Mr. Bennings. His words had been too kind, too encouraging. Whether he distanced himself from his employees as a matter of professionalism or if this was just his personality, it didn't really matter. I'd decided he was a good man. And though his intensity of presence left me not really knowing how to act around him, I was sure I would get used to it. His behavior may have seemed way too stiff and formal for someone his age, but as I followed him from his office into the drawing room, I felt that it suited him nonetheless. It certainly gave his words more weight. This was not a man who said things lightly.

Once back on the stairs, he led me upward, stopping on the landing between the second and third floors.

He pointed toward the third floor. "The first door on the left is my bedroom, so you don't have to photograph that. Also up there is our largest guest room and the ballroom."

Instead of heading up, he turned to the paneled wall beside us. Placing his hand on the wall, he pushed, and a secret door clicked and popped open. Pulling the door ajar, Mr. Bennings gestured for me to head in first.

I entered the dark space, which was illuminated a moment later as he flicked a switch near the entrance. The windowless room was almost as large as Mr. Bennings's office. There were long shelves stacked with clean linens and racks with hanging clothes.

He gestured toward the racks. "Pick out whatever you like. You are expected to wear these uniforms from now on everywhere except the dormitory. Don't be shy; make sure you choose at least a week's worth. I will head down to Miss Geller now, so feel free to try anything on to make sure it fits. You can drop the rest in your room before returning to Mr. Wright." He turned to me. "Do you have any questions?"

I shook my head. "No, thank you, Mr. Bennings. I'll try to be as quick as I can."

He simply nodded and left me to my task.

CHAPTER XIX.

SILENCE DESCENDED as Mr. Bennings closed the door, the type of silence where my ears strained to hear anything at all. I breathed out, and the rush sounded much too loud. A shiver ran over my skin, and my muscles stiffened.

"Let's pick out my uniform and move along," I said, just to hear my own voice.

I thought that being in Mr. Bennings's presence was overwhelming, but I found myself wishing he hadn't left me alone in this stuffy closet by myself.

My boots thumped heavily on the creaky floorboards, the effect more like someone was following behind me than my own feet.

I approached the first rack of dresses, which were arranged by size, then color. The cut was all the same—ankle-length with round necks in what felt like cotton. I grabbed a black one first and began undressing to try it on. I felt vulnerable taking off my clothes in that large, dim space as if something were watching me from a dark corner. I hurriedly pulled on my new uniform. It fit well enough, and I wished there was a mirror to see how it looked. But I would have to settle for waiting until I got back to my room.

Beside the dresses, there were aprons—all white—and kerchiefs of varying colors. I put on an apron next, then chose a light blue kerchief, which I tied around my neck with a square knot.

I was starting to feel a bit jittery, glancing around as my heart pounded in my fingertips. I grabbed four more dresses in my size—two black, a plaid baby pink, and a deep purple. I added four aprons to my pile and a few kerchiefs. Then I made my way to the men's uniforms. I picked out two suits—both black—complete with shirt, trousers, waistcoat, and tie. To top everything off, I chose a cap like I'd seen Lucero wear and a bowler hat.

My arms laden, I wondered how I would open the door. But as I approached, I saw that the magnets that held the door closed were connected but hadn't been pushed in. I turned my back to it and nudged it open with my butt. I carefully shut the door with my foot and clicked it closed with another nudge from my backside.

"Whoa, you need some help there?" a warm voice asked from below, the speaker unseen due to the pile in my arms.

Before I could answer, my load was lifted from me. I looked up to meet Watt's amber eyes on the landing, a friendly smile gracing his face.

"Thanks," I said. "But at least let me take half."

Watt shook his head decisively. "Now, I can't allow that. My pride is on the line here. Don't you think I'm capable of carrying all this for you?"

"Don't you think I'm capable of carrying it all for myself?" I said by reflex.

He didn't miss a beat. "I saw that you were. But you're new, and I'm trying to be friendly. Won't you let me?"

As I stared at his congenial expression, I felt immediately at ease. "All right. Thanks."

He flashed me a smile. "Thank *you*. Besides, now that pretty dress of yours isn't obscured by all this stuff."

I blinked, my eyes flicking to his. But I found just a friendly warmth, nothing suggestive or heated.

"It is a pretty dress," I agreed, starting down the stairs. "I like its simplicity."

"Sometimes simplicity is the most flattering," he stated, following after me. "So you're a photographer, huh?"

"Yes."

"I'd love to see your photographs. I'm sure I'll see tons of the ones you're going to take of the hotel. I mean the ones you're really proud of, passionate about."

As we reached the first-floor landing, I glanced at his earnest face. "Sure, I don't mind…if you're really that interested."

He nodded. "I am. I may not look like it, but I love the arts."

"What does someone who likes the arts look like?"

He chuckled. "I'm not quite sure. Certainly not a blue-collared donkey like me."

I couldn't help but laugh, and the tension I'd been carrying with me drained away. I didn't know if it was Watt's friendly demeanor, his ready smile, or what, but it was easy to talk to him. I couldn't remember the last time I'd had this light of a conversation, especially with a stranger. I'd been too tired, too run-down, to have these light-hearted discussions with my previous coworkers. Even with Cecily, I'd been just too worn out to muster the effort. Alia was nice. But she had so much personality, I felt more comfortable just letting her light shine on me. Something was different about Watt, or maybe I was finally easing up a little now that I was actually here, starting my new life, staring ahead into a bright future I'd never dared to hope for.

"Aw, I like donkeys. When I was a kid, my dad used to take my sister and me to the petting zoo whenever my mom went to get her hair done. I liked visiting the donkey the best. Everyone always paid attention to the goats, but here was this guy, just chilling like, 'Here I am, I'm a donkey, what do you want?'"

He listened to my story intently as if he would be tested on it later. "I've never seen a donkey in real life."

I tilted my head. "No? Maybe there's a petting zoo nearby, you can go visit. They're really cute and very sweet."

"Maybe you'd like to come with me then?"

I smiled. "Maybe." I started toward the front door, but Watt stopped me.

"It's still raining. Why don't we take the tunnel?"

"Oh, right. I haven't seen that yet."

"Follow me." Watt led me down the stairs.

The temperature dropped at least ten degrees as we stepped into the food cellars. The rough, grey, stone walls were lined with wooden shelves full of cans and Mason jars. The naked bulbs overhead were weak and barely pierced the darkness.

"This way." Watt's warm voice seemed entirely out of place in the chilled air, and I followed close behind him.

As we turned a corner, a tunnel stretched out before us, its yellow lights much brighter than those of the cellar. Our scuffling steps echoed off the stone walls.

A shiver ran up my spine, and I got the distinct feeling that something was behind me—a heavy presence, like the feeling just before someone lays a hand on my shoulder. My heart jumped, and I spun around, gasping in surprise. But there was nothing there, only the yellow light of the tunnel ending in the shadowed cellar beyond.

"You all right?" Watt asked, stopping at the sound of my distress.

"Y-yeah, I just felt a sudden cold chill."

He grinned. "You sure?" In the lights of the tunnel, his amber eyes took on a mischievous glint, and I wondered if he would tease me about this later.

"I'm fine."

He shrugged, and we continued on our way.

At the very end, there was another set of stairs, which led to a door. Watt pushed the door open, and we stepped into the dormitory common room near the kitchenette.

CHAPTER XX.

AS I ARRANGED my uniforms neatly in my dresser drawers, Watt watched me from the chair in the corner. I don't know why he'd decided to sit down, but he didn't seem in any rush to leave me to my task.

"Mr. Bennings wants me to take pictures of the guest rooms first. He told me to coordinate with you. I got the impression that you're doing work on some of them. Are any of them ready to be photographed?"

Watt nodded lightly. "A few. If you want, I can give you a tour of the place, show you which ones are ready and what I'm still working on."

I shut the final drawer. "Yeah, all right. That'll be helpful. I probably should go talk with Dominick first though."

Watt shrugged. "Sure, no rush. If we can't get to it today, I can walk you around tomorrow morning."

I grabbed my cap and turned to him. "Thanks." I wanted to go to the bathroom to see how I looked in the mirror and put my cap on properly, but I didn't know how to ask him to leave, or what his plan even was.

He rose from the chair and took a step toward me, not invading my space but certainly closer than what felt normal for someone I'd just met. He reached out and fiddled with the kerchief around my neck.

My breath caught at the intimate little gesture, but he met my eyes and smiled nicely.

"The end of your scarf was tucked under."

"Oh," I breathed, glancing to the side. "Thanks."

He stepped away from me. "Well, I better get back to work. You can find your own way?"

I nodded. Then he raised his hand in farewell and left without another word. I let all of my breath out as if clearing my lungs and filling them with different air would rid me of the strange feeling he'd left behind.

I entered the adjoining bathroom, which was simple but equipped with everything a modern person would need. There was a bathtub and shower, a toilet and sink, and a full-length mirror. As I stared at my reflection, placing the cap atop my head, I couldn't help but notice my flushed cheeks.

Watt may be friendly and easy to talk to, but is that all he is? He didn't cross a line exactly, and he didn't make any overt offers. Is he interested in me, or am I reading too much into it?

I pictured his bright eyes and ready smile. I reached up and touched the end of the kerchief he had so recently adjusted.

Do I want him to be interested in me?

As I'd told Alia, I hadn't been with anyone in a long time. I'd barely had enough time to sleep let alone date. And not having a phone or a computer had hindered that even more.

He's certainly attractive.

I shook my head at my reflection.

I'm definitely getting ahead of myself. I literally just met him. I don't know anything about him, and I just started this job. I need to worry about work and getting my feet under me.

Still, I thought that it must be a good sign, an indication that my life was really turning around, if I even had the time and energy to think about men.

Pushing the thoughts from my mind, I focused on making myself presentable. It really was a pretty dress, and it did accentuate my bust and waist. The rich darkness of the fabric brought out my naturally pale complexion. I wondered what the hotel's policy on makeup was as I had the sudden urge to return to my days of heavy eyeliner and black lipstick. It had been so long since I'd worn makeup, and the small bits I had left were probably long expired.

I imagined that Mr. Bennings would say that makeup, that kind in particular, was not period-appropriate. But the color and style of the dress were too much for me not to feel the urge, and I smiled into the mirror. I almost felt like myself again.

With a spring in my step and a confidence I hadn't felt in a long time, I shut my bedroom door to head back to the hotel. I hesitated only for a second in the common room before deciding to go outside rather than face that long, stone tunnel alone.

It was still chilly outside, but the rain had stopped for the moment. I held my cap down as the wind tried to carry it away. My heart lightened with every step, and I smiled with abandon. I felt good.

I found Dominick alone in the office. He looked up at me as I entered. "All settled?"

I nodded and approached his desk. "I think so."

He smiled. "Good. That desk over there is yours." He pointed to the desk farthest from his. "All of your photography stuff is in there or that cabinet." He nodded toward a tall, metal cabinet in the corner, which looked entirely out of place in the elaborate room. "Pull up a chair, and I'll show you what I've been working on."

I did as he asked, angling my chair to be able to see his

computer screen around his shoulder. He walked me through how far he'd gotten on the website, and I told him what Mr. Bennings wanted me to work on first.

"Oh, is this your family?" I pointed to a picture frame on his very clean desk.

He smiled warmly and pulled the photo toward him. It featured him and an Asian woman at the beach, the sun setting behind them. He was holding a little girl in his arms, and the woman carried a younger boy. They looked like the perfect, happy family. "Yeah, that's my wife and our kids. My son turns three next week, and my daughter just started the first grade."

"They're cute. Do you live close on the mainland?"

He replaced the frame. "Not too far. It's about an hour's commute total with driving and taking the boat. We moved here from Chicago; that's pretty standard in that area."

"Oh? From Chicago? Were they happy to move here?"

He bobbed his head in something between a nod and a shake. "It's taken some getting used to, but we were happy to get out of the city. We love nature, so we go camping a lot. There are some really great parks in upstate New York."

"I've heard that."

My heart warmed to hear Dominick talk about his family. He clearly loved them. It was nice to see that not all families were as messed up as mine. I wondered if we would still be that happy if my father hadn't died.

CHAPTER XXI.

JUST AS I'D RESET my password on my work email, Alia came into the office. She wore a navy-blue dress with a bubblegum-pink kerchief around her neck, and she'd tied a pink ribbon above the ruffles of her cap. The effect made her blue eyes stand out even more.

She grinned when I looked up from my computer.

"That looks great on you," I said.

She struck a dramatic pose. "There was never a doubt. Stand up, let me take a look at you."

I rose from my desk to show her my outfit.

"Gorgeous. Beautiful. I'm loving how dramatic the dark fabric is against that porcelain skin of yours."

I smiled as she drew nearer. "I was even thinking about breaking out some of my old goth makeup," I murmured confidentially.

Alia nodded enthusiastically. "Oh! I love that for you, very Wednesday-Addams-all-grown-up. Though, I do like this little pop of color, too." She pointed at the blue kerchief tied around my neck.

To his credit, Dominick let us gush and didn't say a word though I thought I saw a little smile just in the corner of his mouth at our exchange. But I couldn't swear to it.

Our conversation was interrupted when Lucero popped her head into the office, a tray with a domed cover in her hands. "Lunch is ready in the kitchen." She left just as fast as she'd come.

Dominick rose from his desk, buttoning his jacket as he did so. "Have you two seen the kitchen yet?"

We shook our heads at his question.

"All right. I'll show you the way."

We followed Dominick out of the office, where he led us down a hall along the side of the stairs and through an unobtrusive door. I didn't know what I was expecting, but it wasn't the gleaming white kitchen I entered. Everything was modern, as up-to-date as any high-end restaurant with stainless-steel counters, gas stove tops, and huge ovens. Shiny pots and utensils hung above the burners at the center of the space, and knives clung to a magnetic strip to one side of a counter.

We passed through the kitchen to another door, which opened into a small dining room. The room was much cozier than the kitchen, with cream walls and an oblong table at the center. Nora was placing plates before two women I hadn't met yet. The older of the two was perhaps a decade older than me with blonde hair and rosy cheeks. She was quite busty, and I wondered how the buttons of her dress held on so well. The younger was a lighter-skinned black woman closer to my age, maybe a little younger. She was skinny, not a curve on her.

They both smiled as we entered.

"Finally! Newbies!" the younger woman chirped.

"Welcome," the other said. "I'm Emmaline, and this is Gwynn. We take care of all the cleaning."

I immediately felt for these women, having just left that line of work myself. "I'm Wren, the photographer." It was getting easier and easier to say each time I uttered the heavy title.

I sat across from them, and Alia sat beside me.

Alia thanked Nora as she placed a chili dog and fries before us. "Alia. I'm a writer. So how long have you been here, Gwynn?" Alia asked, draping a napkin neatly onto her lap.

"Oh, I started about a month ago. Auntie Emma put in a good word for me."

Emmaline smiled over at the younger woman. "What wouldn't I do for my favorite niece?"

As I looked more closely at the women, I saw that their features were similar. They had the same eyebrows, same mouth, and the same cheeks.

Gwynn grinned. "Anyway, I'm so glad you're here. Maybe now Watt won't tease me for being the newcomer."

"Not likely," Watt added, coming in with Lucero.

Gwynn scowled at him as he sat on my other side. Lucero frowned and also took a seat. Once Nora sat down, everyone began to eat.

I looked around at the group. "Won't Mr. Bennings be joining us?"

"Mr. Bennings is a busy man," Nora said. "He takes his meals in his office."

I thought about that large, chilly office and wondered if he was lonely eating all by himself. Then again, maybe he welcomed solitude. I could more than identify with that feeling.

As we ate, Alia asked those who lived off-island about what it was like to commute and whether they had any recommendations on available rentals. She was particularly interested in Lucero's apartment building. Apparently, it was close to the harbor.

I simply enjoyed my meal. I couldn't remember the last time I'd had a chili dog. If I had to guess, I would say it was probably during some fundraiser my university's clubs put on. There was usually someone selling something on the quad to raise money for some cause or club activity, and it was often cheaper to eat whatever they were selling than in the cafeteria.

"Do you want some?" Watt asked, offering me a bottle of ketchup with an easy smile.

"Yes, thank you." I took the bottle and squirted it next to my pile of fries.

Before I could pass it down to Alia, Lucero said, "I'd like some as well." Her tone was sharper than expected, but I chalked it up to her wanting to say it quickly before the condiment got farther away.

"Oh, sure." I passed it back to Watt, who gave it to her.

Lunch didn't take very long, and we were soon back in the office with full bellies.

Alia was just saying she'd like to know more about the history of the manor and the art and furniture within it to inform her writing when Watt entered. He tilted his head at me. "Are you wanting that tour now?"

I looked over at my team. "Actually, we're kind of in the middle of a planning meeting right now. Why don't we do it tomorrow morning as you suggested?"

"Sure, no worries."

I could feel Alia's blue gaze on me as I watched him leave, but I couldn't read the expression on her face when I turned my attention back to her. "I'm sorry. What were you saying?"

CHAPTER XXII.

ABOUT MID-AFTERNOON, Mr. Bennings came into the office. I looked up from familiarizing myself with the camera he'd provided for me.

"Miss Mabry, Miss Geller, you two started early this morning, not to mention you've been traveling the last few days. You're free the rest of the day. I'm sure you want to get unpacked and settled. I'll see you in a few hours for your welcome supper in the dining room."

We both thanked him before he left.

Alia stood up from her desk and stretched her arms. "You want to head back to the dorms?"

"Yeah, but I need to send a few emails first, so you can go ahead."

"All right. Have a good night, Dominick. See you tomorrow."

Dominick wished Alia good night as well, then she left the office.

Now that I was off the clock, I opened my personal email account and started a new message.

Izzy,
I've arrived at the hotel all right. I just wanted to drop you
a message to let you know I'm safe. I'm still settling in,
so I will have a lot more to say when I've been here a bit
longer.

It's beautiful here, and everyone seems nice.
I'll send you a more detailed note later.

Love,
Wren

After hitting the send button, I started another message.

Cecily,
I'm here at the hotel, alive and settling in. Thanks again
for all your help and support.
You're the best.
Wren

I sent my promised email to Cecily and then shut down my
computer. "All right, Dominick. I'll see you tomorrow. Have a
safe trip back."

Dominick nodded with a little smile. "Have a good night."

The air felt warmer as I stepped out of the main door, and
I wondered if a warm front was moving in. Perhaps it would
actually feel like spring the next day. When I'd first gotten rid
of my phone, it was the weather app I had the hardest time
letting go of. But now, I found even that small bit of unknown
exciting. What would happen? Would it storm? Would it be
sunny? Perhaps I had too little excitement in my life.

When I reached the dorms, I could hear Alia humming in
her room.

"Hey, I'm back," I announced at the threshold of her open door. "I'm going to unpack."

She waved her hand in acknowledgment, not even pausing in her song.

Once in my room, I shut my door and took my time unpacking my things. Still, it didn't take me very long at all.

The springs of the bed squeaked as I sat down, though the mattress itself was comfortable. I glanced around my space. It still didn't feel like mine, even though my books were neatly lined up on the dresser along with my hairbrush. My alarm clock blinked 12:00 at me from the nightstand, and I looked at the cheap watch on my wrist so I could set it properly.

I squinted down at the white face, its small hands stuck at 11:37. I brought my wrist to my ear, but I heard no ticking. I pressed the knob on the side in case it had been pulled out by accident. It didn't budge.

I clicked my tongue and sighed. I didn't want to face another boat ride to go into town just for a watch battery. I wondered if it was too early in our acquaintance to ask Dominick to pick one up for me if I gave him the money.

I rose from the bed and opened the door to stick my head into the hallway. "Hey, Alia?"

"Yeah, hon?" she called back from down the hall.

"Could you tell me what time it is so I can set my alarm clock?"

"It's 5:39."

I set my clock and walked down the hall, stopping at Alia's room.

"Thanks for the time. My watch died."

Her space had been completely transformed. It looked like she'd lived there for a year with all of her personal things hanging on the walls and arranged on surfaces.

"Wow. I thought you were considering living off-island.

Won't you just have to pack everything up again?"

She shrugged. "I like to live in the space I'm in, make it my own. I even unpack my clothes when I stay at a hotel."

I chuckled. "Do you want a cup of tea or something? I'm about to see what we have in our little kitchen."

"Coffee would be divine if there is any. Thanks."

Leaving her to her unpacking, I walked over to the kitchenette in the common room to take stock of what our options were. There were tea bags and sugar packets neatly lined up in a wooden tea chest beside an electric kettle on the counter near the sink. There was a tin of ground coffee, and I found a glass pour-over coffee maker in a cabinet next to some mugs. The other cabinet held packets of chips and peanut butter crackers, but I wasn't sure whether those belonged to someone or if they were for the taking. The kitchenette even had a full-sized refrigerator, which held cream, bottled water, and soda stuffed among Tupperware, take-out containers, and yogurt cups.

I filled the kettle with water and set it to boil. Then I pulled down two mugs from the cabinet, put a teabag in one and settled the glass cone atop the other. By the time the water was boiling, I'd put a paper cone and coffee grounds into the coffee maker.

My tea was ready well before Alia's coffee, but that was to be expected. She emerged from her room just as I was stirring sugar into my cup. I wanted to get really wild and use cream as well, but I didn't know if I was stealing it from someone.

"Do you want sugar?" I asked.

"Nope. Just black for me." She flopped onto the couch that faced the television and tucked her feet under her, her slippers falling the floor as she did so.

I brought over her cup and set it on the table beside her.

She glanced up from her phone for only a second to thank me. I settled beside her, relaxing into the feeling of the glass warming my hands.

CHAPTER XXIII.

I WASN'T EVEN halfway done with my tea when Watt joined us in the common room, entering through the tunnel door.

"You look cozy," he said. "All settled in?"

I nodded, but Alia ignored him, smiling down at her phone. I wondered if she was texting Phil.

Watt dropped into the chair nearest the side of the couch I was sitting on. "How are you finding the place so far?"

"I like it," I answered.

His face grew serious, though he seemed to be fighting a smile. "You just be careful going around alone, especially at night."

I tilted my head.

He leaned forward, resting his elbows on his knees. "This place is haunted, you know," he whispered.

I scowled at him.

He raised his eyebrows. "Don't believe in ghosts?"

"No."

"Then you don't want to hear the story?"

To my surprise, Alia put her phone down. "I do."

Watt smirked. "It's true. The locals in town talk about it all the time. Apparently, our dark and broody leader, Mr. Bennings, is an orphan. And it's his parents who haunt the place."

My heart squeezed to hear about Mr. Bennings having lost his parents. And to have people gossip about it, people who probably didn't even know him, made me even more sad.

"His mother was actually the heiress to this place, and her family was very particular about whom she could marry. They wanted her to marry this one man, who was from a pedigree family that had lost most of their wealth. But she fell in love with one of the men who worked on the supply ferry."

"I can understand that," Alia said.

"Her family was totally against him. But when she got pregnant, she planned to run away with him. She went to the spot they'd agreed to meet. He never showed. She was heartbroken, and being in a bind, agreed to marry the man her family approved of."

My stomach sank.

"When she gave birth to the ferryman's baby, her new husband sent the child away. He was a jealous man, and he wasn't going to raise another man's bastard. Her heart was broken for a second time. All that she had left of the man she'd loved was gone. Still, she tried to live up to her responsibilities and became pregnant with her husband's child not long after."

I bristled at the word *responsibilities*. Maybe I was just too much in the lower class to understand that kind of pressure. If these were Mr. Bennings's parents, this wasn't that long ago, so it wasn't really a different time.

"She gave birth to our Mr. William Courtland Bennings."

Alia was leaning forward in her seat, raptly listening to the tale. "But how did they die?"

"It seems that even after all of that, she still held onto her love for the ferryman. Her new baby wasn't even six months old when she heard that her ferryman had died, had actually been killed by her now husband."

"No," Alia said incredulously.

"That very night, she came home, put the baby to sleep, and hung herself."

I gasped. "How awful."

"That's not the half of it. Turns out that the ferryman was never killed to begin with. The man who had become her husband had gotten wind of their plan to run away, and he had driven him out of town before he could meet up with her. All that time, he'd been trying to find a way back to her. Eventually, he got back to town and found out about everything that had happened. He hadn't even known she was pregnant with his child. So he came out to the island and shot the husband right in the heart."

My stomach rolled.

"Did they catch him?" Alia whispered. "The ferryman."

Watt shook his head. "They never did. But they say, the mistress still wanders around the place, waiting for her ferryman, chased by her jealous-crazed ghost of a husband."

"What nonsense," Nora huffed from the doorway to the tunnel.

I squeaked, nearly jumping out of my skin at her sudden appearance.

"Don't speak of things you have no knowledge of, Mr. Fitz," Nora scolded severely. "I was here when the master and mistress died. They were two of the most generous people I have ever known, and they loved each other dearly."

Watt shrugged, unperturbed by Nora's reproach. "That's just what I heard in town."

"Well, I will thank you to keep such tales to yourself in the future." Her face was flushed with anger, and she stomped over to her bedroom, shutting the door with a loud thud.

Alia glanced over at Nora's door before turning back to Watt. "Have you seen them? The ghosts?" she whispered.

He smirked, and I found myself swallowing a lump in my throat. "A lot of strange things happen around here. The sound of struggled breathing when no one is there, blasts of cold and hot, thuds and footsteps, I've even had to replace a few burst light bulbs."

Alia shuddered. "Oh God, I've got goose bumps. Look." She held out her arm to me, and all the hair was raised on it.

Watt met my eyes. "I hope I didn't scare you."

I very much doubted that; the glint in his eyes told me he'd wanted to get under my skin. Too bad for him. I wasn't scared. His story was tragic, not frightening. I was left with a feeling of great sadness.

Mr. Bennings grew up an orphan, and everyone around him whispered such horrible things about his parents.

If nothing else, I felt like the story gave me insight into why Mr. Bennings was so distant with everyone.

"You didn't scare me," I told Watt. "I'm not afraid of ghosts because ghosts don't exist."

"Speak for yourself," Alia said. "I'll be looking over my shoulder every moment I'm alone in this place."

"You have nothing to worry about," I assured her.

She turned her big blue eyes on me. "If I call for help, will you come hold my hand, Wren?"

I snorted a laugh. I wasn't trying to be insensitive, but she just looked so vulnerable that it was cute. "Sure. You just scream as loud as you can, and I'll come running."

"I got a set of lungs on me. They'll probably hear me on the mainland. Hopefully, Mr. Bennings doesn't mind if his guests are woken up in the middle of the night by my shrieks."

I thought back to the blog post I'd read about Moonseed Manor and how eagerly the writer had wanted to stay at the haunted house. "It will probably be good for business. There's a market for everything."

CHAPTER XXIV.

———

A FEW MINUTES after Nora had arrived in the dormitory, she emerged from her room, all trace of her irritation gone. "I came to tell you all that dinner is ready. Mr. Bennings will be joining us in the dining room shortly."

We obediently followed her through the tunnel into the kitchen. The trip felt a lot less intimidating this time. I don't know whether that was because I'd already been down there once before, or if it was because I wasn't alone with just Watt.

In the kitchen, Nora grabbed a covered platter. "Everyone, please take something with you to help set the table."

I took up a large salad bowl, its vinaigrette dressing so strong it made my nose tingle. Each of us laden with a dish, we followed Nora out to the stairs and up to the second floor. Then we walked down the gallery and entered the dining room.

The dining room was made entirely of arched windows with paned glass. There were doors on either side of the long room, which led out to a planked balcony. Beyond the balcony, on the north side, there were the brick paths of a carefully tended garden, its inhabitants just springing to life in little shoots of green. And past the garden, there was a pavilion overlooking the northern shore. The ceiling of the dining room was ribbed, like most of the ceilings in the place so far, in honey-colored wood. There were square tables set around the room with four chairs at each. Two of these tables had been pushed together near an upright piano by the entrance. There were only five chairs at the table, enough for everyone since the others had returned home to the mainland. Beautiful white china had been set on the white tablecloths, and candlelight flickered in polished silver candlesticks.

Nora arranged the food we brought as she saw fit, taking our dishes from each of us in turn.

"Good evening." Mr. Bennings announced his presence just as Nora was fixing a slightly askew fork on the table.

We all returned his greeting, and he gestured for us to take our seats and begin serving.

Nora had made roast beef, mashed potatoes, gravy, carrots, and salad. As soon as she removed the covers from the dishes, all the delicious smells filled the room.

My mouth watered, and I breathed deeply. I eagerly spooned the food onto my plate when it was my turn.

I was only a few bites in when Mr. Bennings picked up his wineglass. "Are you settled in?" he asked from beside me before sipping at his wine, a dark red as it swished in the bowl.

"I'm almost done unpacking, but I have everything I need," Alia answered.

I glanced up into his dark eyes, obsidian in the candlelight. "Yes, thank you."

He inclined his head in a nod of acknowledgment and returned to eating for a while. "I didn't mention this before, but every employee is permitted to stay in the hotel at least once. It will give you the experience of what guests might expect. So while you wander around, think of what room you'd like to stay in."

Alia paled at Mr. Bennings's offer. Perhaps Watt's earlier tale still rang in her ears. But my heart thrilled at the idea. Getting to stay in this beautiful mansion in one of these gorgeous rooms? It was awesome enough to get to work here, but to live in such a historic work of architectural art, even for just one night, was an experience I very much looked forward to. It would be like living in one of my favorite novels.

"Thank you," I said excitedly.

Mr. Bennings paused to look at me before bringing his fork to his mouth.

I tucked back into my meal, and the conversation stilled for a long while with only the sounds of forks and knives clinking against plates interrupting the quiet.

I hesitated as I placed my silverware on my empty plate. But remembering Mr. Bennings's earlier words of kindness, I pushed that feeling aside. "Maybe it's too early to ask this, but what is the hotel's policy on staff having visitors?"

Mr. Bennings's eyebrows raised ever so slightly, and he frowned in a thoughtful way. "Are you wanting to invite a guest?"

"Well, I have a younger sister. She's sixteen, and I was just wondering what the policy was."

His expression seemed to say that he'd never given the idea much thought. "I suppose it wouldn't be a problem for your sister to stay in the dormitory for a few days provided that it's your day off. You could, of course, go to the mainland to visit and stay there as well."

My chest warmed, and I gave him a smile. He didn't know what this meant to me. A chance to see Izzy after so long? I knew she'd love it here. "I don't see myself going to the mainland very often. I get seasick. Which reminds me. Nora, how often do you go into town for supplies?"

"Once or twice a week, depending on what I need."

"Could you let me know the next time you're going? My

watch battery died, and I need to get a new one."

"Oh, me too. There are some things I need to get as well," Alia seconded.

"I may have an extra battery you can have," Watt said. "I can check to see if it fits your watch anyway."

"Could you? That would be great. I don't really want to get on a boat again if I can avoid it."

"Sure." Watt nodded. "We'll go check it out after dinner."

I thanked him.

"Mr. Bennings." Alia drew our boss's attention to her. "Have you ever seen anything strange here?"

Mr. Bennings flinched. "Strange how?"

Alia's voice was light as if she wasn't asking anything of consequence. "Well, you know, this house is really old, right? A lot of places like this have complex histories. If there were rumors of the house being haunted, for instance, I could play that up as a marketing gimmick on the website. People love that kind of stuff."

I watched Mr. Bennings's face closely. He didn't move, didn't even change his expression. But it seemed to me that his skin had lost all of its color.

I admonished Alia internally. She'd heard the story. Did she not believe it? Was she trying to reassure her own fears? Or did she just want to see how he'd react? Either way, I felt it was an insensitive question to ask.

"I don't want that to be the focus of our marketing efforts," he said simply. Then he rose from the table, placing his napkin beside his plate. He bowed his head slightly at us. "I wish you all a good night, and welcome again to Moonseed Manor."

I frowned, my chest tightening as he left the room.

CHAPTER XXV.

I STARED DOWN at the brick path before me. I couldn't get the look of Mr. Bennings's pale face when Alia had asked about ghosts out of my mind. Did he believe this place was haunted by the ghosts of his parents? Or had the mention of the town's insensitive gossip upset him?

"This way," Watt said, leading me onto a path, which branched out from the one that led to the dorms. "What are you thinking about?"

I looked up at the sky. The grey clouds overhead weren't nearly as dark as they had been throughout the day, though I could only barely see the sun slowly approaching the western horizon. "I'm thinking about Mr. Bennings."

"Oh, jeez. Ouch. Here I am trying to get a little time alone with you, trying to get to know you better, and you're thinking about another man?" His tone was playful, so I didn't know whether to take what he said seriously or not.

"But don't you think that it's just too sad?" I asked, pushing his words aside in favor of the subject that was niggling at me. "I mean, not only to lose your parents at such a young age but to have people whisper about it."

Watt led me past what appeared to be a small, white house. I could see lines of laundry machines through the windows. Then he slid open the door to a large work shed.

"I wouldn't feel too bad for him." He flicked on the lights. "All that inheritance certainly makes his time easier than ours."

I frowned. I understood what it was like to work just for a crust of bread, but even I knew that money wasn't everything. I would work just as hard as I had been for the rest of my life if I could get only a few minutes more with my dad. And I wouldn't have had the strength to even do what I had been doing if it wasn't for Izzy. It was those bonds of love that mattered most, and money couldn't buy that.

Watt's workshop was just as modern as Nora's kitchen, with tools and yard equipment that would make any suburban dad feel like he was at Disneyland.

He held out his hand. "Can I see your watch?"

I unbuckled the wristband and placed the watch in his palm. He took it to a long workbench and pulled a prying tool from a wooden drawer set into the bench. I watched his practiced movements, so precise, almost gentle, as he removed the back and carefully took out the battery.

"Were you serious before?" I asked quietly.

"About what?" He squinted at the battery, then walked over to a chest of drawers and opened one with a little squeak of metal on metal.

"Were you really trying to spend time alone with me?"

He paused, his hand hesitating in the drawer before pulling out a pack of flat batteries. "And if I was? What would you say?"

I licked my dry lips. "I would say that there's no harm in us getting to know each other better. That's how friendships start, isn't it?"

Watt placed the batteries beside my watch, his amber eyes

fixed on mine. "Just friendships?" His voice was low and warm.

I glanced away. "For now."

He smiled, and I saw that my words had encouraged him more than tempered his interest. And it was clear to me now that he was interested.

Turning his attention back to my watch, he put in a new battery, snapped the back closed, and set it to the right time.

I thanked him as he approached, holding my hand out for it. But instead of putting it in my palm, he buckled it on me himself. His fingers were calloused but deft, warm against the sensitive skin of my inner wrist. I stifled a shiver at the feeling of his touch, and he smirked down at me—fully knowing the impact he had.

Still, he didn't linger. After my watch was securely on my wrist, he pulled back and kept a friendly distance. He seemed to respect my words at least.

"We better be heading back." I moved toward the door. "It's been a very long day for me."

He followed behind without a word, flicking off the light and closing the door after us.

I wanted to go to bed early. But as I stared up at the unfamiliar ceiling of my room, tucked under the same blanket I'd taken to college, I couldn't quiet my mind. It was an unusual occurrence for me. I was so used to falling asleep from exhaustion. My mind never had the time or energy to wander while I waited for sleep to take me.

But here I was, my thoughts swirling like a primordial galaxy of celestial bodies I had yet to discover and explore. My life had so completely changed from what it had been a few weeks before. I hadn't gotten my first paycheck yet, hadn't even properly started working. But, for the first time in a long time, I was excited, looking forward to the next day.

Those thoughts led me right to Mr. Bennings and the

chance he'd given me, which morphed into his sad story—true or not—and his reaction to Alia's question. And then I hopped over to Watt, protesting at the idea that I would be thinking of Mr. Bennings instead of him. And on and on it swirled, flowing from subject to subject and back again.

As my eyes lost focus of the ceiling overhead, the springs of my mattress squeaked softly. I gasped, quickly sitting up and clutching my knees to my chest. My too-full brain lost all traction as I held my breath, staring at the foot of my bed, where it felt like someone had just sat down. My heart pounding in my ears—drowning out the sound of the wind whistling outside my window—I squinted into the darkness. But, of course, there was nothing there.

With a heavy sigh, I shook my head at myself. *How ridiculous. I'm clearly delirious from lack of sleep.*

I settled back down, forcing my eyes closed and evening out my breaths, but restlessness wouldn't allow my limbs to relax. With another sigh, I sat up and climbed out of bed. After shoving my feet into my boots, I pulled on a hooded sweatshirt over my pajama pants and oversized T-shirt and quietly slipped out of my room.

CHAPTER XXVI.

I CREPT DOWN the hallway, past Alia's and Nora's closed doors, and out into the night.

The air was cold but calm, and the clouds had broken apart enough for me to pinpoint where the moon was in the sky even if I couldn't see it clearly.

Without making the conscious choice, my feet followed the brick path toward the greenhouse. And as I entered, the warm, humid air relaxed me. *A while in here should make me tired enough.*

I walked the circuit of the space, strolling through the lush green leaves to the herb garden and back. Finally, I settled on a bench and leaned back on my hands to look at the sky through the glass roof.

My mind was just starting to lull when a shuffling step and the rustle of leaves announced that I wasn't quite alone. I froze and flicked my gaze to where the sound was coming from, my eyes widening as Mr. Bennings came into view.

"Oh," he said, his voice soft in the hushed space. "I'm sorry to disturb you." Then he turned to leave.

"You're not disturbing me," I assured him, rising to my feet. "I just couldn't sleep. I can leave if you want this space to yourself."

"Is your bed uncomfortable?"

I blinked at his assumption. "No, not at all. It's just I'm in a new place, and I'm overly excited, like the night before the first day of school." I huffed a self-conscious laugh. "I guess I just gave myself away. I was that kind of a nerd, the one who got excited when summer break was over."

Mr. Bennings watched me, neither agreeing nor refuting. "I wouldn't know," he said finally. "I went to boarding school, and I didn't leave even during breaks."

"Oh," I breathed. I didn't know what else to say. I could infer that he went to a boarding school because he was rich and alone. I wondered if he didn't have any other family—aunts, uncles, or grandparents—who would have taken him in. But if he spent even breaks at school, they clearly didn't want anything to do with him if they existed at all. Still, I took this little nugget of information he'd shared about himself as a sign that perhaps he wasn't as unapproachable as I'd thought. "Did you also have a hard time sleeping tonight?"

He was silent for so long that I bit my lip, worrying my question was impertinent and prying.

"I always have trouble sleeping," he answered at last. "I often take a walk at night to ease my mind. When the sky is clear, the stars are quite beautiful way out here."

I nodded slightly. "I look forward to seeing that."

Silence fell again, heavy and thick.

"Have you seen the tower room yet?" he asked.

I shook my head.

"Would you like me to show you?"

My eyes widened at his offer. "Right now?"

He hesitated. "Unless you would prefer not."

"No, I'd love to see it. Please, show me."

He turned his back on me but not quickly enough that I didn't see the small smile on his lips. "Follow me."

Cold air blasted into me as we left the greenhouse and headed toward the manor. We entered via the kitchen door and passed through to the reception hall. We didn't speak as we walked.

Mr. Bennings glanced back at me only for a moment when we started up the stairs. Then we began to climb. Each floor looked relatively the same—a landing with a long gallery stretching out ahead—until we reached the fifth floor. More precisely, there wasn't a fifth floor, just a short landing with two more flights above it. On the sixth floor, a door halted our progress. Mr. Bennings opened it and entered.

The room at the top of the stairs was breathtaking. The carpet was that same cobalt and gold that covered the stairs, and the walls were large, peaked windows. There was a canopy bed, draped with sheer, burgundy curtains. At the corner of the room, there was a walled-off area, and I guessed that must be where they had added the bathroom. In another corner, there was a rounded pillar, paneled in wood.

Mr. Bennings walked toward the pillar and pulled on a knob I hadn't noticed. A curved door opened to reveal a spiral staircase. "Would you like to see the roof?"

I nodded and followed him up the metal stairs.

Upon reaching the landing, I gasped at what I saw. We were on the very top of the tower. There were low battlements that acted as a safety wall and spires on each corner. But it was the sky that really took my breath away. Up here it was so big, so open. With the wind blowing at my clothes, it almost felt like I was flying.

"It's really beautiful up here when the sky is clear. It's just you and the stars." His voice was soft, gentle with a sort of longing that felt like the pain of unrequited love.

I looked over at him, his face turned upward, his hair ruffling in the breeze. And he looked so very human to me. Gone was the cold and unapproachable man who kept his professional distance from everyone. Even his intensity had dulled in the sheer vastness of the unending sky.

He was just a man. A man who nobody truly knew, who nobody cared to know.

I don't know for how long I stood staring at him, but he eventually met my eyes in the darkness. And after a heavy moment, his cool demeanor slipped back into place.

"Perhaps we should head down now, Miss Mabry. It's getting late."

I didn't like that distance that returned to his voice, and I pushed against it. "You can call me Wren."

"Yes, but I won't."

My heart squeezed, and I felt like a puppy that had been scolded for jumping up on the couch. As I climbed down the spiral staircase, I wondered if it wasn't that nobody cared to know him, but rather that he didn't want to be known. Did he not want to be close to people? Did he just prefer his own company? Had he been hurt somewhere along the way? Or did he have something to hide?

CHAPTER XXVII.

I SLEPT restlessly that night. I couldn't remember my dreams, but whatever had happened in them left me with a feeling of dread when I awoke.

It was early when I slipped out of bed though I could see the sun was up and shining already. Still, I was used to getting only a few hours of sleep, so by the time I opened my bedroom door—already dressed for the day—my mind was clear and ready to work.

I found Alia in the common room in a thick bathrobe with her hair up in a towel, fuzzy slippers in front of the couch where she sat. She had already done her makeup, and she was sipping from a cup of coffee. The news on the television was on mute, closed captioning running in black and white along the bottom of the screen.

"How long have you been up?" I asked her, making my way to the kitchenette.

"I've been up for a while. I know our suggested start time is eight, but I'm still used to getting up from that long D.C. commute. Oh, Nora told me last night that all the stuff in the cupboards and fridge is for us unless it's clearly marked."

"Okay. Thanks." I felt so luxurious when I stirred cream into my tea and poured hot water into a bowl of presweetened, peaches-and-cream oatmeal.

I was happily chewing my oatmeal from the chair beside Alia when she stared over her coffee cup at me. "So how are you finding it so far?" she asked.

I shrugged. "It's a lot different from my life before, but it's good so far. You?"

She was less forthcoming than I expected her to be. "I'm withholding judgment for the time being."

"I'm looking forward to seeing the rest of the manor. I'd like to start taking pictures today if I can. Watt's going to show me around the house this morning."

Alia pursed her perfectly pink lips. "Do you mind if I come? I didn't get to see a lot of it yesterday."

"Of course I don't mind."

I could feel her blue eyes analyzing me. "What do you think of Watt?"

I nearly choked on my oatmeal. "I don't really know him to have a fixed opinion," I hedged.

She tapped her painted nails thoughtfully on the glass of her mug, and when she finally spoke, her voice was hardly above a whisper. "There's something off about him. I feel like he's hiding something."

"You think so?" *He's not the one who I feel like is hiding something.*

She nodded. "I do, and I'm going to find out what it is."

After finishing her coffee, Alia went back into her room to get dressed. It wasn't long before Watt emerged from the men's hall.

He smiled brightly when he saw me sitting there. "Good morning."

"Morning." I watched him cross to the kitchenette and grab a banana from the fruit bowl on the counter. Alia's warning still whispered in my ears. "Alia's going to join us on our tour this morning. I hope that's all right."

He didn't say anything, but his eyes seemed to be disappointed. I took my dishes to the sink and washed them.

Watt leaned closer to me, his hand on the edge of the counter near the sink. "You wouldn't be trying to avoid being alone with me now, would you?"

I didn't look over at him, concentrating on drying the cup in my hands. "Should I be?"

He put his hand on the cup I held, and I looked over at him. "I would never do anything you don't want me to do."

I stared at him for a while, and he didn't look away. His eyes were earnest and open, and I couldn't imagine why Alia thought he was hiding something. I dipped my head in acknowledgment of his words.

Satisfied, he took the mug from me and put it away in the cupboard.

Before he could turn his attention back to me, Nora came into the common room. We exchanged morning pleasantries, and Watt and I moved out of the kitchen to give her some space.

I watched her go about making herself some tea while I leaned against the back of the couch. Curiosity bubbled up inside me, and I couldn't stop myself from giving it voice. "Nora, you said yesterday that you have worked here for a long time, right?"

"Yes."

"And you said that you knew Mr. Bennings's parents before they died."

She didn't respond but waited for me to continue, her profile to me.

"Has he always been sort of distant?"

"What do you mean?" she asked cautiously.

"Well, I asked him to call me by my first name yesterday, and he told me he wouldn't. I got the impression that he likes to keep a distance between himself and others. But then I remembered that he called you by your first name."

She bowed her head, and a look of sadness made her face droop. "Mr. Bennings can do as he wishes." Her voice was soft despite her words of reproach.

"Why are you worried about what he calls you anyway, Wren?" Watt said. "He's our boss after all. Wouldn't it make sense for him to keep a professional distance between himself and us? Besides, we're only lowly workers to him. Think about it."

I frowned. What he was saying wasn't exactly wrong. There was just something not quite right about how Mr. Bennings acted. I couldn't put my finger on it.

Before I could get a grasp on the elusive thought, Alia entered the common room. "All right, I'm ready. Is it too early to start the tour?"

"I'll get my hat," Watt muttered, trudging toward his room.

Alia watched him go, a sharp look in her eyes.

I raised an eyebrow. "Do you really think he's hiding something?" I whispered so Nora wouldn't hear me.

"Absolutely. I told you before—I'm great at reading people."

CHAPTER XXVIII.

"OH MY GOD. I'VE died and gone to heaven," Alia said as we entered a room on the first floor between our office and the kitchen.

The room was paneled in dark wood with bookshelves all around the walls. There was a set of double doors, which led out onto the porch that wrapped around the back and north side of the house. Two cozy, wingback chairs sat before a heavy, stone fireplace, a standing lamp between them and small reading tables on either side. The rug, which covered most of the wood floor, was a dark green with a Greek-style border.

I sat down at the small desk in the corner, imagining what it would have been like to write a letter here over a hundred and thirty years ago.

Alia immediately went to one of the shelves and opened an old book. She gasped. "This is a first edition Robert Louis Stevenson," she breathed. "I shouldn't be touching this." She carefully returned the book to the shelf as if it might explode.

I leaned back in the chair, then tilted my head when I saw

one of the desk drawers hadn't been shut all the way. Curious, I opened it.

"Don't worry about it," Watt said. "All guests and employees are allowed to borrow any books from the library."

I pulled out a small book with a fabric cover of dark blue. It was scuffed and torn at the corners, and I carefully opened it. From the cover, I'd thought it was an old book, but it was a journal, and the paper inside was clearly modern—white with printed lines.

"That's not the point," Alia choked, scandalized. "Are there any other precious works of literature I should look out for when I decide to casually pull a book from the shelves?"

"No idea."

The contents of the journal I held were handwritten in dark ink. The letters were clear but seemed a little hurried. Given the format of the first page, I surmised that this was a book of poetry.

"Let's move on to the parlor," Watt suggested.

I closed the desk drawer, taking the book with me. I was curious about its contents, and Watt had said we could borrow books from the library.

We followed Watt past the office and entered a large room at the other end of the house. The ceiling was ribbed but all white, and the chandelier overhead was simple with electric lights covered with glass lamp chimneys. On one end of the room sat a couch facing a fireplace with a low table in between. A large mirror, blackening with age, hung above the mantle. The couch looked more about style than comfort, with stiff cushions and spindly legs. The room was completely symmetrical, the other side looking exactly the same down to the couch, fireplace, and mirror. The only thing that it had that the first side didn't was a white tarp folded on the floor, a bucket of paint and a paint pan on top of it. Between the two halves were small, round café tables, only two or three chairs at each, also with tight cushions and spindly legs. Directly across from the entrance was a set of glass doors, clear on the bottom and stained above, which led out to the porch.

"It isn't quite finished yet," Watt told us. "I have some painting to do, and I need to resilver the mirrors."

"Are these pieces original?" Alia asked, pointing at the chairs.

"Some are."

She turned to me. "Wren, when you take pictures of these rooms, could you send them to me as well? I have a friend who works in antiques, and he might be able to give me some interesting information that I can include in my write-ups."

I told her I would put them in the shared drive as Watt led us out.

"What have you seen of the second floor?" he asked.

"We saw the dining room last night, and Mr. Bennings's office," I said, following him up the stairs.

He glanced back over his shoulder. "So you saw the men's drawing room too then?"

"Was that the one with the moose head?"

"Yeah."

"Then yes."

"What about the ladies' drawing room?"

I shook my head.

"All right, we'll go there next."

Upon reaching the second-floor landing, Watt headed down the gallery. Arched windows on the outside wall illuminated the paintings opposite, all depicting pastoral themes. I slowed as one painting in particular caught my eye. It featured a shepherdess, her lamb lying at her feet, sitting beside a young man on a log. The man had his arms encircling her, his fingers on a flute, which he held up to her lips as if teaching her to play. I don't know what made me stop to look at it, perhaps it was the man's bright red coat. But as I stared at the painting, I decided there was something almost lewd about it.

Alia passed me in the hall, and I tore my eyes away from the painting to catch up with her and Watt.

They entered a door just before the one that led to the dining room.

The furniture in the ladies' drawing room looked exponentially more comfortable than that of the parlor. Each couch and chair was upholstered in white featuring a red floral print. The cushions were thick and plushy, and the short legs were modestly covered by pleated skirts of the same fabric. Even the round tables had long tablecloths with tassels all along the hems. The carpet was a deep red with swirls of crimson.

A grand chandelier, sparkling gold in its candle-style lights, hung from the gilded, ribbed ceiling—geometric designs in blue between the ribs patterned like a kaleidoscope. There were more tables and lamps than any room needed. But there was a conspicuous lack of paintings. Instead, one wall was taken up by a huge stained-glass window. Its carefully constructed shards depicted a large tree, colored ribbons hanging from its branches and wild grape vines climbing up its trunk. Beneath the tree, women danced—their hair loose and their feet bare.

My mind raced at the possibilities of how to capture the room's beauty. I wondered what time the sunset would hit the window and if I could even hope to photograph the effect it would have on the space.

"What will the hotel use the two drawing rooms for now that times have changed?" Alia asked.

Watt shrugged. "No idea. I just fix things. That's a question for Bennings."

CHAPTER XXIX.

ON THE THIRD floor, we passed the door Mr. Bennings had said was his bedroom.

The gallery in this hall featured paintings of the sublime art movement: ships ravaged by the unforgiving sea, a storm gathering over the mountains, a volcano—all smoke and lava. The works were so violent, so vivid that I felt dread creep over my skin.

Watt opened a door farther down and waved us in ahead of him. "This is the only guest room on this floor."

I looked up at the vaulted ceiling, which was squared off and featured a teardrop, stained-glass window near the top. The heavy headboard of the bed stood before an arched window in yellow and blue. Despite how large it was—and how high the ceiling—it felt cozy and warm. The bedspread, settee, even the cushion on the vanity chair were a dusty orange, and the rug was a warm combination of sand, yellow, and orange. Beside a heavy armoire, a door led to a bathroom.

"I still have a few chairs to reupholster for this room," Watt said. "So you should probably wait to take pictures. I'm going to set up a little dining table over there. But it's finished enough to sleep here if you choose it for your one-night stay."

Alia walked behind the bed to look out the window. "This catches the setting sun?"

Watt confirmed that was correct.

I ran my fingertips along the marble top of the vanity, the mirror above tall and framed in dark wood. I followed one of the veins running through the cream-colored marble, the cool stone sending a shiver up my arm and into my chest.

As I stared down at the lines, like cracks in a sheet of bedrock, my eyes lost focus and the rest of the room seemed to fade away. My head felt heavy—my restless night catching up with me.

From my peripheral vision, I saw Watt walk behind me in the reflection. The movement brought my eyes back into focus, and I shook the sleepiness from my head.

"I'll show you the ballroom next," Watt said from his place near the door.

I looked over my shoulder. Watt was still near the door, not two feet into the room, and Alia was at the window.

Who did I just see behind me in the mirror?

My heart leapt into my throat; the hair on my neck and arms stood on end. I stared at my own reflection, scanning the mirror for any smudge or spot that might explain my mistake.

I found none.

I shook my head, forcing myself to sigh out the breath I'd been holding. *It must have been a trick of the light, a bird flying past the window that reflected in the mirror.*

I ignored the fact that the mirror didn't face the window and that the movement had looked very much like a man in a flat cap walking from one side of the room to the other—a man I had mistaken for Watt. I scolded myself for being so shaken even as I quickly left the room.

Watt tilted his head at me while I passed him, and I wondered what expression I wore.

"The ballroom?" I asked.

"Right there." He pointed to the door at the end of the hall.

With every step I took away from the guest room, I felt more and more silly at having been so alarmed. And as I crossed the threshold into the ballroom, I forced any lingering feelings of unease away.

Even though it was called a ballroom, there wasn't space enough for more than seven couples to actually dance. It looked more like a concert hall with a musicians' gallery looking down on the nearly empty space. There were arched windows all down the long wall and a simple, wooden chandelier hanging from the dark, vaulted ceiling. I would have believed it was a chapel before it was a ballroom. I stared up at the high ceiling and imagined the acoustics were pretty good. As I analyzed the room, my earlier moment of fright completely faded.

"We probably won't use this as a ballroom," Watt said. "We might set out chairs and have a concert, but I think Bennings is planning on using it more for wedding-related things."

"This would be a great space for a wedding," Alia agreed. "I'll have to ask him about his plans in more detail so I can market it properly."

"Is this space ready to photograph?" I asked.

"Yeah, I didn't have to do much in here."

"What exactly do you do?" Alia asked, her tone more curious than accusatory. "You've mentioned that you paint and reupholster and resilver mirrors."

"I do a bit of everything. I'm a little bit handyman, little bit gardener, even a restorer if it isn't beyond my capabilities."

"That all takes a lot of varying skills. You're pretty young to know how to do all that."

I could see where Alia was going with this. She was prying,

trying to get any hint at what Watt might be hiding. But he wasn't playing along.

He just shrugged. "I've always been good with my hands, and I'm a quick study."

Alia hummed her acknowledgment.

He meandered back toward the door. "Are you ready to see the other guest rooms?"

While we followed him out, I saw Alia purse her lips at Watt's back, squinting as if she could read his mind if she tried hard enough.

As we passed the guest room to return to the stairs, I quickened my steps even as shame heated my face.

We headed up to the fourth floor next.

"This floor has taken the most work," Watt said from ahead of us on the stairs. "We even had to hire contractors to help out. It used to be the female servants' dormitory; the male servants lived out where we are now. So before last year, it was one big room with beds all in rows and only one bathroom."

The long gallery of the fourth floor had only one door, with nothing above the ballroom at the far end of the hall. The door led to a hallway with two doors on the left and three on the right.

"They're all pretty much the same," he said.

We entered the first door on the left. It was small, much smaller than the tower room and the third-floor guest room, but it didn't feel cramped. This was the first room I'd entered without a vaulted ceiling though it did have a molded square pattern. There was a bed with a simple headboard, nightstands on either side, and a dresser in the corner near the paned window. The attached bathroom was even smaller than the one in the dormitory with only a sink, toilet, and shower stall. The most luxurious part of the room was the oriental rug, which was dark grey with purple flowers.

"Are all these rooms ready to photograph?" I asked.

He nodded at me from the threshold. "Yeah, these ones were finished first."

"So there are six guest rooms total?" Alia asked.

"No, seven. There's also the bridal room in the tower."

For some reason, I could feel my cheeks flush as Watt mentioned the tower room. I pictured Mr. Bennings's expression as he gazed up at the sky in the hushed darkness. Looking back on it in the light of day, going to the tower with him in the middle of the night had felt like a very intimate experience.

CHAPTER XXX.

"HEY, WHERE are you going?" Watt pointed up the stairs as I started heading down. "The tower room is this way."

"Oh, Mr. Bennings showed it to me last night. I'd like to go grab my camera and get to work. Thanks for giving me a tour."

Watt frowned, his amber eyes looking severe in the colored light that filtered through the stained-glass windows of the tower. But a moment later, his expression shifted as if the frown had never been there. "No problem. I'll let you know when the rooms I'm still working on are ready for you."

"All right. Thanks."

Dominick had yet to arrive when I walked into the office. I flipped on the lights and made my way to my desk. After turning on my computer, I sat in my chair and opened a drawer to put away the book I'd borrowed from the library.

I blinked in confusion and pulled my wallet from the desk drawer. *I don't remember putting it there.* But then I shrugged and put the book in the drawer with my wallet.

I checked my work email to see if there was anything I needed to address; there wasn't. Then I went over to the wall to retrieve the camera battery I'd started charging the day before. I was just sliding it into the camera when Alia entered the office.

"That was quick," I commented as she dropped her bag on her desk.

"I'm telling you—there's something wrong with that guy. The minute you were gone, he just pointed me up the stairs and told me to find it myself. And did you see how he dodged my questions in the ballroom?"

I didn't really see that as dodging her questions, but I did think that refusing to show her the rest of the tour was kind of rude. I wondered what that was about.

Alia turned her blue eyes on me seriously. "Has he said anything to you that was suspicious or off-color?"

I thought about it for a moment. "Not that I can think of. He was a little forward about wanting to get to know me, but that's not so suspicious as it is surprising."

Alia crinkled her eyebrows. "Why is it surprising?"

I shrugged. "I guess it isn't. I'm just not used to guys being so frank. But then again, I haven't dated since college. Maybe men get more unambiguous as they get older."

"How did you feel about that, him coming onto you? Did you get any warning vibes?"

"I wouldn't say that… I mean, it's flattering when someone attractive pays attention to you. But I don't think I know enough to feel one way or the other about it. I told him we could start getting to know each other as friends."

Alia nodded. "That's smart, very sensible." Then she sighed heavily. "Maybe I'm wrong. Maybe he just doesn't like me, and I'm picking up on that. Not liking me isn't a crime…yet." She snorted at her little joke. "You're a grown woman. I'm sure you know what you're doing. Just…be careful. Okay?"

I knew Alia's heart was in the right place, and she was looking out for me. I smiled over at her. She was proving herself to be a good friend, even if we hadn't known each other for very long. I appreciated her concern. "I will," I promised.

Alia sat at her desk and crossed her legs. "So did you see anything spooky while we walked around?"

I froze. *Did she?*

"I know I'm a big wimp, but I was almost disappointed at how mundane everything was after he made such a big deal about that ghost story yesterday. I was so worked up last night that I was going to refuse to do my one-night stay. But after this morning, I'm not worried at all. What room are you going to request to sleep in?"

My jolt of anxiety eased. If Alia hadn't seen or felt anything, it had definitely been my imagination. "I think I'm going to stay in the third-floor guest room." *There's nothing in there, and I'll prove it to myself.* "What about you?"

"I liked the tower room the best, I think. Plus, if we're marketing it as the bridal room, it would be good to get a feel for it before I write about it. You know, see the sun rise and set from the windows and such."

Just then, Dominick came into the office, a kind smile on his face. "Good morning."

We greeted him, and Alia asked him if he'd had a good night.

Hanging the camera around my neck, I rose from my desk and told them I was going to start on the fourth floor in case they needed me for anything.

As I reached the landing between the second and third floors, I saw Mr. Bennings descending the stairs. When his dark eyes met mine, he gave me a cool nod. "Good morning, Miss Mabry."

I flinched as he said my name. Gone was the man who'd shown me the night sky the evening before, gone was the man who'd given me a small smile in the greenhouse—a smile he'd tried to hide.

He looked even more pale than he had the day before, and I wondered if he was coming down with something or if he hadn't gotten any sleep.

"Good morning. I wanted to thank you for showing me the tower last night. The walk helped me sleep." *Though not well.* "How about you?"

"I'm glad to hear it." He didn't sound like he cared one way or the other, and he fully ignored my question.

I tried again. "Watt showed Alia and me around this morning. I'm heading up to the fourth floor now to start on the guest bedrooms. Would you like me to show you when I'm finished?"

"I'll see them when Dominick posts them on the website."

My heart sank. I'd thought for sure he'd want to see my work before then. He'd praised my portfolio after all. And wasn't it normal for a boss to want to monitor his employee's work? Perhaps it was his way of saying he had faith in my abilities, but I couldn't help but feel like he was discouraging me from getting even a step closer.

"All right," I murmured, my tone doing little to hide my disappointment. "I'll get to it then."

CHAPTER XXXI.

———

ONCE I WAS standing in one of the guest bedrooms preparing to take photos, I knew I'd need some equipment. The windows were too small to provide enough natural light in this room, and the bulbs made everything look yellow. I returned to the office to get lighting and reflectors. Then I had to go down again for a step stool.

It took me almost an hour to set everything up just the way I wanted it before ever even pressing the shutter. Then I had to move everything around to get the room from a different angle.

It felt good to concentrate on photography again, to worry about camera settings and composition, lighting and angle. It came back to me so naturally, and my heart lightened. I'd made it. I was doing it for real. This wasn't a dream or even a hope; I was actively living it. I soon found myself so consumed that I completely lost track of time.

"Hey," Alia popped her head into the room, and I jumped at the sound of her voice. "Lucero said lunch is ready."

"Oh," I breathed out my surprise. "Okay. Let me turn all this stuff off, and I'll be right down."

As I descended the stairs alone, I heard a deep voice whisper. I stilled, looking around to see where the sound was coming from.

But no one was nearby.

The man's voice whispered again, and I listened hard, unable to make out what it was saying. A shiver ran over my skin when I heard a giggle.

What the hell is that?

The sounds seemed to come from behind the wall below me on the stairs. I slowly took a step down, wondering how quickly I could get down the stairs without tripping. And then the wall creaked open.

I swallowed a scream, the sound a strangled squeak, and my heart hammered. *It's just the linen closet.* I sighed and clicked my tongue at how ridiculous I was being.

"So stupid," I muttered.

Watt slipped out from behind the secret door before it was fully opened. The top buttons of his shirt were undone, revealing the defined line between his pecs. His hat was askew.

"Hey!" he said much louder than I expected, shutting the door behind him with his foot.

"Hey… What's up?"

"Oh, nothing. I just got something on me while I was working so I came up here to change my shirt." He buttoned his shirt the rest of the way.

"Okay."

"What do you think is for lunch today?" His tone seemed excited. He tilted his head to indicate that we should start heading down to the kitchen.

I eyed him but followed his lead. "How would I know? Does Nora post a menu or something?"

"I've never looked, actually. I'm not a picky eater, so I just let myself be surprised."

"Guess we'll find out when we get there then."

"So how is your stuff going so far?" he asked when we reached the first floor.

"I think it's going all right, but I won't really know until I look at the images on the computer later."

"Don't forget that you promised to show me your portfolio."

"It's not like I'm going anywhere. We've got time."

He followed me down the hallway to the kitchen. "As long as you don't forget."

Lunch turned out to be open-faced roast beef sandwiches, likely the roast beef that was left over from dinner the night before, not that I minded.

Gwynn and Alia were laughing about some new meme that was going around on social media, and Emmaline was asking after Dominick's kids.

Lucero joined us a few moments later, returning from delivering Mr. Bennings's lunch tray. We all started to eat as soon as she sat down.

Rather than moving on to the next guest room after lunch, I plugged my camera into the computer to see whether what I'd shot so far was viable.

Toggling through the RAW files, I quirked my mouth. *Not too bad. A few minor tweaks in Photoshop should do it.* After uploading the files to my computer, I spent the rest of the work day touching them up.

"I put the finished images on the shared drive," I told Dominick as he pulled on his coat to leave for the evening. "Let me know what you think of them tomorrow. I still have a few left to tweak. I'll do that tomorrow morning. I want to get them to you room-by-room so you aren't waiting on me to get to your stuff."

"I appreciate that. Thanks. Have a good night." He gave us a wave and headed out.

Nora, Watt, Alia, and I had dinner that night in the kitchen dining room. Mr. Bennings did not join us, and I was under the impression that was the normal state of affairs.

Despite not sleeping well the night before, I wasn't very tired when I changed into my pajamas that evening. I glanced over at the bedside table, the brass headboard digging into my back as I sat up in bed. My wallet rested atop the poetry book I'd borrowed from the library, both of which I'd grabbed before leaving the office for the day.

Scooting off the bed, I took the book to the common room, thinking the couch would be a much more comfortable place to read. The common room was deserted. I tucked myself into the corner of the couch nearest the lamp, resting the book on my knees.

There was no title or name written inside to tell me who it belonged to or who might have written it. Turning to the first page, I read.

Oh, what cursed fate is mine,
Last of a damned bloodline.
Born to die an early death,
Closer with each strangled breath.

Stalked by shadows of the past;
Their revenge they'll have at last.
Ticking, clicking, the clock goes,
Heedless of my pressing woes.

Do I deserve to know cheer,
Or only sorrow and fear?
I exist to pay the price
For my forebears' wicked vice.

Quietly, I endeavor
To bear my fate whatever.
Hold my tongue and close my eyes,
Swallow my desperate cries.

Some are meant to live in light,
Others in the darkest night.
Settle now and wait for death;
Be grateful to have drawn breath.

A thrill ran through me as the fear and sorrow of the writer seeped into me. Every pen stroke, every line screamed an anguished cry of unavoidable fate. I was captured, enthralled. It felt so real, so vivid. *Who wrote this?* I wanted to reach out, to grab hold of the narrator and shelter them from the storm of their inner turmoil.

CHAPTER XXXII.

PULLED BY A sense of urgency, I turned to the next page.

What relief I feel
At finally departing
This torment that is life.
And starting
My eternity with you—
At last starting!

For now—after so long!—
My dearest love,
We can finally meet
Whether below or above—
I have kept you waiting
High above.

Were you fair
In your life
However long ago?

My sweet wife—
You do not mind that I presume
To call you wife?

For I know
In my soon dead heart
That you, my destined one,
Are waiting for me to depart.
Be patient, my love,
For I will shortly depart.

You will know me,
When together at last,
Though we have yet to meet.
But gentle and fast,
Whisper your name to me now
So I might find you fast.

I let out a shaky breath. I could feel the writer's longing, could see the unsteady strokes of his trembling hand. The utter sense of hopelessness resonated within me to my deepest core. Why was he dying so soon that he had yet to have the chance to find love in this life?

My nose began to burn as my eyes filled with tears. He was in so much pain, yet he still found that little silver thread—that even when he died, an unknown love would surely be waiting for him in the void.

My soul trembled and tears spilled down my face as a sob caught in my throat. I tried to stifle the sound of my crying, my chest screaming at the effort. Was it silly to cry for someone I'd never met, someone I would never meet? It was entirely possible that this person didn't even exist; writers didn't always write about themselves after all. Even so, his words spoke to me, stroking my heart in a way it had never been touched before.

Eventually, my tears abated, and I wiped my face on the long sleeves of my nightshirt. Though the sweet sorrow of his words still sung within me, I felt lighter than I could ever remember feeling. My heart-wrenching cry had washed away all the stress, all the exhaustion that had piled on top of me over the last few years. I smiled down at the little book, a warm glow shining within me.

Just as I was turning the page to the next entry, Watt came into the common room, an empty glass in his hand. He wore pajama pants with cartoon tacos on them and a V-neck T-shirt.

He pulled up short upon seeing me nestled in the couch. "Whoa, you scared me there for a—Hey, what's wrong?"

I sniffled, my nose somehow both stuffed and running. "Nothing."

His amber eyes lit with concern, and he sat beside me on the couch, putting his cup down on the table and angling his body toward me. "What do you mean 'nothing'?" he asked gently. "You've clearly been crying."

I gave him an embarrassed smile. "Yeah, but it was over something stupid. I was just reading a sad poem."

His answering chuckle enveloped me in warmth. "You artists are so sensitive. It's adorable. What were you reading?"

I offered him the book, and he took it from me. "I don't know. I found it in the library this morning. It doesn't have a name on it, but it's really incredible... The words moved me to my very soul."

He flipped through the pages, his eyebrows rising. "You found this in the manor's library?"

"Yeah, is that so surprising?"

He met my eyes seriously. "Yes, it is...because I wrote it."

"*You* wrote it?" I shouted before cringing at how loud my voice came out while others were trying to sleep.

Watt frowned. "Are you that surprised? Don't you think I'm capable of writing good poetry?"

"N-no…I mean, yes. I mean, it's not that. You just…don't come off as having such dark tastes. I guess I wouldn't have thought you'd be carrying around such longing and sorrow."

"We all have darkness in us. Don't you agree?"

I gazed into his eyes, no longer warm but hardened like stone. "I do, actually. I think the darkness is where we face our true selves. Everything starts and ends there… You really wrote these?"

"You don't believe me?"

I searched his expression, and my face flushed, my heart pitter-pattering in my chest. "I do…" I lowered my eyes to the book in his hands. "I'm a little dumbstruck that I'm even able to talk to the person who wrote something that touched me so deeply. I feel a little embarrassed to be honest."

Watt reached out and placed his hand over mine. A jolt ran through me, and I looked up at him again. "You don't have to be embarrassed with me." His voice was low and intimate. "I'm glad to hear my words touched you deep inside… Are you a little less hesitant to get close to me now?"

I stared at him. His mussed hair was brassy in the yellow light of the lamp, and his lips looked pink and soft. The expression in his eyes was one of hope, and I couldn't help but hear the echo of the words he'd written—longing for a love he would not meet in this life.

"Y-yes," I whispered.

I wanted to know him, wanted to know the man who could move me so thoroughly with just a few lines on a page. And I wanted him to know me.

His thumb stroked the back of my hand, and warmth spread through me. He gave me a gentle smile. But as he leaned slowly toward me, my chest tightened.

"Do you mind if I read the rest?" My voice came out rushed and a little frantic.

He pulled back, and my flash of anxiety eased. "Of course not." He removed his hand from mine and offered me the book.

I crossed my arms, holding it to my chest. "Thank you. Do you mind if I ask you where you got your ideas? I mean…do you really feel this way?"

Watt shrugged and rose from the couch, grabbing his glass. "Here and there. It's all my imagination."

"Oh." I don't know why, but I was a little disappointed at his vague answer.

CHAPTER XXXIII.

THE NEXT morning, I went to the office early to send Izzy an email. I wanted to give her the good news—that she was allowed to come for a visit. I told her I wouldn't be able to buy her a ticket until after my first paycheck, but I asked her to consider when she would want to visit during her summer break.

My work email had a message from Mr. Bennings, in which Alia had been copied, asking us to let Emmaline and Gwynn know which rooms we would like to stay in that evening.

By the time Dominick and Alia came into the office that morning, I was already done fixing the photographs I'd taken the night before.

"You're an eager beaver this morning, aren't you?" Alia commented.

"Oh, I understand. Sometimes I come in early so that I can get off early, too," Dominick said.

That wasn't why I had come in early, but I didn't argue. The fact was that when I'd finally crawled into bed the night before, I'd slept like a rock. I wasn't used to getting more than six hours, so I was up and ready way too early and itching to get moving.

It seemed I had yet to acclimate to the slower pace of this new environment, so used to the mad hustle just to survive.

I spent the rest of that morning in another guest bedroom on the fourth floor. Just as Watt had said, this one was much the same as the other, but with a red and black rug rather than grey and purple.

Again, Alia came to get me for lunch, and again I spent the afternoon fixing the photos I had taken in the morning.

I hadn't planned on getting off early when I'd started before everyone else, but Alia shamed me into not working over.

"What time did you get here this morning?"

"Seven."

"Then you need to leave."

I hesitated; I still had photographs to fix.

"Look, we're living where we work. If we aren't careful, our whole lives will become the job. Go on, it's sunny outside. Go for a walk or something."

I looked out the window at the blue sky beyond the covered porch and grabbed the camera.

"Leave it," Alia said firmly.

I pouted, and I could see the turmoil in her blue eyes.

"Don't look at me like that… I'm trying to watch out for you. It will be sunny again, and you can take all the photographs you want."

I drooped. "I know. You're right." I left the camera on my desk and wished Dominick a good evening.

I went outside via the parlor doors, stepping onto the wraparound porch. To my surprise, not only was it sunny, but it was also very warm.

I squinted into the bright day, staring past the still-budding garden to the pavilion. The garden was set up in a grid pattern with nine large beds cut through with brick paths. The inner three beds held tiny shoots of spring flowers just coming to life. Large weeping willows grew in each of the six outer beds, yellow flowers cascading from their picturesque branches.

I breathed deep, the warm air smelling of cool lake water as seagulls called overhead. Then I stepped off the porch onto a path through the garden. I strolled slowly amongst the blowing trees, their yellow petals raining down and covering the ground. It was beyond pleasant, and I hadn't realized how much I'd really needed leisure time. Sure, I didn't really know when to let go, but with that little push, Alia had given me a wonderful gift.

I continued on to the pavilion, which was constructed in Gothic revival style like everything else. It had spires on its peaked roof and arched openings between every delicately carved pillar. I rested my hand on the spiraled wood as I stared out at the lake beyond.

The blue waters of Lake Ontario sparkled in the sunshine, and I couldn't help but smile. I'd spent so many summer days at various lakes and rivers growing up. I could hardly think of a happy family memory where we weren't at some cabin, lake house, or campground. And while I never ventured into the boat with my dad and Izzy, I'd loved to walk on the sand or dip my feet in the water off the dock. I remembered the smells of sunscreen and hot dogs roasting on an open flame. I remembered my dad playing the guitar as my mom sang songs in that same red flannel she always wore when the sun went down.

She'd been so different then, like an entirely separate person. I'd often wondered how someone could change so much. Had it only been grief of losing my dad that had made her who she was now? If she had loved him that much, then why had she remarried so fast? But then even when we were happy and whole, she'd never been a particularly independent person. She'd relied on my dad for almost everything. Maybe it was just in her personality to mold to whatever would best reflect the man she was with.

Despite who she was, or maybe because of it, my father had always taught Izzy and me to follow our own paths, to be independent and self-reliant.

The scraping sound of a heron's call drew my attention to the rocky shore. Standing on a boulder near the water was a great blue heron, its yellow bill pointed skyward as it continued to vocalize its opinions.

I smiled to myself. Herons had been my dad's favorite birds. We'd kept a count of how many of them we saw every year. It was as if me thinking about him had conjured the bird into existence. As sad as it was that I hadn't had much time with him, he'd taught me so much. He'd been wise and loving, and I was lucky to have had him for as long as I did.

As I watched, the heron spread its massive wings and took flight.

"I hear you, Dad," I whispered, my words stolen by the wind. "Don't worry about me."

CHAPTER XXXIV.

CONTINUING my walk, I followed a path from the pavilion toward a long outbuilding made of the same grey stone as the manor. It also featured the same peaked roof and arched windows, the top half of which were stained glass.

Curious, I pulled open one of the beveled-glass doors and stepped inside.

"Whoa," I whispered, my voice echoing off all the stone surfaces.

Carved stone pillars ran through the center of a deep, rectangular hole in the floor, wide steps leading down into the unfilled pool. A separate square, walled in with its own walkway, had been cut out of the rectangle. I assumed this was a hot tub. High on one wall were three spouts, and I wondered what they would look like if turned on, sending streams of water into filled pools.

I'm going to have to ask Mr. Bennings when we will be filling this pool. The pictures in here will be incredible.

Feeling optimistic about my work ahead, I left the building by a door on the other side and stepped onto a short path that led to a gorgeous beach. This wasn't the rocky shore the pavilion overlooked. It was all soft sand and would be easy on bare feet. The beach stretched all along the western part of the island, and I told myself to return to get pictures of the sunset.

Not wanting to get sand in my boots, I walked through the grass at the edge, eventually meeting back up with a brick path, which ran between the manor and a group of trees. I headed toward the trees.

Though I knew that I was still close to the shore, the trees dampened the sound of the waves. If they had been fuller, I might have thought the distant sound was their leaves rustling together. The new leaves did manage to filter much of the harsh sunlight. Birds chirped their spring mating calls, and my boots made little sound on the pavement.

It was peaceful here; I might have believed that I was alone on this island had I not known otherwise. This quiet walk felt almost sacred. I looked up into the many branches and wondered how long these trees had stood on the island. Had they been here when the house had been built?

The path eventually ended in a round overlook, stone benches set into the wall. The trees had opened enough so that I could see the lake, but the spot was still shaded by their limbs. The overlook seemed to float above the lake as if there wasn't a shore between me and the body of water. The wind off the lake nearly blew the cap from my head. It was cool and fresh, and I breathed deeply.

Sitting in the shade on the wrap-around bench, the wind on my face, I watched the sun sparkle off the water. The clouds were white and fluffy in the distance and held none of the ominous darkness they'd held upon my arrival. I sat there for a long time, rising reluctantly when I glanced at my watch and realized I would be late for dinner if I didn't leave.

Alia was excited about our stay in the manor that evening,

particularly about seeing the sunset from the tower room. "You can come up and watch it with me if you want," she offered as she passed me a bowl of sweet peas.

"I might do that," I said. "But I also want to see how the setting sun hits that window in the third-floor guest room."

She nodded. "That's true. Well, it's not like the sun won't set tomorrow and the next day."

As I slowly chewed my meatloaf, I wondered if the sky would be clear enough to see the stars that evening. *Does Alia know about the roof of the tower?* Since Watt hadn't properly shown her the room, I didn't know if she'd found the inconspicuous knob in the pillar that hid the spiral staircase.

But just as I was about to ask her, something within me hesitated. That place was secret, a special moment between Mr. Bennings and me. Did I really want to share that with anyone else?

I scolded myself internally. *That's pretty selfish of me. It's not like telling her about the roof will erase that memory. And besides, who says it was a special moment? I shouldn't give more weight to things than they deserve. In any case, she should know about it for work.*

"Did you see the spiral staircase up to the roof?" I asked her. "I bet the stars are amazing up there when it's a clear night."

"No, I didn't see that. I'll have to check it out when I get up there," Alia answered.

"They really are beautiful," Watt agreed, directing a smile at me. "I'll take you up there one night and show you."

Conflict tugged at my heart. It didn't feel right to go up to the tower with Watt. But then I remembered the feelings the words of his poetry had evoked within me. He wasn't just the too-forward man I'd initially taken him to be. He was a man with a depth of feeling that pulled me under and drowned me in sweet darkness.

With the thought of what beautiful words being enveloped in a starlit sky might elicit from him, I smiled. "I'd like that."

After dinner, Alia and I went to the dormitory to gather just a few things for our overnight stay. Then we headed back to the manor.

My arms full of clothes, a few toiletries, and Watt's book, I separated from her on the third-floor landing. "Have a good night," I called to her as she continued up the stairs.

My heart hammered in my chest as I made my way to the room I'd be staying in that night, passing by the paintings of nature's most violent expressions. I stopped on the threshold, my hand on the knob, and looked down at the door I'd just passed. I'd forgotten that my room would be beside Mr. Bennings's.

<h1 style="text-align: center;">CHAPTER XXXV.</h1>

———

I WATCHED the sun set while lying atop the dusty-orange blanket, staring at the ceiling from the bed. The light coming through the stained-glass window had bathed the room in shards of blue and yellow, and it was even more beautiful than I'd imagined it would be.

As the day faded, all was quiet in the house, peaceful, and I felt even sillier for having been startled upon my first visit to the room.

I took a shower and prepared for bed. The rug was stiff but soft beneath my bare feet as I padded from the bathroom to the bed. It was still much too early for me to sleep; I wasn't a bit tired. So I turned on the bedside lamp and picked up Watt's book.

As I leaned my back against the cushioned headboard, the soft mattress yielding to my weight, I suddenly felt stifled—the air too thick and too hot. I puffed my cheeks out and blew a heavy breath, then walked around the back of the bed to open a window. The metal latch dug into my palms as I tried to pry the window open, but it just wouldn't budge.

I must be overheated from the shower. I'll take my book down to the library and leave the bedroom door open to let some of the humidity out.

As I grabbed the book from the bed, I made a mental note to tell Watt about the stuck latch before any guests came to stay.

But as I neared the door, I hesitated and looked down at myself. I wore short pajama shorts and a cami. Needless to say, it wasn't an outfit Mr. Bennings would have called period-appropriate.

"Oh, whatever," I muttered. "It's not like he's going to see anyway. And besides, is he going to tell guests what kind of pajamas they can wear?"

I reached for the doorknob and stopped, squinting as a shadow broke the line of light coming from below the door. My heart jumped, and my breath caught in my throat.

Then I sighed out my surprise. Mr. Bennings was just next door. He was probably passing by. "Hello?" I asked. "Mr. Bennings?"

The shadow moved away without a sound.

"Wait!" I called, pulling open the door and thrusting my head into the hallway.

But there was no one there.

My mind spun, and I blinked in confusion. I'd been sure there was a shadow, and there was no time for anyone to get down the hallway to another room, especially without me hearing footsteps.

Unease crept over me, raising goose bumps on my skin. I rolled my shoulders against the feeling, thinking I should kick Watt for telling me that stupid ghost story.

By the time I reached the library, I felt back to normal. I hadn't encountered anything on my descent, as was to be expected.

I turned on a reading lamp and settled into one of the wing-backed chairs that faced the empty fireplace. It was much cooler down here, and I sighed with relief, opening Watt's book and flipping to the next poem.

On the wet and slippery bricks, I stood, a shivering boy of six,
Waiting, cold and lonely, on this island I'd heard tell.
Never had I been here since I'd been born the cursed prince,
Born to cursed parents, parents whom in this house did dwell,
But, sent away as a babe, where I never did dwell.
      Finally returning to this hell.

Now my father, being dead, had a will that needed read.
Thus, I waited for admittance in a gloom I couldn't dispel.
Though I'd never met my sire, now but ashes from the fire,
He would sometimes write me letters, letters that would wish me well,
Rambled, scrambled, were his letters that always wished me well,
      And of my fate did he foretell.

Brought inside and wrapped up tightly, while the fire flickered brightly,
A servant served me cocoa with a sweet and soothing smell.
Not 'til morrow would we meet in my father's study suite
With the lawyer and my guardian, my guardian Maybell,
The only mother I'd ever known, my sweet guardian Maybell.
      And of my fate did it foretell.

What of my mother? You might inquire, of whom many did admire,
Before she perished young and beauteous while crying her farewell.
Her face I could not remember, too small when she died in cold November,
Still I called for her many nights, nights I'd ask her story to tell,
And though a tot, easily moved to fright, my guardian would tell,
      And of my fate did she foretell.

Cursed blood she said I had, which would one day drive me mad,
When I returned to the house where my forebears did dwell.
These stories I did appraise near that brightly flickering blaze.
Up my spine ran a shiver, a shiver I couldn't quell.
Lightning flashed and thunder rumbled in a storm that wouldn't quell,
          And of my fate did it foretell.

Pulling closer my wrapping, I closed my eyes against the clapping,
Tensing tightly while I swallowed my childish yell.
All sense did I lose when another flash of storm alighted on a form
In a room where I was alone, alone where my forebears did dwell.
On whom could have joined me my thoughts did dwell.
          And of my fate did it foretell.

"Oh, you gave me a start," says I, clutching my heart,
My hands trembling with a fright I couldn't dispel.
But with a sigh, I peered at my visitor who'd quite suddenly appeared,
Smiling to reassure him, reassure him all was well.
His response, or lack thereof, did not bode well.
          And of my fate did he foretell.

In the flickering of the blaze, stood the man as if in haze,
His eyes sparkling beads of black like the deepest pits of Hell.
Shimmering, foggy was his shape, with a mouth that hung agape.
Gasping, rasping, soundlessly, soundlessly unable to tell.
His hand clutching his throat but still unable to tell.
          And of my fate did he foretell.

As a boy of merely six, my understanding was nix,
Terror clawing at my mind like a beast one can't repel.
To my great increasing fear, this visiting specter came near,
Reaching out his ghostly fingers, fingers tightening on my throat's swell.
Dread mounted every second while my lungs refused to swell.
          And of my fate did this foretell.

Not another moment thereafter, with a dark but silent laughter,
Did my harasser cease his assault though why I could not tell.
And just as he'd formed, vanished in a flash of storm.
Trembling with tears, tears which unabated fell,
I recalled all the tales and prophesies of how my family fell,
   And of my fate did they foretell.

I could feel the narrator's terror, the ghostly hands upon his throat, and a shiver ran over me.

"Miss Mabry," a voice whispered from behind me.

I let out a high-pitched shriek.

CHAPTER XXXVI.

"MISS MABRY!" Mr. Bennings shouted, gripping my shoulders as he stood in front of my chair.

I sighed heavily, dropping the book to the ground and covering my face with my hands. "Oh my God, I'm sorry. You scared the living crap out of me."

He pulled his hands away. "Are you all right now?" he asked softly.

My heart still hammered in my chest. "Yes, I'm fine. I was just reading this scary story and was surprised when you called out. I'm sorry I screamed."

I dared to peek up at him. His dark eyes were lit with concern, and his pale brow was puckered. For some reason, his anxious gaze made him look very much his age. But before I could wonder why that was, he stepped away, his expression closing off.

"It's nothing to apologize for." He knelt to pick up the book I'd dropped. "What were you reading?" As he rose, he looked at the book, and his eyes sharpened. "Where did you find this?" His voice was barely above a whisper.

"Oh, I found it in that desk over there. Watt said that we could borrow anything from the library, and then when I found out he'd written it—"

"Who did you say wrote it?" he demanded, cutting me off.

I blinked. "Watt said he wrote it…"

He frowned severely, and I found myself babbling to make it stop. "W-would you like to read it? It really is excellent. I haven't read anything this good in a long time."

He closed his eyes and took a slow, deep breath, and when he opened them, his usual expression had returned. He held the book out to me. But when I took the other end, he showed a little resistance in giving it back. Still, I pulled it from his hand with little effort.

"Are you interested in dark poetry and stories?" I asked him, holding the book to my chest.

His gaze slid to mine, and he raised an eyebrow. "Are there any other kind?"

I huffed out a laugh, but his stony mask didn't change. I sobered. *Oh, maybe he really only reads that kind.* "Did you come down here for a book or…"

"Actually, I was going for a stroll, and I saw the light on. I'm sorry to have disturbed you. I'll leave you to your reading."

He turned to leave, and I shot to my feet. "Would you mind some company?" I blurted out.

I could already tell he was going to refuse by the look on his face, and I prepared myself for the lash of disappointment. But as he opened his mouth, his eyes shifted to over my shoulder. His face drained of all color, and pure terror shined in his black eyes.

"No," he said in a strangled voice. "I'm sorry. I—" His words were cut off as he gasped for air. He doubled over, clutching at his throat as if he couldn't breathe.

"Mr. Bennings, what's wrong?" Panic raised the pitch of

my voice, and I surged toward him. "What's going on? Are you okay?" I rested my hand on his lowered shoulder. "Are you choking?"

His eyes shone with a desperate plea for help.

My heart hammered out the call to action. "I'll go get you some water."

But as I started to move toward the kitchen, he firmly grabbed me by the wrist, his fingers cold and bloodless. "Air," he choked out.

"You need fresh air?" Taking his hand, I pulled him toward the double doors, which led outside.

The moment we were on the porch, he began coughing, sucking in the cold air that whipped around the corner of the house.

"Mr. Bennings…are you all right?" My hand trembled in his.

As he continued to take deep gulps of air, I thought the worst of it was over. But the longer he didn't answer, the more anxious I became.

"Mr. Bennings?"

Still nothing. He didn't look at me as his breathing slowed.

"W-William?" I murmured, unsure.

His dark eyes met mine in the light of the waxing moon. There was no more panic in them, no more cool distance. There was only gentleness and sorrow. "Corey," he said quietly.

I blinked at him.

He squeezed my hand, and I was suddenly very aware of how close we were standing. "I never went by William. I was always called Corey."

My heart tapped out a little rhythm. "Okay, Corey," I whispered back. "Are you all right now?"

"Yes, thank you."

I hesitated, not wanting my words to break this moment.

But then I went ahead anyway. "What happened? Did you have a panic attack?"

He frowned and pulled his hand from mine, stepping away from me. "Not exactly."

I wanted to cross my arms and click my tongue. I wanted to sigh and walk away. I wanted to point a finger at him and demand to know why he was purposely putting distance between us again, why that cool, unwelcome expression was back on his face.

Had I asked so much? Was it such a big deal? Was he embarrassed over something like this? Or was I so untrustworthy that he wouldn't even talk to me? Was he worried about keeping a professional distance even after what I'd just seen? Wasn't it natural to get closer the more time and experiences we shared? Why was he trying so hard to stop that from happening?

I pursed my lips, Watt's words echoing in my head. Perhaps Corey really did look down on me, maybe I wasn't on the same level as him because I worked for him.

But the moment that thought crossed my mind, I knew it wasn't true. He'd never really given me any reason to believe that he thought he was better than me or that I wasn't worth the same as he was. Maybe I was wrong, but I still got the feeling that he didn't want to get close to anyone. It wasn't just me.

I wanted to know why. He was such a peculiar and intriguing man. His intensity pulled me in closer, demanding my full attention whenever his black eyes met mine. But his professional distance pushed me, and everyone else, away. With every little detail about himself that he let slip to me, I wanted to know more. And the more he closed himself off, the more curious I became. What was he trying to hide? What did he so desperately want to keep to himself?

Something had happened that night. That much was clear. Something was bothering him, something he wanted to handle alone. But with the image of his terrified and pleading eyes still in my mind, I wasn't going to let that happen. He needed help. I didn't know what with, but I was going to find out. I wasn't going to let him face something so terrible alone. Not him.

"Good. Then would you like to go for a walk with me?" I gave him the friendliest, most carefree smile I could muster.

CHAPTER XXXVII.

COREY STARED down at me for a heavy moment. "Perhaps another time. It's chilly since the sun went down, and you aren't even wearing shoes."

"It's not that cold," I argued just as a gust of wind made me shiver.

He snorted and hid his smile a little too late.

"Okay," I relented. "It's a bit cold. But I can go change."

His answer was obvious. He was going to refuse.

"I'm still a little shaken," I pushed before he could say anything. "I…don't really want to be alone right now, and I think a walk will help me calm down before bed. Won't you come with me?"

It wasn't a complete lie. Sure, I wasn't as shaken as I said, but I wanted to stay in his company, and I likely wouldn't be able to fall asleep if I went back to my room now.

The more I watched him, the more I noticed the subtle changes in his expressions. The tiniest twitch of his mouth, the slightest arch of an eyebrow, the faintest glint in his eye. Overall, he still appeared cool and distant, but I was paying much too close attention to not see what lay underneath.

"All right," he said, still using his professional tone.

"Okay. Great. I'll be right back." I turned to rush inside, looking back over my shoulder. "Stay right there. I won't be a second."

From his stiff posture, it didn't look like he was going anywhere.

I ran upstairs as quickly as I could, my footsteps thumping on the carpet. I pulled on the dress I'd worn during the day but left my cap and kerchief off. I was back on the porch within five minutes.

"Thanks for waiting," I gasped, my heart still pumping from the exercise.

He inclined his head in a polite nod.

"Is there anywhere you would like to walk?" I asked.

"Pick wherever you like."

"All right. This way then." I pointed to the path that headed to the overlook I'd seen earlier in the day, then stepped off the porch.

Corey easily matched my strolling pace.

The night closed in around us. The cool wind blew my hair into my face, and I tucked it behind my ear as I stared down at the bricks before us. The moon was out, and it did a decent job of illuminating our way. An owl hoot-hooted from the trees ahead, and another answered back. It was the perfect evening.

I peeked over at Corey while he walked beside me, his hands clasped behind his back. He didn't look like he would be starting a conversation anytime soon. We entered the trees, and a heavy hush insulated us.

"Why do you go by Corey?" I asked, my voice sounding quiet but close.

He turned his head away from me, staring into the trees on

his other side. "It's a shortened version of my middle name," he answered after a long pause.

"Ah." There wasn't much else I could say, so I fell into silence again. I pursed my lips, trying to think of anything that might further the conversation. "You said you like dark stories before. Who's your favorite writer?"

"Poe," he answered without hesitation. "He has such a way of recognizing the darkness that lives within us."

"I agree. I feel like reading 'A Telltale Heart' changed the entire direction of my life. I used to get in trouble in high school because I would hide a collection of his works behind my other textbooks. I have no idea how I managed to pass algebra."

"He does captivate readers."

But just when I thought we'd found a topic to talk about for some time, the conversation lapsed again.

"Why did you decide to call the hotel Moonseed Manor?" I inquired, truly out of ideas to find out more about him.

"Because that's what the house has been called since it was built. Would you like to see why?"

He stopped walking. We were right in the middle of the path between the house and the overlook, surrounded by trees.

"Yes," I responded, hoping he wouldn't lead me back to the house just yet.

He held out his hand to me, and my heart skipped a beat.

"The ground is uneven, and the moon isn't very bright through the trees," he explained. "I don't want you to trip."

Swallowing against the dryness in my mouth, I gently placed my hand in his. I was surprised at how warm it was, given how frozen it had been in the library. His fingers were long and uncalloused.

With a soft tug, he led me off the path and into the trees. He kept our pace slow, likely to avoid a falling incident, and I was in no hurry to get wherever we were going. I couldn't hear the rustle of last year's leaves beneath my feet over the sound of my heart pulsing in my ears.

"There. Do you see that tree over there?"

I peered into the darkness and found the huge poplar, its branches far overhead. Vines crawled and twisted around its trunk, clusters of flowers growing from them.

"Those vines are called moonseed. Later this fall, it will grow berries that look remarkably like wild grapes. But they're poisonous. The only way to tell the difference is that the pits of moonseed berries are shaped like crescent moons. When my family bought this island, the place was nearly covered in the stuff, so they called it Moonseed Manor."

"That's really interesting," I said, glancing up at him. "I should come back here when it's light out and take a picture for the website. I think people would like that story."

He nodded and turned to start back to the main path.

But I held my place, and my arm tugged him to a stop. "Corey..." I could feel my face flush at the sound of his name on my lips; it sounded so soft, so intimate in this secluded place. I continued on, ignoring the feeling. "What happened earlier, in the library, does that happen often?"

"With greater frequency as of late," he admitted in a tone that said he didn't want to talk about it.

"You don't have to tell me. But I want you to know that if you need any help, if you want to talk about it, or if I can make it better in any way, you can come to me."

I couldn't see his face, couldn't see what expression he was making as he looked away from me, but I could feel his hand tremble in mine. Still, when he spoke, his voice was firm though quiet. "Thank you, but I'm fine. It's no more than I deserve."

I scrunched my eyebrows. "What do you mean?"

He paused so long that I knew he wasn't going to answer.

"If you wouldn't mind, Miss Mabry, could we head back? I'm exhausted."

I flinched at his use of my formal name. Were we still so far apart? "All right. I'll let it go if you'll call me by my given name from now on. Deal?"

He frowned. "Very well."

It's a small win, but it's still a win.

Corey led me back to the brick path and released my hand the moment we reached it. My limbs felt heavier as he pulled away. But as disappointed as I was by how very little I'd gotten out of him, I did feel a little closer to him. And as he said goodnight at his bedroom door, I felt even more determined to uncover the mysteries of Mr. William Courtland Bennings.

CHAPTER XXXVIII.

ONCE TUCKED into the bed of the guest room, I took up Watt's book to read one more poem before sleep.

I.
Breathe in the fresh air—
Clean air!
What a breeze, so soft and fair!
How it drifts, drifts, drifts,
In the chilly mountain morn.
And my spirit how it lifts
When the hollow's mist shifts
Amongst the oak and thorn.
As we walk, walk, walk,
All us miners in a flock,
To the dark and stifled lair
With no air, air, air, air,
Air, air, air—
Where the deep and cramped mine has no air.

II.

Breathe in the closed air—
Heavy air!
What an unfortunate place this is we share!
Through hour upon hour,
Below the surface scour,
For but lumps of dirty coal.
Just for pennies and some blisters
Do I climb down in this hole,
Never minding the toiling toll.
For my mother and my sisters,
For my family I do care.
I do risk; I do dare!
And I whisper a hushed prayer
That I'll see my wife so fair
And my children in a pair,
Just as many a forebear.
Always sweating, always fretting
In this thing that we call air
In this air, air, air, air,
Air, air, air—
In the thick and laden air.

III.

Breathe the thin, fleeting air—
Fiery air!
What a scene of horror shadowed that flash of flare!
In the cramped and quiet cave
That will no doubt be our grave,
Did the firedamp ignite
Though the boss said all was right.
Some souls are lost already,
Taken swiftly by the flash—

With that unexpected flash!
          When gas and flame did clash,
          And now they're smoldering to ash.
     But few of us are left,
     Trapped by stone we cannot heft.
As my breathing comes unsteady,
          In the dwindling, smoky air,
          With singed flesh and burning hair,
          I think of my poor mother
          And how she'll take the news
          That her only son left, she did lose.
My tears I will not smother.
          My chest heaves with pain
          While I'm gasping,
          While I'm rasping,
          Trying to breathe in vain.
          What's little left of air—
     All is hushing
          No more rushing
Of air.

As I finished the poem, I just stared at the page, the words blurring as my eyes lost focus. My body sagged with the great sense of hopelessness and loss the narrator felt, desperately clinging to his last gasp, knowing it would soon be his death.

Wow, Watt is amazing. As the rhythm of his words played in my head, I think I fell in love with him a little bit. It was clear that he had a great sense of empathy.

I thought about how he'd leaned in to kiss me the night before. *Why did I pull away?*

And as I lay in bed, staring up at the vaulted ceiling while I clutched his book in my hands, I told myself I wouldn't miss my chance next time.

After waking up and dressing the following day, I took my things and headed back to the dormitory for breakfast.

Alia was already there, sitting on the couch with her cup of black coffee. "Good morning," she said cheerfully.

I returned her greeting and put my things away before coming back to the common room.

"How was your evening last night?" I asked her as I went about making my oatmeal and tea. "Did you sleep all right?"

Now that I was thinking about it, it was strange that Alia hadn't come down in all the commotion what with me screaming and Corey having "not exactly" a panic attack.

"Yeah, no problem. I took a sleeping pill and was out like a light." She snapped her fingers for emphasis. "I would never get a full night's sleep without one."

Ah. That explains it.

"But oh my goodness, did you see the sunset last night?" she continued. "It was absolutely gorgeous from those upper windows."

"Yeah, the effect it had on the stained-glass was beautiful, too."

"What was beautiful?" Watt asked, coming into the common room.

I glanced over at him, then looked again. He wore jeans and a black T-shirt, which really accentuated his muscular form. I fully took in the sight of him in modern clothes, and when I met his eyes, he grinned at me.

I felt my face flush at having been caught checking him out. "What's this? Casual Thursday?"

He chuckled. "I wish. No, I'm heading into town today for supplies. Do you need anything while I'm there?"

I thought about it for a second. "I don't think so."

"What time is the ferry coming?" Alia asked.

"Seven," he answered.

Alia looked down at herself, frowned, then rose from the couch. "I need to change."

Ten minutes later, she returned looking even more fabulous than she had before.

The weather was very nice that morning, sunny but not too warm. I decided to walk down to the dock with Alia and Watt rather than head into the office early.

"Are you sure I can't get you anything?" Watt asked while we waited for the ferry to show. "I could bring back a pizza."

My mouth watered at the suggestion. I couldn't remember the last time I'd had pizza. "But won't it be cold by the time you get here?"

"Chinese food then? It keeps its heat better, and it tastes great even if you have to reheat it."

That's true, and that does sound delicious. I gave him a smile. "I'm good, but thanks. I'd rather you come back early. I read some of your poems last night, and I'd like to talk to you about them."

He blinked in surprise but then smiled. "I'll come back to you as soon as I can."

"There it is!" Alia pointed as the ferry came into view.

"You're just in time," Watt said, glancing behind us.

I turned toward where he was looking to find Corey a few steps away. He wore dark, straight-legged jeans and a sweater over a collared shirt, one flap of which hung out the bottom. He looked like the sort of guy I'd see reading at a bookstore coffee shop, the guy who might look up and smile but always returned to his book.

"Good morning," I greeted.

But Corey didn't return my smile, he just dipped his head at me with the same expression as usual.

"Hey." Watt touched my shoulder to get my attention. Then he grinned at me. "I'll see you later. All right?"

"Yeah, see you later."

Watt and Corey walked toward the boat as it moored on the dock. I went to stand beside Alia. She waved excitedly at Phil, who returned the gesture.

"So you two have been texting?" I asked her while she watched him go about his duties.

"Yes, he is very sweet but a little shy. I'm hoping to set up a real date soon."

Phil gave her another wave goodbye as the ferry pulled away from the dock. Watt also gave us a wave, but Corey didn't even glance our way, heading into the cabin instead.

CHAPTER XXXIX.

IT WAS BUSINESS as usual for the rest of the day. Since I'd gotten the hang of my equipment, I was able to photograph two upper rooms before lunch. Of course, that meant I'd be spending twice as long editing them, but I'd likely get faster at that too.

When I returned to the dorms before dinner, I found a handwritten note had been slipped under my door. I bent down to pick it up.

Meet me in the greenhouse tonight.
Midnight.

My heart gave an excited leap, and I smiled. *Maybe we've gotten closer than I thought.* For the first time in a while, I thought about what I should wear for my moonlit rendezvous. *Should I wear work clothes? Pajamas? Or something cute and modern? It will be after-hours. Will he mind?*

I didn't speak much at dinner. My mind too full of questions. *Why does he want to meet so late? It can't be work related, or he would have just called me to his office. Does he want to talk to me about something? Maybe he's going to open up about what happened last night.*

After dinner, I returned to my room. I was too amped to sit still. I went through my meager wardrobe and settled on wearing a short, pleated black skirt over black tights with a tucked-in T-shirt featuring a chibi cat with bat wings smiling mischievously, its ears poking out of a witch's hat. I also pulled on a pair of wrist-warmers with Poe's "The Raven" printed on them.

I frowned at my reflection. It was a cute outfit, but I again wished I had just a little bit of eye liner. With a sigh, I settled for my dollar-store lip balm.

I got to the greenhouse ten minutes early and began walking the paths, watching the door that was closest to the manor. I glanced down at my watch for the fourteenth time. It was five minutes past midnight. I bit my cheek.

But just as I was wondering if he'd accidentally fallen asleep, the dormitory-facing door opened, and Watt rushed in.

"Sorry I'm late. Nora was in the kitchenette for whatever reason, and I wanted her to go back to bed before coming out."

I blinked at him, tilting my head. A moment later, my excitement dimmed. *The note hadn't been signed. Watt had sent it.*

He smiled down at me. "Is this how you normally dress on the mainland? Very cute. I like it."

His eyes lit with appreciation, and my face heated. Whether it was in shame or pleasure, I wasn't quite sure.

I murmured my thanks.

"I'm sorry to ask you to meet so late, but I don't know when we'll get another chance. Bennings is still on the mainland."

My chest tightened. "Another chance for what?"

He stared at me seriously, and the expression looked strange and foreign on his face. "Do you remember that story I told you the first night you were here?"

How could I forget? It's had me jumping at every sound and shadow. "The ghost story?"

"Yes, but more specifically the part when I said that Mistress Bennings had been in love with the ferryman and how her husband had sent their child away."

I nodded.

"Well…I'm that child."

My eyebrows scrunched, and I blinked in confusion. "What?"

"I know it sounds crazy, but hear me out. I never knew my family growing up. The only clue I even had as to who they were was a baby blanket with the initials EB embroidered on it. I can hardly remember who raised me before I went to school. And then I was sent to all these very expensive boarding schools. Anything I needed was provided for me through a trust. But when I turned twenty-one, all that money just stopped. I went to the office of the lawyer who'd always taken care of everything, but they wouldn't tell me anything. I hadn't prepared for anything. I never went to college. I thought I'd be provided for my whole life. I started taking odd jobs in construction, in groundskeeping, learning from plumbers and handymen. Eventually, to find out what was going on, I broke into the lawyer's office."

I didn't know what expression my face was making, but he lowered his head.

"I know it wasn't the right thing to do, but I was desperate. My file was pretty bare, mostly a history of all the payments made on my behalf. But there was one document that was useful. It set up the trust, and it was signed by Elizabeth Bennings. I had no idea who that was though it didn't take me long to find out. I knew that she had died from her obituary, so I came to town hoping to find out more about her. And the story I told you before is all I heard from the locals. It makes sense, right? She would have wanted her child provided for. In any case, I tried to get onto the island, but Bennings didn't even live here then. Eventually, he came back and decided to turn the house into a hotel. So I applied as keeper to try to find out more."

"And have you?"

He shook his head. "I haven't really had a good chance. I've looked around the best I could on the sly, but I think the records must be in his office. And this is the first time he's left the island for any real amount of time."

"You want to break into his office?" I didn't like the sound of that at all.

His eyes pleaded with me. "What choice do I have? All I want is to find out the truth. There has to be a birth certificate somewhere, right? And besides, if I'm right, then I'm actually the heir to all this. I would have been born first. Isn't it only right that I should have a say at least?"

I bit my cheek. *He isn't wrong. If he really is Elizabeth Bennings's son, he at least has the right to know about his own parents.*

"Come on, Wren. I need help. You've seen how many filing cabinets are in that place."

"Why don't you just ask him? Why do we have to sneak around like this?"

"If he wanted anything to do with me, don't you think he would have found me before now?"

That didn't sound right, didn't sound like the Corey I knew. Then again, what did I really know about him at all? Maybe he wasn't the person I took him for. The thought made my skin prickle with curiosity. I could find out a lot about him if I helped Watt with this little task. If he was as bad as Watt said, I wanted to know. And if he wasn't, I wanted to clear his name.

"All right. I'll help you look."

CHAPTER XL.

———

"I'M GOING to start over there," Watt said, pointing his flashlight toward a row of filing cabinets.

"All right," I murmured.

He smirked at me. "You don't have to whisper, you know. He's not here. The house is empty."

I knew what he was saying was true, but I couldn't help but feel like we weren't alone, that someone could pop up anytime and catch us in this dishonest act. I pushed the thoughts away. I was here now. I might as well get this done as quickly as possible.

I swept the flashlight Watt had given me across the space, and it reflected off of something on Corey's desk. *That's as good a place to start as any.*

Watt was already opening file drawers, and I winced while they clinked and squeaked in the silent house.

It turned out that the light had reflected off the only picture frame on Corey's neat desk. My nervous heart pounded in my fingertips as I picked up the frame, shining my light near the edge to get a good look. My brow puckered. It was clearly an old photo, yellowed with age. It looked like an albumen print to me, likely from the second half of the nineteenth century. The photo was of a group of miners standing before the opening of a mine, their serious faces staring out beneath their caps. There were even some young boys, clad in similar attire, standing at the front, their coworkers' hands resting on their shoulders.

It was the type of photo I'd seen many times in history books and old newspapers, but it seemed out of place framed on Corey's desk.

I replaced the picture where I found it and slid open the top drawer of his desk, gritting my teeth in anticipation of a squeak that never came.

The drawer appeared to hold a stack of papers, seemingly unrelated as I flipped through them. Perhaps they were papers he had yet to file. There were receipts for things he'd purchased for the hotel, my and Alia's personnel papers we'd filled out upon arriving, and other miscellaneous things. But just when I was about to put the stack back in its place, I paused at a letter from the IRS.

Dear Applicant:

We are pleased to inform you that upon review of your application for tax exempt status we have determined that you are exempt from Federal income tax under Section 501(c)(3) of the Internal Revenue Code.

I squinted at the letter, bringing it closer to my face. *501(c) (3)? That's the code for a nonprofit.* I glanced at the top of the letter. It was addressed to Descendants of Mount Blessed c/o William Courtland Bennings.

What's that? Is Corey also running a nonprofit somewhere?

I made a mental note to look up the organization later and

put the papers carefully where I'd found them.

I glanced over at Watt; he was quickly making his way through the filing cabinets and not at all being quiet about it.

If he does have Watt's birth certificate, it's much more likely to be filed away than in his desk. I moved to join his search at the other end of the room when my flashlight suddenly flickered out. I shook the thing, banging it against the heel of my hand. In the process, it slipped out of my grasp and fell with a loud clatter onto Corey's desk, flickering back on as it hit.

I clenched my teeth at the sound, then glanced over at Watt, who had the audacity to put a finger to his lips to tell me to be quieter. I pursed my lips at him. *He's got to be kidding.*

Reaching out for the flashlight, I paused. The beam of the light had fallen onto a rather flat box, one of those fancy papier-mâché ones that I'd seen during cultural art festivals. I lifted the lid to find a long-yellowed piece of paper. The ink was a reddish-brown and was written in a messy, uneven hand, with splotches and pools in odd places.

I picked up the box rather than the paper, afraid to damage it as it was clearly old.

On this land, bought with blood,
In this house of brick and mud,

"You've got to be fucking kidding me," Watt growled.

His words interrupted my reading, and I looked over at him and the bright stream of light flowing into the window.

"What's that?" I asked.

He peered out the window. "We've got to go. Fucking Bennings is back."

I nearly choked on my heart as it leapt into my throat, hurriedly replacing the lid on the box and grabbing my flashlight.

I looked around frantically. "How are we going to get out? He'll have to pass this floor to get up to his room, and what if he comes here instead?" My voice cracked with whispered panic. *I knew this was a bad idea. I never should have done this.*

Watt crossed the room quickly, grabbing my hand and pulling me after him. "Come on." He led me to the opposite wall from where he'd been searching and started to feel under the ledge of the fireplace.

My heart screamed, and I bit back the urge to vocalize it.

There was a little click, and the panel beside the fireplace opened like the hidden linen closet. He pushed me through the opening onto a set of stone, spiral stairs. "Go," he whispered, closing the door behind us.

The spiral staircase traveled both up and down. I clenched my jaw against the soft scuffle of my shoes on the steps as I headed downward, the sound echoing too much for my liking. My unsteady hands and the movement of my descent shook the beam of my flashlight. The staircase stopped in a corner, two doors creating the sides of a right angle.

"Which one?" I asked, unsure of where each door would lead us.

Watt reached around me, his chest firm against my back, and pressed a button that opened the door on the right. We stepped into the kitchen.

Without a word, he closed the door and grabbed my hand again.

He led us into the night, and I breathed a guilty sigh of relief as the cool wind blew the hair from my face.

CHAPTER XLI.

"GOD DAMN it!" Watt growled, running his hands through his hair.

I could feel the anger rolling off of him. His back was to me, his shoulders tense.

"It's all right," I said, trying to soothe him. "We can—"

He spun around, his eyes blazing. "How exactly is it all right, Wren? I've been waiting for months and months to get into that room unobserved. Years of work down the drain. What the hell were you even doing at his desk? Why didn't you look harder?"

I flinched as though he'd slapped me. Perhaps I wasn't the best spy or cat burglar, but I didn't deserve his ire. I squinted back at him, reflexive anger bubbling in my gut. "Look, I know you're upset, but that doesn't give you the right to speak to me that way. This wasn't my idea. And if this is how you're going to act, you can forget me helping you in the future."

I turned on my heel and started to stomp toward the greenhouse. He stopped me by grabbing my wrist. I spun around to demand he let me go, but he held up his hands in surrender, his expression drooping and apologetic.

"I'm sorry," he said. "I didn't mean to take it out on you. I dragged you into this, and you agreed to help. I'm grateful. I'm just frustrated. Why the hell did he come back so soon? Why didn't he stay on the mainland and come back in the morning? That's what any normal person would do."

I sighed out my anger and shook my head. "I don't know. But really, can't we just ask Corey for his help? It doesn't feel right snooping around his things. And if we get caught, we could both lose our jobs. I don't know about you, but this job means a lot to me."

He squinted. "You call him Corey now?"

I shrugged, glancing away from his watchful eyes. "He said I could."

"I bet he did." He looked like he was about to spit.

My hackles rose again. "What's that supposed to mean?"

"Nothing." He closed his eyes and sighed. "Look, let's just call it a night. All right? It's late, and we're both tired."

I crossed my arms over my chest. "Yeah, whatever."

But when I changed into my pajamas and crawled into bed, I had a hard time falling asleep. And when I finally fell into fitful dreams, it felt like my sleeping brain was trying to solve math problems. Images from Corey's office swirled in my mind, but nothing about them made any sense. My bed felt too stiff and squeaky beneath me as I tossed and turned, and the wind outside my window howled all night like moans of the restless dead.

I stared at my tired face in the mirror as I dressed the next morning. *This wasn't what I meant by wanting black under my eyes.*

I didn't see Watt that morning, and I was glad for it. I still smarted from our argument. Planning to forget it all by burying myself in work, I headed into the office early.

As I rounded my desk to check my email, my heart nearly

exploded. Right there, sitting before my keyboard, was my camera. Not the one Corey had let me use but *my* camera, the one I had left at the pawn shop.

"What?" I breathed, picking it up with trembling hands. "How did…?" But as impossible as it seemed, it was the camera my father had gotten me. I rubbed my fingertips over the velvety surface of the sticker on the lens cap.

Then I dug into my jacket for my wallet. I emptied it all onto my desk, my license, my debit card, the loyalty card for the place I used to buy makeup. But the pawn ticket was nowhere to be found. I wracked my brain, trying to think of how this could have happened. And then I saw something else that didn't belong on my desk. Sitting beside where the camera had been was a small box of chocolates and a notecard folded in half so it stood on its own. My name was written in neat handwriting on the front. I picked up the notecard and unfolded it.

You deserve an apology for what I put you through. I hope this helps you put the whole incident from your mind.

Tears fell from my eyes. I couldn't believe it. He said he'd gone into town for supplies, but somehow, Watt had managed to get my camera sent here. All of his words of anger and accusation were forgotten. He was just as kind and empathetic as his poetry had suggested to me. Even the thought of him looking in my wallet didn't bother me, so touching was his sweet gesture.

I dropped the card on my desk and ran from the room in search of him. I checked the parlor first before remembering that he had mentioned some things he wanted to work on in the third-floor guest room. I rushed back to the entrance hall, nearly clashing with Lucero as she approached the stairs with a covered tray.

"Sorry!" I called to her, running past her as we both headed up the stairs.

My chest heaved by the time I reached the third floor, and my feet thumped loud on the carpet while I raced down the hall.

And there he was, kneeling before a pair of chairs, dusty-orange fabric folded nicely near his knee. He looked over at me and rose to his feet.

I must have looked wild, cheeks flushed and cap askew. Without a word, I threw myself at him, wrapping my arms around his waist and burying my face in his chest. "Thank you," I whispered, my voice thick with emotion.

He returned my embrace, and I could hear his smile when he said, "I guess you found my present. I'm really sorry about last night."

I pulled back just enough to look up into his warm, amber eyes. He smiled down at me, clearly pleased to have made up.

"You don't know what this means to me," I told him.

He shrugged a little. "It's not that big a deal."

"It is to me." I raised myself onto my toes and pecked him right on the mouth.

He grinned. "You caught me off guard. Let me try that again."

"Okay. But then I have to go to work."

"You're a tease."

"You want it or not?"

"Oh, I want it." And with that sultry little comment, he pressed a kiss firmly to my lips.

CHAPTER XLII.

DESPITE OUR kiss not being a long one, I could still taste Watt on my lips as I skipped down the stairs to the office. My heart was light, and I looked forward to getting to know what else he was capable of.

The rest of the day was much the same as the ones before. I took photographs, I ate lunch, I fixed the photographs and dropped them in the shared drive for Dominick and Alia. So far, I had finished all of the upstairs bedrooms and put my equipment in the ballroom, which I would start on Monday.

The cherry on top of my cheerful day came when I checked my personal email before leaving the office.

Dear Wren,

I'm so excited to hear that I'll be able to come for a visit soon! And when I mentioned it to Mom, she seemed almost relieved. I know I still have a few weeks before summer break, but now I have something to look forward to.

I've got two whole weeks between spring and summer crew, so I can stay for a while. I've attached my regatta schedule and the information for summer registration.

I'm sorry if I came off as unsupportive before. It just took me a while to get used to the idea of you being farther away… But now that I know I'll get to see you more often, I'm glad.

I'm really happy for you, sis. I know how hard you've worked for this and how much you do for me.

So tell me about your new job. Do you like it so far? How does it feel to be working as a professional photographer? Is it everything you hoped for?

What about the hotel? Is it gorgeous? I was surprised that you took a job in the middle of a lake. Is your seasickness not as bad as before?

What about your coworkers? Are you getting along? Are there any cute guys there? Maybe now you'll have more time to date. Then again, maybe you should wait a little bit. You fall in love too easily. You artists are too romantic.

Anyway, tell me all about it. I want to know everything before I come to visit.

Love you.
Izzy

I scowled at the screen, then smiled. I wasted no time in writing my sister back.

Dear Izzy,

When did I ever fall in love too easily?

Exempting Camron. He doesn't count because I fell in love with his music, not him. And Gerrit doesn't count either. How was I supposed to know that he was only using me for his paintings?

You know what? Whatever. You just hush. :P

I should get my paycheck next week, and I'll have enough money to pay for your summer crew fees and your travel expenses. I'm excited for you to come for a visit too though I don't think it will be for as long as you're hoping for.

How is crew going? Are you winning?

I love my new job so far. It's so beautiful here. What is it like being able to work as a professional photographer? I feel like my soul is singing. I feel like I can breathe again.

No, my seasickness hasn't gotten better, but I don't plan on going to the mainland very often.

My co-workers are great. I can't wait for you to meet Alia. I already know you two will hit it off right away. My boss started out all cold and mysterious, but I think I'm wearing him down. And then there's Watt… You know what? Given your earlier remark, I'm going to wait to tell you about him. See? Maybe I'm learning.

Anyway, I'll be in touch soon.
Good luck at your regattas!

Love,
Wren

Just as I was about to close out of my internet browser, a stray thought rose to the surface of my mind. I pulled up a search engine and typed "Descendants of Mount Blessed nonprofit."

The first hit was the organization's website. I clicked on the blue hyperlink. The website was simple but effective. There were only two pages, which were titled "Who We Are" and "How to Help."

I read the Who We Are page.

Descendants of Mount Blessed is a 501(c)(3) nonprofit that benefits the descendants of the 1894 Mount Blessed Mine disaster.

We support these descendants in a variety of ways— from helping them with college fees and medical bills to helping them secure home loans and plan for their futures.

The nonprofit is funded by a combination of private donors and profits from <u>Moonseed Manor</u>.

Moonseed Manor was hyperlinked. I clicked on it, and it brought me to the hotel's website. *The hotel is a nonprofit? And everything above expenses goes to this organization?*

I pulled up the search engine again and typed "1894 Mount Blessed Mine disaster." I skimmed the search results and clicked on a site called "Fatal Mine Disasters." It took me a few minutes, but I navigated to the entry for the Mount Blessed Mine disaster of 1894.

Bennings Mining Co.
Mount Blessed No. 1 Mine Explosion
January 27, 1894
No. Killed—128

My chest tightened. *Bennings Mining Co.? Corey's family owned the mine?* His words from the other night echoed in my ears. *"It's no more than I deserve." Does he blame himself for this tragedy even though he wasn't born yet?*

Below the stated facts of the tragedy, there were two hyperlinks—one for the state mine inspector's report and the other a list of fatalities.

I clicked on the report.

It was pretty dense for someone like me, who didn't have any knowledge of how coal mines worked. But it was clear that the miners had raised concerns about leaking gas. The fire-boss checked it and said everything was fine, and—not long after the miners went back in—the mine exploded. To my surprise, the report concluded that there was no negligence on the part of the fire-boss or the company.

A great sadness made my limbs heavy and my heart sore. "Oh, Corey…" I whispered.

What had happened to these miners was terrible. But it was clear to me that Corey was carrying the guilt of his ancestors' mistakes. *How much is he tortured by this? Enough to set up a nonprofit to benefit the descendants of those killed, obviously. But what else? Are his feelings of guilt enough to make him have panic attacks? Are they enough that he won't let anyone close to him?*

CHAPTER XLIII.

MY MIND WAS full of thoughts at dinner, and I hardly spoke a word. I could see that Watt was trying to engage my attention, but I just couldn't get what I'd read out of my head.

Before I knew it, I was alone at the table, a cold plate of food before me.

"You seem preoccupied," Nora said, coming in from the kitchen. "If you aren't going to eat, may I have your plate so I can wash it?"

I looked down at the food I'd only picked at and shoved a forkful into my mouth. "Sorry. I'll be done in a minute."

She hovered in the doorway, leaning against the jamb with her arms crossed. "You should be more careful," she murmured.

I swallowed around a huge bite and tilted my head at her.

"Not every man is as trustworthy as he seems."

My eyebrows shot up. *Whom is she talking about? Watt? Corey?*

The look on her face was serious and sad, and I wondered who had hurt her in the past.

"What do you mean?" I asked.

She shook her head. "Never mind. I'm just rambling. I'll take your plate."

I wanted to press her for answers, but she closed the discussion when she turned her back to me and went into the kitchen.

I didn't much think about Nora's words after I crawled into bed that night. I was tired from not having gotten enough sleep the night before, so I slept soundly.

Despite my reluctance, Alia somehow convinced me to go into town over the next two days. It was the weekend, and she asked for help looking for apartments. When she smiled and turned her big blue eyes on me, I wasn't going to say no. I didn't mind helping her at all. I actually liked the idea of getting to know the town closest to us. I just wasn't keen on the boat crossings.

Still, I survived. And come Monday, she had gotten some good leads on apartments though she would have to wait a few weeks before one was available to rent. She was particularly disappointed that the building Lucero stayed in had no vacancies as it had a beautiful view of the lake.

I spent Monday morning photographing the ballroom. I looked up from editing photos in the afternoon when Alia stormed into the office.

"Ugh, how frustrating," she grumbled, plopping into her chair.

"What's going on?" I asked.

She clicked her tongue. "Mr. Bennings is being obstinate. I just met with him to talk about writing a short history of the manor for the website. Customers like that kind of stuff. But he wouldn't tell me anything other than the architect and what year it was built. How am I supposed to market this place without knowing anything about it?"

I frowned. *That is strange.* "Well, I mean, it's still a gorgeous place, right? And it has historic architecture at least. So people will want to come just for that, won't they?"

She puffed her cheeks out in a rush of breath. "Yeah, I guess. It would just be way better with that stuff too. In any case, he did agree to my other idea."

"What's that?" I asked.

She propped her chin up with her hand, her elbow on her desk. "I convinced him that we should at least run stories, newspaper articles, and blogs about what we're doing to get this place ready for customers and other things that make this place special. All that should generate some buzz."

I wondered if they had pictures of the rooms before they'd been renovated to go along with those stories. "How are you going to do that?"

"Well, one idea I had was to partner with some local businesses for products we use at the hotel. For instance, there's a nearby farm that makes artisan bath products using goat's milk from their goats and honey from their bee hives. There's also a local coffee shop that roasts all their own beans. I thought we could use their products exclusively and you, Mr. Bennings, and I could make a sort of field trip there and write some stories about it. That would give us a lot of good press— free advertising from local newspapers. And the businesses would also talk about it, I'm sure. Plus, we'd have excellent products for our customers."

"He agreed to that?" Dominick asked incredulously.

Alia nodded. "Yeah, I just have to reach out to the businesses and set up a time that works for them. It's a good idea, I guess. But it would have been better to have the historical stuff too."

I hummed my sympathy for her frustration and wondered why Corey didn't want to talk about the history of Moonseed Manor. "Oh, I did hear something you might be able to use." I told her about the moonseeds Corey had shown me the week before, and she assured me that it was a fun little tidbit she could use. I promised to go out and take pictures of them while they were still flowering, though they wouldn't bear fruit for months yet. Dominick also seemed interested in utilizing that knowledge for the website's design.

Despite the island being rather small, I hadn't seen Corey in a few days, not since the night I'd stayed in the house. As I moved my equipment to the guest dining room near the end of the workday, I wondered if he was avoiding me for some reason. Was I being too sensitive?

I glanced around at the unoccupied space, assessing the lighting and layout. It wasn't nearly as picturesque as Nora had made it our first night. *Maybe I should set the tables properly with linens and stuff before I take any pictures tomorrow. That will be much more inviting.*

I set the light I'd just carried up on one of the dining tables, frowning down at it. *Will I even need it with all these windows? Natural light will be better.*

I stared out at the dark clouds gathering on the horizon. The willows in the garden swayed in frenzied shivers, their yellow petals snatched from their branches and swirling in mini twisters.

The glass and wood dining room creaked as gusts of wind hit the sides, and a shiver ran through me. I didn't really notice just how quiet the house was most of the time. When I was off photographing by myself, it almost felt like I was completely alone on this island. The mostly glass room suddenly felt very exposed as a heavy dread settled into me. *A storm must be brewing.*

Just as I wrapped my arms around myself, a low thrum echoed through the room. I jumped, nearly choking on my own gasp while I spun around to look at the piano behind me.

There was no one there.

Panic crept over my skin and crawled down my throat, my mundane thoughts long gone from my mind.

I scanned the space, my heart hammering much harder than the hammer had struck the piano wire.

I'd heard it, heard it clear as if I'd been sitting in the front row of a concert hall.

"H-hello?" My voice was wispier and more ghost-like than the reverberation of that note, still ringing in my ears.

I tried to swallow around the lump in my throat but failed. I wanted nothing more than to get out of here. But there was only one inside door, and I would have to pass the piano to go through it.

Despite my logical mind scowling at me, everything in me told me not to go that way. I backed slowly away from the entrance and slipped through the nearest door leading to the outside balcony.

A cold wind blasted my face, whipping my skirt like the sails of a ship. The day had started out warm, but a cold front had moved in, the electric air promising no regular storm.

I walked with purpose, my boots thumping on the wood planks of the wrap-around balcony beneath my feet. The next door I came to was the one that led into the ladies' drawing room, but it was locked. Praying I wouldn't have to go back to the dining room, I tried the double doors that led into the men's drawing room. I sighed as the knob turned easily. Then a gust of wind blew them wide open.

CHAPTER XLIV.

———

"P-PLEASE, STOP tormenting me," a voice from inside the men's drawing room pleaded. "Just end it already."

I stepped into the room to find Corey, his face pale and his eyes wide as he stared at me. He sat on the floor like the wind from the doorway had blown him over. His breathing was ragged, and he didn't seem to recognize me at first.

A moment later, he sighed, and his whole body sagged as if that one breath was the only thing keeping him inflated.

"Of course," he said bitterly. "It had to be you. As if I didn't look pathetic enough in your eyes."

I knelt in the space created by his long, spread legs. "That's not true. I don't see you that way at all. But I am worried about you."

I knew he wouldn't want to talk about it, especially not in his current mood. Though my mind burst with questions—*What's going on with him? Who is tormenting him? Is he hallucinating terrifying things? Is he sick? Then again, didn't I just hear something impossible? Does that mean I'm going mad, too?*—I didn't give them voice.

"Corey," I murmured gently.

My tone had the desired effect when he met my eyes.

"Would you stay with me for a while?" I asked. "I think I might have just freaked myself out a bit in the dining room."

He didn't ask me what had happened, he just nodded slowly. I don't know if my presence was as much of a comfort for him as his was for me, but he did seem to calm down as the moments ticked by. The color returned to his face, and his breathing evened out.

And right when I was becoming aware of just how close we were sitting, just how suggestive our positions were, Lucero burst through the door at a purposeful pace, a covered tray in her hands.

She froze, her dark eyes wide when she saw us sitting on the floor, me still kneeling between Corey's legs. She let out a little snort and smirked.

"I'll just leave this on the table, shall I?" she asked, her tone nonchalant. She didn't wait for a reply but placed the tray on the nearest table and left.

I knew what the whole thing would look like to her, but I didn't much care. It's not like Corey and I were doing anything wrong. Still, I could feel Corey's gaze on my face, watching to see how I'd react, whether I would be worried about the optics of the situation.

"Well, I guess that's my cue to leave," I said easily. "Your dinner is here and mine will be waiting for me in the kitchen."

I stood with effort, the blood rushing back to my legs when I rose. I fixed the fabric of my skirt, looking up only when Corey cleared his throat.

"We could share if you like." He stared down at me, having stood to his full height. "Nora always gives me too much."

I blinked at him, surprised by his sudden invitation.

"That is…you can, of course, return to the others if you

would prefer. They can provide you with the company you were after much more effectively than I could, I'm sure."

I never would have guessed that I would look at Corey and think that he was cute. Even when vulnerable, he seemed mature. I might have called him handsome, intense, mysterious, maybe even alluring. But as he stood, awkwardly inviting me to share in his meal, clearly self-conscious about what I would choose and whether I wanted to eat with the others instead, I couldn't help but see him as cute too.

I smiled. *Is he doing this for me, or has he disliked eating alone all along?*

"I wonder what Nora has made for us today." I moved to the table where Lucero had placed the tray and lifted the lid. The warm, buttery scent of chicken Kiev and creamy mashed potatoes drifted to my nose.

Corey had been right. Two large, crispy chicken breasts sat beside each other on his plate, his potatoes in a huge mound beside them. I thought about the respect with which Nora always spoke of Corey and decided she must have a great deal of affection for him.

"Well?" I raised an eyebrow at him, hovering near the table. "Why don't you sit so we can eat before it gets cold?"

I couldn't be certain, but I thought I saw a little twinkle in Corey's black eyes.

Our shared meal was pleasant overall though pretty quiet. The only thing we talked about was Nora's cooking. Corey said her beef bourguignon was his absolute favorite, but he enjoyed her stroganoff as well. I told him I looked forward to trying them both. Still, our silence didn't seem so loud as rain began pelting the windows and thunder rumbled in the distance.

At the end, with no food left to concentrate on, an awkward air settled between us.

"Well"—I stood from my chair—"thanks for the food. I'll,

uh, take the tray down to the kitchen on my way back."

"You don't have to do that. I can take it in the morning when I go down for coffee."

I covered the tray and picked it up. "It's no trouble, I'm heading that way anyway." But as I took a step toward the door, I hesitated and glanced back at him. For some reason, he looked so lonely sitting there at the small table in such a large room. I thought of the fear, the agony in his eyes when I'd first entered. *Will he be all right?* I could just picture him drifting around the halls, unable to lie down from fear of what he might dream. I could see him wandering in the rain, his coat flapping as lightning flashed in the distance.

"I hope you have a restful night," I said sincerely.

He frowned, looking like he knew that would never happen. "Thank you. I hope you have a good night as well."

CHAPTER XLV.

I LEFT COREY'S tray on the kitchen counter and headed back down the hall to take the stairs to the tunnel. As I neared the reception desk, a flash of lightning lit a silhouette in the dark library door. I gasped, stumbling and only regaining my footing just in time to avoid a fall.

"There you are," Watt said, stepping into the light, his face cold and serious. "You missed dinner. Are you hungry?"

I flinched at his icy tone. "No, I happened to be with Corey when Lucero brought his dinner, so I ate up there with him."

He scowled, and his amber eyes looked severe. "Well, at least you didn't bother to lie about it."

I scrunched my eyebrows. "Why would I?"

"So this is normal behavior for you then? Kissing me one minute and cuddling up with Bennings the next?"

"I didn't 'cuddle up' with him," I protested.

Watt stepped toward me, his towering height menacing even before his tone came out dark and low. "Lucero told me what she saw before she left for the night. Do you think I'm a fool?"

I straightened my spine and glared back at him in indignation. "Lucero was there for only a moment. She doesn't know what did or didn't happen, and I resent the accusation. If you'd rather take her word over mine, then that's your concern. In any case, a few kisses don't give you the right to demand anything from me."

He opened his mouth to say something, but I was done talking to him at the moment.

"I'm going to bed. You can talk to me when you've got your head on straight." Turning my back to him, I stormed down the stairs, through the cellar, and into the tunnel.

But as I closed my bedroom door a little louder than I should have, I already felt bad. It was true that Watt and I had made no promises to each other, and I hadn't done anything to break even unsaid promises. Even so, it was clear that Watt was feeling self-conscious about where our relationship stood. Instead of pushing back so hard, I probably should have reassured him. If I was being honest with myself, which I wasn't, I probably felt a little guilty underneath it all for how I felt toward Corey. My mind dwelled on him quite a bit, and I was clearly drawn to the mystery that surrounded him. But as I changed into my pajamas, I didn't think of all that. I just thought of Watt's anger and how I hadn't handled it very well.

I wanted to apologize to him right then, but I leaned my back against the wall, my feet dangling off the side of my bed. I told myself that I would apologize and talk it out with him in the morning; maybe I was just too much of a coward to revisit it that night. *At least I can feel close to him through his writing.* Frowning, I took his book from my nightstand.

What I expected when I left that devastated and distraught town I'd dwelt in since my youth, I cannot say with any degree of certainty. But having departed with a destination in mind and a heart heavy with so recent sorrow, I set out in search of answers.

For weeks I traveled in bitter February cold, as icy winds cut to my tired bones, to stand on the shores of this near-frozen lake. I waited with patience, having come so far, for a boat that would carry me on to the island where the moonseeds fruit on autumn trees. Or so I was told, for I had never been to such a place as where my betters dwelt.

On those shores, I paced, moving so my limbs wouldn't freeze beyond use before I could reach my purpose. What would they say? I wondered, pondering the answers I may be given to the questions I could not keep straight in my thoughts.

Finally, as luck would have it, a vessel docked whats destination matched my own not far from where my frost-bitten feet held me aloft though swaying as I might in the frozen air. Piteously, my face must have looked to the captain of the little boat, sent ashore for supplies. For well my voice did crack with emotion when I asked if I might board, the very sound frightening even myself in its dead and hollow tone. In truth, I had not used it for some time but to weep and wail.

The captain, soft-hearted man that he was, was moved by my hushed plea to ride with him upon his return though I had not elaborated to him the purpose of my desire to be taken thither.

I did not feel the wind, biting as it was, on my face and hands while I sat amongst the crates and boxes of the boat, so warm was my aim in my belly. The waves were rough, and I had to reach out and grab the rope, which tethered the goods, so I was not thrown from the vessel by Mother Nature's enthusiasm.

As we approached the island, blanketed in virgin snow,

my marvel at the grandeur of the dwelling turned sour in my gut. Was this what the lives of my husband and sons had bought? I raged in my mind, the rushing blood warming my extremities that it might be high summer for all they knew.

Upon landing on the roofed dock, I thanked the captain, who offered his hand to assist me in climbing onto solid ground. I did not wait for him to show me the way to the dwelling, if so vulgar a word is acceptable to a mansion such as it was, but moved my numb feet, toes likely blackened by then, along the clear, paved path.

I have to admit the house was inviting, still cheery in its Christmas trimmings, its garlands and tinsel fresh and sparkling like the snow that covered every surface and eave.

With my hand, chilled and thin and speckled with the years I had seen, I grabbed the great knocker beside the door, the iron so cold that it burned like the gates of Hades. But the cavernous echo was not so great as the pounding of my own broken heart in my hollow chest.

I could see in the sharp, flashing eyes of the butler that the likes of me were not welcome at a noble house such as this when he opened the glass door. But I would not be turned away so easily after so long a journey, not without satisfaction.

"I find myself here"—I told the stiff man—"to call upon Mr. Bennings and his wife. He is not expecting me, but he'll see me nonetheless for I have pressing business that he must address."

The man huffed a snort, his breath coming out in a frosted puff that seemed to mock the very cold for its nature. "Very well," said he, his tone lacking in polite manners. "I will tell the master that you are here. He may be feeling charitable."

"Charity is not what I seek, sir." I corrected his assumption. "I would not have come all the way here for a

thing such as that. I wish to speak of his mine, some thirty and a hundred leagues thence, and of the tragedy that has occurred there."

The man frowned severely, the lines etching deep, but he did not speak further. He simply turned on his heel and strode into the warmth, expecting me to creep in after him. So fast were his steps that I stalled in my pursuit, settling in the front hall to wait.

A quarter of an hour I stood in that place, my fingers and toes tingling and burning as they thawed to something resembling the temperature of human flesh. When finally, the man returned, he did not speak a word but inclined his head in such a way as to bid me to follow.

Through rooms larger than every shack back home, glowing with electric lights, I followed the man across the fine rug, the mud on my boots leaving crusts and crumbles in my wake. Stopping at a polished wood door, the butler turned the silver knob and motioned me in.

I was greeted with a scene from a Christmas illustration—the master with his pipe and the dog at his feet; this well-mannered dog hardly noticed my entrance for he didn't even lift his tufted ears. The mistress, round with child, sat near the fire, knitting things for the life yet to enter.

Tears welled to my eyes at the sight of the little socks, so much did they remind me of the pairs I'd made for each of my fine sons.

"Why have you come?" Mr. Bennings demanded, his mustache not twitching as he spoke.

"Sir," I said meekly despite my long journey. "You have no doubt heard of the tragedy in your mine. Some twenty-eight and a hundred souls were lost."

"I have," says he, his voice clear and devoid of sympathy. "A terrible accident."

"But, sir," I countered. "A neighbor of mine, one blessed to have survived, says the fire-boss cleared the new tunnel as safe the very morning it went up in flames."

"What is your aim?" the man asked impatiently.

At that tone from her husband, the lady looked up, her eyes meeting mine.

"My husband and all three of my sons were lost that day," I said to the woman. "Even if there was a faulty lantern, the shaft would not have gone up if the gas levels were safe."

She blinked her dark eyes, this mother-to-be, soft and slow then shrugged her narrow shoulders.

"You have come here for money." the master accused. "Well, we have nothing for you here." Then he waved his hand with a sweep of his arm, casting me aside as he had all his men.

"No, sir," I said firmly, my face heating with rage. "I but ask for the truth. It would be a comfort to me and to all of the families who have lost someone dear to them."

"I've given you that," Mr. Bennings asserted, his mouth twisting in a sneer. But his eyes could not hold the lie so well.

"The conditions are bad," I argued. "You must have seen it, too."

The man rolled his eyes, dull and pitiless as they were. "If the men do not wish to work, they are free to leave. Others will happily take their places. You are disturbing our peace, and you are not welcome to stay. Return to the boat before the ferryman leaves."

My jaws clicked as they met, blood flooding my mouth where my tongue was bitten. "You will regret this," I vowed, and then I spit on the floor, marking the spot of their destruction.

The kind ferryman left, and despite his insistence, I stayed, watching and waiting for the dark moon to rise.

With his jagged knife, which I took from his boat, the blade on which many a fish had met their demise, I walked with a new purpose through that cold winter's night.

The stars sparkled brightly in the cloudless sky, and the wind blew my hood from my hair until I slipped back into the sleeping house.

Creeping on well-worn boots, I slithered from shadow to shade until that same room I reached.

With the fire just dead, its logs still hissing, there was no one in sight, long tucked into their cozy beds. To the desk near the window, I trod with my knife, a smile of vengeance pulling at my cheeks.

Then with paper and pen before me, I slashed one hand, mixing my blood into the ink of the pot. It did not sting, my wound from the rusty fish knife, for nothing could compare to the agony that already rended my heart, the agony that this man and his greed had caused.

And this I wrote in blood and ink:

On this land, bought with blood,
In this house of brick and mud,
An heir will born,
His features warn.
With hair as dark as blackest soot,
Thus know the curse is afoot.

Every penny, every sou,
Will drain like life of the men slew.
One year for every soul
You sacrificed in search of coal.
And when the years are matured,
The heir will know what we've endured.

The pang of hunger, the burn of thirst,
The sting of poverty is but the first.
When gasping for breath and crying from fear,
When everything lost that was held dear,
The spirits bygone is all he will see.
This is my will. So mote it be.

Every letter, every word, soothed my sore soul, for I
knew what this spell required. Then raising the jagged
knife, I plunged it into my heart, and thus sealed the curse
forevermore.

CHAPTER XLVI.

THE LAST PIECE slid into place, revealing a picture that didn't make sense with the facts I knew. I stared at the words on the page, so neatly written in a clear hand. I shambled off the bed and snatched the note Watt had slipped under my door from my dresser. Placing it on the page of the book, I held them under the light, comparing the handwriting.

They were nothing alike.

But I knew I had seen the handwriting before, and the flicker of an idea shined at the end of a dark tunnel. I clutched the book to my chest while I ran from my room. My muddled mind wasn't thinking properly, following that little flicker out into the night. The rain soaked my skin, seeping into my pajamas, and the chilled wind raised goose bumps all over my flesh. The bricks were smooth and hard beneath my bare feet as I ran through the storm to the main house.

Even when I slipped inside the warmth of the entrance hall, I shivered, my hair and clothes dripping onto the floor between my wet footprints. I moved swiftly to the office, my feet slapping the tiles.

After flicking on the light, I rushed to my desk and yanked open the top drawer, pens and paper clips rattling at my force.

The water from my fingertips seeped into the paper of the notecards I grabbed. Carefully, I opened the book, only spotted with water—my chest and arms having mostly protected it from the pelting rain.

I compared the notecards as I had done with Watt's note. My breath rushed out of me, and I squelched into my desk chair.

They were a match—the notecard with my work email and password and the note that had accompanied the return of my camera—the handwriting the same. Watt hadn't gotten my camera back for me, and he hadn't written these poems. It wasn't Watt's words that had so moved my heart and crept into my soul. It was Corey. It had been Corey all along.

It made so much more sense now that I knew. The fear and sorrow, the mysterious darkness, were much more in tune with Corey's personality than Watt's. How the poems made me feel—drawing me down, drowning me in intense emotion—was the same as being in his presence.

All the other clues were there, too. The poem about the mine accident, the picture on Corey's desk and the nonprofit he'd set up. The old scrap of paper I'd found in the papier-mâché box had the same lines on it as the curse in the story.

Horror closed my throat at the realization. *Does that mean the curse is real? Was that piece of paper the same one from the story? Was Corey writing the real-life events of his family's history?*

It was clear to me that at the very least, Corey believed himself to be cursed. His words in life and on the page spoke of a dark fate, retribution for his forebears' wrongs. I didn't know how much of it was real happenings or just the guilt he carried with him.

My heart ached at the thought that he had been suffering all alone, that he hadn't been given credit for the things he had done and accomplished. I'd kissed Watt for returning my camera. I'd gushed to Corey about the poems that Watt had taken credit for.

I scowled at myself for not having seen it before. It was all so obvious, and deep down I felt like I knew. Had I not pulled away when Watt had tried to kiss me the first time? Had I not kept him at a distance when he'd said he wanted to get to know me? Something within me had clearly known something was off about him, even though I outwardly disagreed with Alia on the subject. And all along, hadn't I been pulled toward Corey at every turn? It was as if my soul recognized him even when my eyes did not.

I clenched my jaw at the thought of Watt's deception. He wasn't going to get away with this. He had lied right to my face, and he was going to answer for it.

The next morning, I stormed around the manor looking for Watt. My face was hot with fury, and my limbs strained with rage.

"Have you seen Watt?" I asked Gwynn in the hall, a bucket of water and a rag in her hand.

Her eyes widened at the expression on my face. "Uh, yeah, he was down in the boathouse when we arrived."

"Thank you," I spat.

My rage built with every step, the morning wind not enough to cool my temper.

But as I neared the boathouse, I slowed my approach when I heard voices. As much as I wanted to let Watt have it, it wasn't necessary to involve any of our coworkers.

"Aw, come on, Luc, don't be like that," Watt said. "I spent the weekend with you, didn't I?"

Nearing the door, I peered into one of the windows. Lucero stood with her arms crossed, her lips pursed in irritation as Watt rested his hands on her shoulders.

Lucero turned her head to the side in a dismissive gesture. "I don't care. I saw your expression yesterday. You were jealous when I told you that I saw her with Mr. Bennings."

Watt's voice was soothing and persuasive. "Why would I be jealous? You know you're the only girl for me." He slipped his arms around her waist, and though she didn't yield, she didn't struggle either.

I curled my lip. *How dare he make such a big deal about Corey when he's actively playing both Lucero and me?*

She laughed bitterly. "The only girl? I'm tired of your lies. Do you think I don't know that the other writer left because of you? And now with the photographer. Who's next, eh? Have you tried Gwynn yet? How about Alia?"

Watt scowled. "Don't be disgusting. That girl has slut written all over her. Anyone that full of herself is probably carrying all kinds of diseases. Besides, I'd have to climb a beanstalk just to reach her."

Bile rose in my throat as my rage hit its breaking point. Watt was clearly the scum of the earth. First lies, then cheating, and now this? He wasn't even worth the tongue-lashing I'd had planned for him.

Turning on my heel, I left him to Lucero. She could do what she wanted with him.

CHAPTER XLVII.

"WHAT'S WRONG with you?" Alia asked when I sat at the desk beside hers, jerking my chair closer. "You look like you're about to chew someone's head off."

I snorted an angry sigh, pressing my computer's on button with more force than necessary. "Let's just say that you were absolutely right about Watt."

She leaned toward me, lowering her voice in an eager whisper. "What happened?"

I shook my head. "I don't want to talk about it."

She frowned but let it go. "All right. I won't push for now, but I'm here if you need me."

My anger eased, and I gave her a tired smile. "Thanks." *She made it her personal mission to find out what Watt was up to. I won't be able to hold her off for long, but I'm still too annoyed to talk about it at the moment.*

"Meanwhile, I have a problem of my own." She pursed her lips.

I typed my username and password into the computer. "What's that?"

She sighed the most dramatic sigh I'd ever heard. "Woe is me. My love is doomed to be star-crossed."

I huffed out a laugh, and she smirked over at me.

"I contacted those two businesses in town, and the best time for us to visit is Saturday, but I have my first date with Phil this weekend." Her bright aura seemed to dim with disappointment.

"Well, what if we just go without you? I mean, I don't want to cut you out or anything, but we only need pictures and stuff, right? I can tell you what's happening in all of them, and if you want to include more information, you can call the places on the phone."

Her blue eyes sparkled, and she clasped her hands together in a pleading gesture. "Would you? I would appreciate it so much. I really like this guy, and I think he really likes me, too."

I was glad I could do something nice for her. "Sure, no problem. In fact, I'll go upstairs and let Corey know the plan right now."

Alia raised one eyebrow. "Corey, is it?"

I stood from my desk, turning my face away from her. I left without another word, her soft chuckle following me out.

Sighing a steadying breath, I straightened my shoulders. I had a lot I wanted to say to Corey even if I didn't quite know where to start. I began a dozen sentences in my head as I climbed the stairs, and each one faltered unfinished. My knock on his office door sounded too loud and echoed in the room beyond.

"Come in," he called from inside.

Despite his clear invitation, I hesitated, my hand resting on the doorknob as my heart pounded in my chest. I suddenly felt so foolish, so embarrassed, for not having realized that everything I'd liked about Watt had been Corey all along. *How could I have been so wrong?*

The doorknob twisted in my hand, and I yelped as I jumped back.

Corey stuck his head out. "Oh, it's you, Wren. Come in."

Was that warmth I heard as he spoke my name, or was I imagining it?

He crossed the room to his desk, and I shuffled after him, ducking my head guiltily at the thought of the last time I'd been in this room. I stared at the papier-mâché box on his desk, the curse from the story hidden under its elaborate lid. *If the curse was real, then what of the other stories? Was the ghost that choked him as a child also real? Are all the strange occurrences I've experienced in this house caused by some otherworldly force? Is that whom he was talking about when he told me to stop torturing him yesterday?*

"What can I do for you?" Corey asked from his office chair.

I flinched at the sound of his voice as it pulled me back into the present. "Oh, um, Alia set up an appointment for us to go to that farm and coffee shop this weekend, but she has plans, so I told her that we could go without her. It shouldn't be a problem for me to collect everything she'll need."

He nodded his acknowledgment. "All right. Why don't you take the rest of the day off then since it seems you'll be working this weekend?"

His words went in one ear and out the other. I couldn't help but stare at him, pale against the dark colors of his suit. I wondered if the black waves of his hair were as soft as they looked, and I wanted to hear his full lips whisper my name in the night.

His dark eyes watched me closely. "Are you all right?"

"Who? Me? Of course." But the more he stared, the more nervous I felt. *Why am I being like this all of a sudden? He's the same Corey he was before.* No matter what I screamed inside my head, I knew that wasn't quite true. Sure, he was the same, but I wasn't, my perception of him wasn't. And not only had all of my feelings been forced to the surface in the light of truth, but he wasn't nearly as accessible as Watt. Corey wasn't open about his thoughts and feelings, and he was my boss. If I misjudged the situation or handled it poorly, I wouldn't only be dealing with a bruised heart. I could lose my job.

But when I met his eyes, even across the room, I could see the concern in them. Even if he didn't feel like I did, I could at least set the record straight about the book and thank him for getting my camera back.

"A-actually, Corey, there are some things I'd like to clear up if you have a minute."

He made a hand gesture that suggested I take a seat across the desk from him. I didn't move toward him. My nerves couldn't handle sitting at the moment.

"The other night, in the library—"

My words were cut off when a loud ringing split the relative quiet of the space. Corey looked over at the telephone on his desk. "If you could just give me a moment to take this."

I backed away, my heart startled by the sudden sound. "It's fine. There's no rush. We can talk about it later."

In the men's drawing room, my back against the office door, I covered my face in my hands. *Jesus, why am I such a mess?*

CHAPTER XLVIII.

MY ANXIETY turned to annoyance turned to irritation. I felt ridiculous. I'd had no problem reaching out to Corey when I'd thought he was just my mysterious employer. But now that I knew he was the poet, now that I knew that he was even more kind and generous than I'd taken him for, now that I had a fuller picture of who he was, I felt shy. The moment I thought of him in that way, I lost my nerve. It was absurd, and I took it out on my lunch by stabbing the pan-fried potatoes on my plate.

Watt had wisely not said a word to me that day though he likely thought I was still angry about our fight the night before. I didn't much care. I'd deal with him when the time came. Right now, I was too frustrated with my own weakness to spare a thought for him even though I could feel him shooting me glances across the table. I could also feel Alia's curious gaze on me; I knew she was itching to know what had happened between us. But if I explained what happened with Watt, I'd have to tell her about everything with Corey too, and my heart was still too jumbled and uncertain to talk about it. I hoped she would be patient enough to wait until I was ready.

I was in a pissy mood for the rest of the day, more with myself than anyone else. When the sun had long set, I sat on my small bed, Corey's book resting on my knees as I reread, caressing the ink strokes with my fingertips.

Knowing they were his words shed an entirely different light on the poems. I could picture his face so easily, twisted in fear and agony, tormented by unseen forces and guilt for things he'd never done. *He's prepared to suffer alone.* I couldn't let that happen. I may not have been overly bold when it came to relationships; my fear of rejection was much stronger than my fear of loneliness. And, as strange as it was, I'd always found the ache of a love unspoken, even unrequited, as beautiful as it was bittersweet. Even so, I couldn't let him face it all by himself. Maybe he would push me away, but I wasn't going to give up without even trying.

I got up from my bed and walked to the window, trying to peer past the trees to see if there was a light on in the manor but to no avail. I slipped on my boots and held his book close to my chest. *Perhaps he will be walking again tonight.*

It was cold and windy when I stepped into the night, but at least it wasn't raining. As I entered the greenhouse, I thought about going back for a jacket. The air was humid and pleasant amongst the plants. I determined to warm up a bit and then go back to the dorms for more suitable clothes before continuing my walk.

A cool breeze drifted down the path toward me, and I spun around to find Watt standing there. I glared at him.

"I get it," he said. "You're still mad, but can't you understand it from my perspective?"

I sighed, and it came out more like a growl. "You can drop the act now. I already know everything."

He tilted his head in confusion, and the gesture just pissed me off.

"You lied to me about this book. You didn't write it. Which, why? Why would you even lie about something like that? You know what? I don't actually care. That's bad enough. But then you got all upset about me getting close to Corey when you were trying to get with both Lucero and me. You've got some nerve."

"I did write it," he insisted. "And where did you hear that? Did Lucero tell you that?"

My mouth dropped open in disbelief. His audacity was remarkable. "Are you kidding me, right now? I saw you two together with my own eyes. And if you're going to try to take credit for someone else's work, you should probably get better at mimicking their handwriting."

He sighed heavily. "Fine. Okay? I didn't write it. But you were so into it that I thought if you thought I wrote it, you would let me in. I really like you, and I didn't know how else to get close to you."

My stomach rolled as if I would vomit. "Yeah? You like me so much that you tell Lucero that she's the only girl for you? Just save it."

He clicked his tongue. "So what? You're allowed to say that a few kisses don't give me the right to get jealous of Bennings, but you're allowed to get jealous of Lucero?"

I groaned. "I'm not jealous of Lucero. She can have you. I just think it's rich that you would get all pissy about Corey when nothing happened while you were actively doing stuff with someone else. But you know what? It doesn't even matter. Ship has sailed. Conquest over." I turned on my heel and stomped back toward the dorms. My mood was ruined, and I was too worked up to talk to anyone else that night.

As I set up my equipment in the library the next day, I decided to wait to talk to Corey once we went ashore that weekend. It would be easier to have an uninterrupted conversation then, and it gave me more time to think about how I wanted to approach the subject. I hoped that I wasn't just losing my nerve in the light of day.

But as Saturday morning dawned and I put on my modern clothes, my determination hadn't wavered.

The morning air was warm and the wind calm as I waited for Corey on the dock. Alia stood beside me, looking as cute as ever in her beret and long jacket.

"So you're meeting Phil in town then?" I glanced over at her, all primped and prepared for her date.

"Yeah, we're meeting for lunch at a little bistro."

"Well, I hope it goes well for you."

She gave me a bright smile. "I have a good feeling about this one." Then she raised her eyebrows, glancing past me.

I looked over my shoulder as Corey started down the planks of the dock. He wore jeans and a black buttoned-down shirt, the straight lines accentuating the broadness of his shoulders compared to his narrow hips.

Lines from his poems drifted up to my mind, echoing in my ears as if he were saying them right to me.

You will know me
When together at last
Though we have yet to meet.
But gentle and fast,
Whisper your name to me now
So I might find you fast.

I wondered what the pale skin of his chest would feel like beneath my lips, and I forced my attention toward the lake. *Oh my God! Get a hold of yourself.*

CHAPTER XLIX.

———

ON OUR WAY ashore, Alia detailed to us again exactly where we were going and who we were to meet. I tried to pay attention to her words, but my queasy stomach made me miss a lot of it. Once on land, she gave us a happy wave goodbye and went on her way.

"Do you need a minute?" Corey asked, staring down at me as I got used to the ground not shifting beneath me.

I planted my feet and took a few deep breaths, then sighed a satisfied sigh. "I'm good." I glanced over at him and blinked in confusion. I didn't know if it was the light or if I just wasn't used to seeing him in modern clothes, but he looked almost like a different person. He no longer looked pale and drained, and his dark eyes were bright and lively.

He smiled easily at me, and I nearly had a heart attack. "Good. Let's go."

I followed after him, my brow scrunched, wondering what had changed during that boat ride. *Was he just tired and needing a change of scenery?* I peeked over at him as he unlocked a black car just ahead of us. *Is he excited to spend the day alone with me?*

I tried to pluck out that hope before it took root in my heart, but I didn't succeed. Corey might not have been overly forthcoming with how he felt toward me, but I was certainly closer to him than the others were. He even called me by my first name now.

With light in my heart, I climbed into the passenger seat of his car and buckled myself in. I arranged my camera bag comfortably on my lap while he typed the first address into his phone.

He shifted the car into gear. "I'm glad we're going to the coffee shop first. I could use a strong cup."

I was a little surprised to hear that. He seemed so energized compared to how he normally was.

We didn't speak for a while, and I looked out the window at the buildings surrounding us. The words I needed to say swirled in my mind. The atmosphere between us was easy and comfortable, which was so unusual that it made me hesitate. Did I really want to ruin it? "Corey, do you recall the other day when I said there were some things I wanted to clear up?"

He hummed his assent.

"Well, I realized that I never thanked you for getting my camera out of the pawn shop. So I want to thank you sincerely from the bottom of my heart." I wasn't about to tell him that I'd thought Watt had done it. I'd already have to apologize for that where the book was concerned. And having someone take credit for your art was far more hurtful.

His eyes flicked to mine for a brief moment, and he frowned as he looked back at the road. "I was worried you were angry. I didn't mean to go through your wallet. You left it on my desk when you were filling out your employment paperwork, and when I picked it up to return it to you, the ticket fell out. I can only imagine how hard it was for a photographer to part with her camera even if only temporarily."

My chest warmed at his self-conscious explanation. "It was.

Thank you very much for getting it back for me."

"You're welcome," he said simply. "And I have to say, your photographs are already better for it. I don't know if your camera is just better than ours or if you're more comfortable with yours, but there's a clear difference in the work posted to the shared drive—not that the earlier ones were bad."

I smiled to myself. He'd said he would look at my work once Dominick had posted it on the website, but he'd obviously been tracking it in the shared drive. "It's likely the latter. The camera you provided is quite good, but I've had this one for a long time. It's very special to me, so I can't tell you how grateful I am that you got it back for me. My…my dad got it for me before he died."

"Oh, I'm sorry to hear that," he murmured. "Were you two close?"

"Yeah, we were."

"I'm sure that makes it more difficult, but count that as a blessing. Not everyone gets to be close with their parents."

My heart panged as I recalled the lines from one of his poems. *Was it true that he lost both of his parents when he was very young?* Watt had said as much too, but Watt was a liar. When I glanced over at Corey, I didn't want to ask. His expression teetered between moods, and I didn't want to push him back into melancholy. "Did you really go all the way to Philadelphia that day to get my camera back?"

His silence told me that he did.

"What a kind and generous thing to do. I really can't thank you enough." My tone held all of the warmth and affection I had for him.

But he didn't look like he appreciated it. The glance he shot me was serious; his cheeks flushed as he gripped the steering wheel. "Don't," he said low and urgent. "Don't put me on a pedestal."

I flinched, a little gasp escaping me. *What could he mean?* I stared at his profile as he drove, and he didn't look at me again. *Was I doing that again?* Though Izzy had teased me about falling in love too easily, I knew it was a bad habit of mine, especially when it came to creatives. Of course, this time I hadn't known that Corey was the poet. I frowned and cast my gaze out the window. *Am I putting Corey on a pedestal? Is he not as good, honest, and kind as he seems? Am I ignoring something that will be obvious to me later?*

I wasn't sure, and his words seemed a warning to re-examine my own impressions and feelings. I still wanted to apologize to him for giving credit to Watt for his writing. I still wanted to be there for him in whatever harrowing situation he was clearly dealing with at the moment. But perhaps now was not the right time to bring up any of that. We had a day of work ahead of us, and his mood had started so warm and refreshing.

"I've never seen anyone roast coffee beans before," I said lightly. "But I'm more excited about going to the farm if I'm honest. Animals are always fun to photograph. Do you think they'll let you get involved? The pictures will be that much better if you interact in the process."

The little worry that had crept into me eased when he answered in that easy tone from before. "We'll just have to wait and see."

CHAPTER L.

THE DAY WAS as pleasant as it could be. The people at the coffee shop and farm were kind and welcoming and were very excited about partnering with Moonseed Manor. I got great pictures of all their processes and even some fun shots of Corey with the animals and in a beekeeper suit.

As we climbed into his car for the long drive back to the harbor, I hoped that I'd made enough mental notes for Alia to do her part.

I sat in the passenger seat, toggling through the photographs I'd taken that day and smiling at a job well done.

"That doesn't look good," Corey muttered.

I looked up from my camera, following his gaze to the dark storm clouds we were driving toward. The thought of getting on a boat in those conditions made my stomach twist. "Do you think we'll pass through it? I mean, they won't run the ferry if the conditions are bad, right?"

He frowned, ducking his head to get a better look through the windshield. "No, they won't run the ferry if it's dangerous. But I'm more worried about driving through it at the moment.

Hold on." He pulled over to the side of the road and took his phone from the dashboard.

I anxiously watched his face.

Finally, he shook his head. "It's not a good idea. Look."

I stared at the storm radar map on his phone. There was a lot of dark red, even some bright pink, from where we were all the way to the shoreline and into the lake.

"What are we going to do?"

He looked down at his phone and started typing. "We'll have to find a place to stay for the night—and quick by the way those clouds are looking."

After a few heavy minutes, Corey turned the car around and headed away from the storm. And ten minutes later, he pulled into a little roadside motel.

"Wait here," he instructed before getting out.

I stared at the motel out the window, wondering if it would hold up if that bright pink on the radar should bring hail down on us.

Not long after, Corey returned and opened the passenger door. "Here, pick whichever room you like better." He handed me two keys. "I'm going to go down the street and get us a pizza before we're stuck for the night. Anything you want on it?"

I shook my head, climbing out of the car with my camera bag.

"All right. I'll be back soon. Get inside."

I squinted against the wind as it whipped my face and nearly knocked me over. All I could think about was how glad I was that I wouldn't be getting on a boat tonight.

The two keys Corey gave me were for rooms two and three, and there wasn't much difference between them. I chose two just because it was the second one I looked at.

The room was similar to those I'd cleaned at my previous job, and I was glad to see that the housekeeper was just as meticulous as I had been. In some ways, it was nicer than the place I had worked at. They'd put a small table and some chairs near the door, which beat eating on the bed.

I stood by the window, watching the parking lot for any sign of Corey's return. When twenty minutes turned into thirty, I started to worry. The wind menaced the nearby evergreens, and I could hear the wood creak under the pressure. I wondered if I shouldn't get a cellphone after all. This waiting and being unsure was nerve-wracking. But ten minutes later, he pulled into the nearest parking spot, and my tension eased.

I opened the room door for him, and he hurried in, two small boxes in his hands. He placed one on the table, took up the other room key, and then turned to me.

"I'm sorry about this inconvenience. I'm sure you'd rather be back in your own room."

The door to room two was still open, and I could hardly hear him over the wind. I shook my head. "It's not your fault there's a storm. I'm just glad I won't be on those choppy waters. Thanks for all this, the room and the pizza, too. Do you want to shut the door so we can eat?"

He glanced over his shoulder, then back at me. "I better not. You have a good evening. I'll see you in the morning."

I frowned but nodded. "You too."

With a hard slam, likely only because the wind was so strong, he shut the door and passed by the window. I sank into the chair at the table, the scent of pizza wafting to my nose.

Mechanically, I opened the box and started to eat. Somewhere in my mind, I registered that the food was good, warm and gooey in all the best ways. But all I could do was stare at the empty seat across from mine. *Couldn't he have eaten with me at least? Was there any harm in that? Was he so tired of my company?*

I knew that last one wasn't true, though I couldn't stop myself from thinking it. It was far more likely that he was trying to give me space. That he didn't want me to feel uncomfortable. Or maybe he was pulling away as he always did after we'd gotten just a little bit closer.

I frowned at the thought and shoved the rest of the slice of pizza into my mouth. *Not this time.* Rising from my chair, I marched to the door and stepped outside. The rain had started. It pelted my arms like pebbles as the wind tried to splatter me against the wall. But that wasn't going to stop me either.

I pounded heavily on Corey's door to ensure he heard me. He opened it a few moments later, holding the door firmly against another gust.

"Can I come in for a second?"

CHAPTER LI.

————

ONCE I WAS inside with Corey's dark eyes watching me, I didn't feel quite as bold. I lowered my head but forced myself to speak, though my voice was much quieter than I would have liked. "I'm sorry."

"What for?" His tone was compassionate and encouraging, and it gave me strength.

I stood up straighter, meeting his gaze. "I want to apologize for giving Watt credit for your poems. I feel very foolish for thinking that he wrote them, even if he told me he had. I'm embarrassed enough to have gotten it so wrong, but then I went and said it to your face."

He shook his head. "There's nothing to apologize for. You were lied to, and they aren't that important. They're just words."

"They aren't just words to me," I insisted. "I…I can't tell you how much they moved me. I'm not as good with words as you are, so I'll probably get this wrong. But they spoke to me on such a level… It's like they reached deep inside me and pulled all my emotions out. Sorrow, despair, longing, love, fear, horror. I could feel everything you felt, hear your heartbeat in every word. It was as if all the world was just a mirage, and this was the only thing that was actually real. I'm getting it wrong. I can't say it right. I'm sorry. But, you see, they aren't just words to me. They are you, your soul, your thoughts, your feelings. And I gave them to someone else, which just feels wrong and dirty somehow."

He let out an unsteady breath, and a war seemed to brew in his eyes. "I shouldn't have hired you."

My heart felt like he'd reached inside my chest and crushed it like some naked, skinless tomato. I couldn't even take a breath. I'd gotten it wrong. I'd ruined everything. Lightning flashed outside the window, the rumble of thunder right on its tail.

He took a step closer to me and lifted his hand to my face as if he would stroke it though he stopped short of touching me. He licked his lips. "I knew I shouldn't do it, but I couldn't stop myself. Your photographs just spoke to me, gnawed at me. I knew that you saw the world the same way that I did, felt it just as keenly. And even though I knew it was a bad idea, I brought you here. I had to meet you, had to know you, if only for a short time. But now, I see the horrible mistake I've made. When you say things like that to me, when your eyes look at me like that, how am I supposed to face my fate?"

I managed a shallow breath, uncertain how to take this mixture of emotions he was sharing with me. "What fate?"

He shook his head and started to pull away, but I snatched his hand and pressed it to my cheek.

"Corey, please. Tell me."

"I'm dying," he said clearly.

I started to tremble, my knees wobbling—only just holding. "You're sick?"

"No, I'm slowly being murdered. You've read the stories. I know it sounds crazy, but it's all true. There is a curse on my family, brought on by the greed of my ancestors. After so many years, a child would be born, a child who would suffer for their sins. First, all of our money would be drained away, then this child would endure the fear and agony of his forebears' victims. That's me. I'm that child. Seeing the mark of the curse upon my head, my own mother went mad with sorrow and killed herself. My father followed, his heart finally giving out after years of grieving her loss. And the moment I returned to that island, the spirits have slowly taken their revenge. First, they frighten me, then torment me, and finally, they will kill me—suffocate me the way they were."

His words were absolutely mad, and I believed every one. The strange sounds and shadows, the incident in the library where he appeared to be choking. "If it only happens on the island, why don't you just not go back?"

"I've tried, but somehow, I always find myself there. It's like I'm compelled to return. I've long accepted that this was my fate. What happened to those people, those miners? It was too awful, and they deserve justice. And besides, there's nowhere else for me to go."

"But you didn't do that to them," I protested. "You never could have done something so horrible. Why do you have to pay for their sins?"

He stroked my face with his thumb, his eyes sad. "This is why I shouldn't have brought you here. If I hadn't let you get close, if I hadn't wanted to let you get close, then only I would be suffering now. I'm sorry."

"No," I said firmly. "I don't accept this. There has to be a way out of this curse. I have a friend named Cecily, she's a wycche. She knows about curses and stuff. Maybe she can help."

"Please…don't give me hope. It will only be that much worse when it's dashed."

"Corey." I rested my fingertips on his chest. "I don't want

to make anything worse for you. But you said you brought me here because you wanted to know me. Well, I want to know you, too. I want to get so lost in you that I don't know how to find my way back. Won't you let me try to save you? And if I'm wrong, and if this curse is unbreakable, I'll be here with you until the end. I don't want you to face this alone."

"Are you a blessing sent to save me in my darkest hour? Or are you but one last torment?"

"Which would you have me be?" I whispered.

"I'd have you either way." Lowering his face, he brushed his lips against mine in the sweetest, saddest, most desperate kiss of my life. The electric air of the storm as it raged outside seemed to make our exchange that much more intense.

It was far too brief, and he pulled back only enough to take in my reaction.

"What do you want?" he murmured, his words like soft kisses on my skin.

"I want to hear you call my name even above the crash of thunder."

Leaning down, he brushed my hair aside and pressed a kiss to my neck, and my whole body hummed. "I will if you will."

I let out an uneven breath as I trembled against him. He felt warm and solid, no longer just pen strokes on a page. And as he claimed my lips again, I wanted him to pour all he was into me, to stain my soul black with his ink. I wanted all his longing, all his fear, all his torment; I wanted his everything.

He didn't seem in a rush, trailing his fingertips down the sides of my body. My breath caught as his thumb stroked the skin just under my T-shirt near the waistband of my pants. That gentle touch set me alight, and I knew taking this slow would not work for me.

The storm raged outside, but the one within me was even more fierce.

I clenched my fists, the smooth fabric of his shirt wrinkling as I took a step toward the bed, pulling him along with me so as not to break our kiss.

Picking up on my urgency, he needed little encouragement, releasing my hips only to begin unbuttoning his shirt.

His black eyes, glinting in a flash of lightning, watched me with rapt attention while I removed my jeans and shirt.

And I followed his movements just as keenly while he revealed every inch of himself to me. He was lean, his muscles not as defined as they would have been were he used to manual labor. But he didn't work with his body; he was a poet. And he had the thinness of someone who spent more time agonizing over unearthly torments than enjoying the mundane delights of this world.

And though I wished that he did not carry around such pain, I still thought him beautiful.

As I looked down at myself, standing in that cold motel room in my dingy old bra and the cheapest panties I could find, I did not feel self-conscious. The intensity in Corey's eyes, the intensity that I had once found cold and intimidating, did not leave room for me to feel that way.

I knew that he wanted me. He wanted every flaw and blemish, every hardship, every skipped meal, every sleepless night, and all the tears that had long dried up.

"Wren," he whispered as he closed the distance between us.

And that's all he kept saying, upholding his promise to speak my name while he stripped the last of my clothes from my skin, while he stripped away the last of the barriers he'd put between us.

Never had my name sounded so sweet and yet so painful. For a man full of words, it seemed he needed only the one to make himself understood.

Despite the storm, I heard him just fine, his lips at my ear with his cock deep inside me. As I clutched at his back, his scent all around me, I couldn't accept that he would leave this Earth anytime soon. He was too alive—too real—to disappear.

"Corey," I gasped, breathlessly. "Stay with me."

"Until the end," he promised.

CHAPTER LII.

"I WONDER…" Corey muttered, lying naked on the bed of his motel room.

I lifted my head from his chest and propped it in my hand. The storm outside had passed after raging for hours, and all was quiet.

Corey's black eyes met mine. "Did I plan all this somehow?"

"What do you mean?"

He frowned. "I told you not to put me on a pedestal. I can never be sure of my own motivations. I think I'm doing something good, returning your camera to you, for instance. But then it turns around and benefits me. How can I know that I'm doing good for good's sake? Perhaps it was all some subconscious plan hatched in the back of my brain."

I ran my fingertips over his chest. "Would you have felt cheated if this hadn't happened?"

He raised his eyebrows. "Cheated? No, that makes it sound like you owed it to me. But…I still wanted it."

"Did you? I couldn't tell."

"Wouldn't it have been kind of creepy if you could? I'm your boss. That's an abuse of power."

I snorted a laugh. "I don't think you have to worry about whether this was all some grand machination. Your morals clearly would have gotten in the way of you doing anything too bad."

His brooding expression didn't budge. "I suppose."

I scooted my body up so that my head was next to his. "You hid it so well. When did you want it most?"

"When didn't I? From the moment our eyes met, before you even stepped off the ferry, I've thought of little else. I've been tugged between fear and desire, one moment indulging in feverish dreams of you, the next chased by spirits of the dead. It has been a very harrowing few weeks."

"Oh, come on. I don't believe that, but your words sure are pretty."

He looked me straight in the eyes, his expression the most serious I'd seen from him. "That night atop the tower, I felt like I could spend the rest of my life looking at you watch the sky. And in the library…"

"In the library…?" I whispered, my body heating as my heart raced.

"You wore those tiny little shorts and that thin-strapped top."

"Not very period-appropriate."

"Appropriate fuel for my yearning for you."

I pressed an ardent kiss to his lips, my flesh burning for his touch. Any coherent thoughts in my head fizzled and disappeared as he turned his full attention to proving his words true.

And so it went. The night was spent in bursts of lovemaking and lulls of pillow talk. Neither of us slept as if we shared the unspoken fear that this might be our first and last night together.

When dawn light lit the back of the window's curtains, we turned away from it, cuddling in close with his chest to my back.

"Let's run away," I said, my voice hushed.

He tightened his arms around me. "Do you mean it?"

"Would you if I did?"

"No."

I sighed. "I thought not."

He didn't speak for a long time, and every moment the sun's rays grew brighter and more insistent. "You don't need to put yourself through this, Wren. We can walk out this door and pretend none of this ever happened. I'm good at pretending."

I squeezed his hand. "Don't even think about it. You pretend too well. I might lose my mind and think I imagined the whole thing."

He pressed a soft kiss to my shoulder, and a shiver ran through me.

"You won't push me away once we get back, will you?" I asked, picturing that professional mask sliding back into place like the Victorian clothes he wore so well.

"I don't think I'm capable of that now that I've let you in."

The tension in my chest eased a bit. I hadn't known how much I was worried about that until he'd given his reassurance.

"We should…probably get ready to go," I said reluctantly.

"Probably."

Corey made no move to get up and neither did I.

We might have lain like that forever, clinging to each other, clinging to that moment to try to make time stand still. Unfortunately, the world outside went on without us, and our peace was shattered by the insistent ring of Corey's cellphone.

Slowly, he released me and reached for it on the bedside table.

"Hello?" he said, not quite hiding his irritation.

With his head so close to mine, I could hear the person on the other end.

"Mr. Bennings? This is Madison Winstell with *Travel + Leisure* magazine. I'm sorry to bother you on a Sunday, but my editor is breathing down my neck for next month's issue. I'm calling about the ad you purchased. Do you have a date for your grand opening yet? Are you still wanting to run the ad in June?"

"Yes, Miss Winstell, give me a moment to look at my calendar." Corey rose from the bed, and I smiled at seeing the moon so early in the morning. He walked over to his bag and pulled out his datebook.

I rolled onto my back, his voice washing over me as he spoke into the phone. I didn't pay attention to the words, just let the tones seep into me and soothe me.

I must have drifted off to sleep because I jolted awake when I heard my name.

"Wren." Corey hovered over me, fully dressed with hair damp from the shower. "Do you want to shower before we check out?"

Do I? My tired body didn't really want to move just yet, but I'm sure I smelled of sex and sweat, the traces of which had dried on my skin.

I hissed as I stiffly got to my feet. It had been a while since I'd had sex and even longer since I'd done it all night. My desires may have been satisfied for the moment, but my body was sore.

Corey reached out to steady me when my legs shook a little. "Are you all right?"

"Worth it," I told him, standing straighter with a bit of effort. "It'll be better after a hot shower."

CHAPTER LIII.

"COULD I BORROW your phone?" I asked Corey as he pulled his car out of the motel parking lot.

"Sure." He handed it to me.

As I started to type in Cecily's number, I smiled at the screen. It had been saved as "Wren" in his phone. The call rang in my ear and went to voicemail. "Hey, Cecily, it's Wren. Call me back, please. I have some questions about some wycche stuff, and it's urgent. This is Corey's phone. Thanks."

Corey glanced over at me. "She didn't answer?"

"She never answers numbers she doesn't recognize. She'll call me back when—" The phone started buzzing in my hand. "Right now. Hello?"

"Who's Corey?" Cecily asked on the other end.

"He's…" I shot him a glance. "My boss."

"You slept with him, didn't you?"

My mouth dropped open. "How did you—"

"I didn't. Your reaction just told me." She laughed. "Damn girl, you work fast. So what's going on? What do you need help with?"

"I have questions about how to break a curse. I'm going to put you on speaker. Corey can explain better." I pressed the speaker button. "All right. Go ahead, Cecily."

"Hey, Mr. Bossman, I heard you slept with my girl. Was she wild? I always got that impression given how wrecked Gerrit looked whenever he left our dorm room."

My face flushed. "Cecily!"

"I'm sorry!" she yelled back. "Actually, I'm not. Anyways… What's up? Are you cursed?"

I didn't dare look at him.

"I am," he confirmed, his voice sounding suspiciously like he was trying not to smile.

I peeked over at him and scowled at the fact that I was right.

"Are you sure? Because a lot of people think they're cursed when it's just bad luck or even Karma."

"I'm sure."

"All right. Give me the details. Who? What? When? Where? Etcetera."

He sighed. "It's kind of a long story."

"Give me the short version."

He frowned, staring at the road ahead of us. "Over a hundred years ago, a woman put a curse on my family. We would lose all our money, then a child of a certain appearance would be the sign that the curse was near completion, and that child would be tormented and killed by the spirits who lost their lives in a tragedy that was my family's fault."

"Oh. Damn. That sucks. Do you know how she cast the curse?"

"She wrote it on a piece of paper in her own blood."

Cecily hummed. "Blood curses can be tricky to break. Any idea who this woman was? Does she have any living descendants?"

"I doubt it. She lost her husband and all her sons in the

tragedy, and she killed herself in our house right after writing the curse."

"Well, fuck. Death magic, too?"

My stomach twisted. I didn't like the sound of Cecily's response.

"What are the exact words she wrote down? Do you know?"

"Word for word:

On this land, bought with blood,
In this house of brick and mud,
An heir will born,
His features warn.
With hair as dark as blackest soot,
Thus know the curse is afoot.

Every penny, every sou,
Will drain like life of the men slew.
One year for every soul
You sacrificed in search of coal.
And when the years are matured,
The heir will know what we've endured.

The pang of hunger, the burn of thirst,
The sting of poverty is but the first.
When gasping for breath and crying from fear,
When everything lost that was held dear,
The spirits bygone is all he will see.
This is my will. So mote it be."

"Okay. Do you think you can send that to me? I didn't hear anything in it that sounds like a way out, but I'd like to study it to be sure."

Corey's face was pale and grim. "Yes."

I reached out and took his hand. The smile he mustered was weak and seemed quite devoid of hope.

Cecily sighed heavily. "So…death magic is seriously strong. To give up your own life force to power a spell… Well, it won't be broken by simple protection magic or the like. From where I sit now, your best option is to find a descendant of the wycche who cast the curse. It likely won't be a direct descendant given what you've told me, but who knows? A great-grand-niece or someone might work. In any case, you need that person's blood."

"What are we supposed to do with it?" I asked.

"Worry about finding them first. Sounds like you have a search ahead of you."

My heart sank. This wasn't going to be anywhere as easy as I thought it would be. "All right, Cecily. Thanks. I'll email you that information when I get back to my computer."

"Hang in there, Wren. And Corey?"

"Yes?"

"I'll, uh, look into some things that might ease your pain a bit as well."

"Thank you," he murmured.

"Good luck. We'll talk later."

"Okay. Bye," I said.

She wished us goodbye and hung up.

I lowered my face, staring down at the phone screen without really seeing it.

"Hey," Corey murmured, squeezing my hand. "Even if I could be happy for only this one night, it's more than I'd ever hoped for."

I pursed my lips at him, my nose burning as I fought tears. "Don't come at me with that sort of talk. We still have something we can try. I'm not giving up yet. Do you know the name of the woman who cursed you?"

"I know her first name was Maggie, but I don't know her surname."

"That's a start… Can I borrow this some more?" I held up his phone.

"Sure. But what for?"

"When I was looking up the history of the mining accident before, there was a list of victims. We know that Maggie lost her husband and three sons, so if we search the names on the list for multiple men with the same last name, we can cross-reference against obituaries. They always list those who survive the deceased."

Corey nodded, then tilted his head. "When did you search for the mining accident? How did you know what one to look for?"

I flinched, a guilty little thorn digging into my heart. I didn't want to tell him I'd gone snooping around his office with Watt. "I…got curious after reading your stories and wondered if any of them were based on real events. The company was called the Bennings Mining Company, so it wasn't hard to find."

"Oh."

My chest tightened at how easily he swallowed my lie. *What will it matter anyway? I won't be helping Watt anymore.*

CHAPTER LIV.

THE ONLY impression I got from the list of victims of the mine tragedy was that many of them were related. *This is going to take longer than I expected.* The document, which listed all of their names, had been handwritten and scanned. The handwriting and paper dimensions were awkward on Corey's cellphone screen. I squinted and turned the phone every which way, then gave up with a sigh. I would have to do a proper job on an actual computer.

I gave Corey his phone back and tried to push my anxiety from my mind. There was nothing I could do at the moment.

Corey laced his fingers with mine and brought my hand to his lips. "Don't get so wrapped up in the search that you miss what little time we have. I don't want what could be our last days together to be me watching you fall apart."

He was right, but his words only made me feel more anxious. *How many days will we have?* Still, I didn't want to upset him, so I just smiled and nodded and talked of other things.

Our progress toward the ferry was slow going. The storm had done a number on the roads, with trees and power lines down and all manner of small inconveniences. But I was in no rush to get back on that boat, to return to the island where Corey would be tormented yet again.

We did eventually reach our destination, after stopping for lunch along the way, and the change in Corey was immediate. It was like the very ground zapped the life from him. His complexion paled, and his movements seemed weighed down and sluggish.

"Are you all right?" I asked him, resting my hand on his shoulder as the manor loomed ahead of us.

He gave me a tired smile and nodded. "I better go change out of these clothes."

I grabbed the sleeve of his shirt to stop him from leaving so soon, and he looked back at me. "Can I…can I come to you later?"

He stared down at me for so long that I was sure he was going to refuse. "Sure, but why don't we both get some rest first?"

I nodded reluctantly and headed toward the dorms.

Nora was in the common room when I entered, watching television with an embroidery hoop on her lap.

"Good afternoon, Nora. We just got back. We had to stay overnight on the mainland because of the storm. How did you all fare here?"

She muted her show. "It was a rough night. I think a few limbs came down. Watt was out there cleaning them up this morning. But other than that, we were fine."

"Did Alia make it back all right?"

Nora shrugged. "The ferry didn't dock last night, so she must have been stranded on the mainland, too."

I hope she had as good a time as I did. "Oh, okay. Thanks."

She turned the television sound back on.

I changed into pajamas when I reached my room and fell

asleep as soon as I hit the sheets.

I awoke with a start when a knock sounded at my door. My head was heavy with fog while I shuffled across the floor to answer the call.

"Will you be having dinner with us?" Nora asked. "I just need to know how many to cook for."

"Is Alia back yet?"

She shook her head.

All I could think about was Watt and me staring at each other from across the table as Nora silently ate her meal.

"No, thanks. I'll just grab a sandwich later."

She acknowledged my answer and went about her business.

Moving to the window, I stared at the trees. They were much fuller than they had been when I'd first arrived not very long ago. The leaves swayed gently in the breeze, no trace of the storm that likely ravaged them the night before. Daylight was still holding on though the sun was approaching the western horizon. *Is Corey sleeping well? Are the spirits leaving him alone? Is it too early to go to him?*

I didn't like the idea of leaving him alone in that big house, surrounded by ghosts bent on tormenting him. But he had told me to get some rest. *Well, I did rest though. Didn't I? I'll just sneak over there and tap gently at his door. If he's sleeping, I'll come back later.*

I looked down at the shorts and cami I was wearing, the same outfit Corey had remembered so vividly, and grinned to myself. I pulled on my boots to head to the main house and then thought better of it. It wasn't nighttime, and we were supposed to dress appropriately when outside the dorms. Even so, I left my pajamas on under my uniform and hurried up the path to the manor.

With it being a Sunday, the house was quiet. I'm sure Nora was in the kitchen making dinner, but I couldn't hear her. I crept up the stairs to the third floor and tapped ever so quietly at Corey's bedroom door.

I held my breath, waiting with my heart in my throat for any indication that he'd heard me. Suddenly, the door flung open, and Corey stood there looking like he was prepared to see the Devil himself. He sighed heavily, relief clear on his face.

"May I come in?" I asked, looking around to see if there was any danger I hadn't perceived.

"Please do." He stepped to the side to invite me into his space.

I would have thought that the room slept in by the master of the house would be the grandest. That just wasn't the case. Oh, there were the stained-glass windows and the same vaulted ceiling. But the decorations, the bedding and the rug, were all quite muted and plain. Even the mantle above the fireplace was bare and unadorned. I wondered if Corey had saved the elegant design for the guests or if he just didn't like such splendor. Even so, his bed was something to remark upon—very large with a heavy, carved headboard finished in black.

"Did you get any sleep?" I asked, turning toward him as he closed the bedroom door.

"Not really. They always seem more active when I'm gone for a while like they have to make up for lost time."

I frowned. "Would it help if I laid with you? I could even stay awake if you'd like."

He wrapped his arms around my waist and rested his forehead heavily on my shoulder. "I hope it will be that easy."

CHAPTER LV.

"COME ON," I urged in a soothing tone. I took his hand and led him to his bed. "Get comfortable, and I'll join you in a second."

"What are you going to—" He cut himself off as I unbuttoned my dress, his dark eyes watching my every move.

"Don't worry. I'm wearing pajamas," I said with a smirk.

"Not for long."

I crawled into bed beside him, and he immediately wrapped his arms around me, pressing a kiss to my throat. "As much as I would love to right now, I really think you should sleep."

"I'm not that tired."

I giggled at his insistence, but I still shook my head, stroking his hair in a calming gesture. "The bags under your eyes could fit everything I own. Come on. You can afford a few hours. And when you're all nice and rested, we can tire you out again."

He pursed his lips. "You promise?"

"Just get some rest first." I gently guided his head to my chest, cradling it against me as he settled down. He really didn't need much encouragement. His limbs soon relaxed, and his breathing evened out. I continued to stroke his hair, the black waves softer than I'd imagined, and stared up at the ceiling.

A low rumble jerked me from sleep when I'd just drifted off. It was followed by the loud crash of what sounded like rock on rock. My eyes flew open, and I sat up in bed. I coughed, squinting when they burned as if I'd gotten smoke in them.

I blinked past my tears, and that's when I saw them. Men and boys in miner's clothes, their mouths agape in soundless screams as their flesh slowly burned, charred bits of bones exposed in their faces and hands. Their eyes were haunted and dull.

My lungs stung as I filled them to scream, but a hand over my mouth prevented me from giving it voice.

"Don't," Corey wheezed between coughs, his hand still on my lips. "It's not real. They won't hurt you. They only want me."

I stared at the specters, my eyes nearly popping out of my head. They looked so unearthly; their forms somehow opaque yet fading in and out.

Corey's hand slipped from my face when he curled onto his side, shaking as he struggled to take a full breath.

I could smell the burning flesh and singed hair. It dried my throat and made my eyes water. But under my panic and horror, I could still breathe.

I rose onto my knees and covered Corey's body with mine as if I could shield him somehow. "I'm here, Corey," I told him. "You aren't alone. Just listen to my voice and breathe. Can you hear me?"

He nodded slightly.

I dared to look up at his assailants. "Go away," I ordered.

They glared at me in fury; their eyes no longer dull but blazing. Then they disappeared.

Corey relaxed beneath me, sighing out his tension as if it was his last breath. "They're getting stronger," he whispered.

I stroked his back, and I didn't know whether the gesture was to soothe him or me. "How do you know?" I pulled back to look down at him.

He just stared straight ahead, his eyes fixing on nothing. "You saw them. No one else has ever seen them. Or if they did, they never said. And they can affect more, and they stay for longer. It used to be just a smell or just a sound, but now they can pull me in as if I'm really there with them, trapped in that mine."

"So they just run out of time?" *Me telling them to go away didn't do anything? What happens when they have enough strength to stay until they finish the job?*

"For now."

I swallowed down my dread. I didn't know how he had been living with such horrifying experiences for so long, all alone and knowing that they would one day take him. How had he survived? How had he not gone mad?

"W-we're going to fix this. I won't let them have you." My tone didn't sound nearly as certain as it had before. "I'm—"

A firm knock thumped on the door, and I nearly jumped out of my skin.

"Mr. Bennings?" Nora called from the other side. "I've brought your dinner if you're hungry."

Corey's eyes flicked to mine.

I sprang from the bed, grabbing my dress and boots, and ran to the bathroom.

He hadn't told me to hide; I'd just moved without really thinking about it.

"Come in, Nora," Corey called.

I heard the door open and her footsteps on the floor though I couldn't see her through the crack in the bathroom door.

"I've made stroganoff this evening. I know how much you like it."

"Thank you. That sounds delicious, Nora. I'm sure I'll enjoy it."

Her footsteps headed back toward the door but stopped halfway. "Mr. Bennings, I hope you don't mind me asking, but are you all right? It's just…I've known you all your life, and you seem harried as of late. I know your parents wouldn't have wanted you to open this place up to the public if it caused you so much grief."

Corey's answer was affectionate and warm toward the older woman. "Thank you, Nora. I am a bit tired. But everything will be all right once we've got the hang of things. We're fully staffed now, and it won't be long before we're open. I appreciate your concern, but I'll be fine."

"All right. Well, let me know if there's anything I can do for you."

"I will. Thanks. You have a good night."

"Goodnight, Mr. Bennings." The door shut with a thud and a click.

I crept out of the bathroom, watching Corey as I moved. He still sat in bed, frowning down at the nest of blankets beside him.

"Nora seems worried about you. Does she know anything about what's going on?"

He glanced over at me. "No, and I don't want her to."

"How come?"

"Nora has been with the family for a long time, since before I was born. She's been like a favorite aunt. A nanny raised me for most of my childhood, but every time I had to come here for something, Nora would pet and spoil me. She always made time to tell me stories or play games. I…don't want her to have to worry about this." He moved toward the covered tray that Nora had placed on the table.

"But, if you're that close, don't you think she'd be shocked if you died all of a sudden?"

"Better that she mourns my tragic death than knows I've lived a cursed life."

"Better that we break that curse and you can live happily until you're old and grey."

His answering smile seemed unconvinced to me.

CHAPTER LVI.

I SLEPT IN Corey's room that night. The rest of the night was undisturbed, and he looked more refreshed for it.

"Are you wanting to keep us a secret?" I asked, leaning against the bathroom sink as he turned off the shower.

Steam billowed out of the glass door when he opened it and reached for a towel. He glanced at me, drying his face before wrapping the towel around his waist. "Are you?"

I scowled at him. "That's a fine way to dodge my question."

He approached me and grabbed me by the hips, pressing me to him. The water from his skin seeped into the fabric of my dress, and his hair dripped onto my shoulder. "I'll follow your lead on this matter. I'm putting you in the power position here. You can tell everyone if you want them to know, or we can keep it between us. Whichever you're comfortable with."

His chest was still hot from the shower, and it seemed to burn my fingertips. I looked up at him through my lashes. "Well…I wouldn't say I want to keep it just between us. As much as keeping it a secret seems like fun, it would likely be a lot of effort. And it's not like I'm ashamed or anything."

Corey smirked. "But?"

"But it doesn't really need to be broadcasted either. I mean, if it comes up, then it comes up."

He kissed my forehead. "Very well." He moved to pull away.

I made a small sound of protest, pressing my hands more firmly on his chest. "But, even if we're at work, you can feel free to call me if you need me, okay? I mean, if they're bothering you, I'll drop whatever I'm doing to come help. And I'll stay with you at night whenever you want me with you."

"I hope you won't take that back," he said, dipping his head to kiss me on the cheek. "Because I can be very clingy, byproduct of never really knowing my mother, you know. At least, that's what the psychologists said."

I stood on my toes and wrapped my arms around his neck. "Cling all you like." Then I kissed him deep and long. I smiled as I felt his cock harden against me, digging into my stomach through the fabric of his towel and my dress.

My body warmed, and I broke our kiss to take a proper breath. "How much time do we have?" I gasped as he breathed heavily into my ear.

He grabbed me by the hips and lifted me onto the counter, settling between my legs. "Enough."

There was no clock in the bathroom, so I didn't know how he knew. But when he started to slowly gather the fabric of my skirt, I didn't much care.

He hadn't been correct, or perhaps he had been too thorough in his lovemaking. Either way, I walked into the office a half hour later than usual.

"There you are, Wren. Did you get a late start this morning? How did the field trip go?" Alia asked as I turned on my computer and sat down.

More like I got an early start. "It went well. I'm about to upload the files to my computer. Then we can go through them together and pick which ones we want to send out."

"That works."

"Oh, how did your date go by the way?"

She grinned at me. "Stormy nights are the very best for staying in, don't you think?"

As always, Dominick proved to be the picture of gentlemanly fortitude while we two had our thoughts in the gutter.

Poor guy. We should get him a fruit basket or something for all he puts up with.

I spent the rest of the day editing the many photos I'd taken on our trip to the mainland.

At lunch, I sat on the opposite end of the table from Watt. Whether he looked my way or not, I couldn't say, but he didn't attempt to speak to me. Lucero seemed in particularly good spirits during the meal.

Corey didn't call for me at all that day, and I hoped it was because his time was unaffected by otherworldly antagonists. After work had finished, I stayed behind to print out the five-page list of victims from the mining tragedy. I highlighted all of the names that were shared by at least four miners, cutting out about three-fourths of the list.

That left around thirty names to try to find obituaries for. *At least I know where most of them lived and what year they died.*

I managed to eliminate only one name before Alia popped her head back into the office.

"Are you still here? Are you trying for overtime or what? Come on, time to eat dinner."

Reluctantly, I put the list into my desk and shut down my computer.

After dinner, Alia wanted to tell me all about her date with Phil. And though I'd normally be glad to listen, I couldn't help but stare at the sunlight fading from the dorm windows. *Will*

Corey be all right until I get there? Are the spirits more active when the sun goes down?

"Did you hear me?" Alia asked.

I pried my attention from the window. "I'm sorry. What?"

"I said, Phil helped me find an apartment. They have immediate availability. I expect them to email me the lease by tomorrow, and I should be able to move in a few days."

"Oh, that's great. Will you need help moving or anything?"

"Not right away, no. I put a lot of my stuff into storage before leaving D.C., so that will have to be sent up here. All I have to move right now is what I brought with me. You can come help me when all that arrives."

"But if you don't have any furniture or anything, why don't you wait until you can send for your stuff? Why move so early?"

Alia frowned. "I didn't want to say anything, but haven't you noticed anything weird about this place? Maybe Watt's ghost story just freaked me out, but I do *not* like being here after dark. I'm probably just a big wimp, right?"

"Of course not," I reassured her. "If you aren't comfortable here after dark, you should follow that instinct."

Alia leaned in closer and dropped her voice though I couldn't really figure out why. "You should think about leaving too, Wren. Hell, you can camp out with me on my living room floor until you find a place if you want."

I admired Alia's intuition. It was really something else. But I wasn't going to leave Corey alone no matter what. I tried to give her a smile. "I like it here."

CHAPTER LVII.

BY THE END of the week, Alia had moved out of the dorms, and I was spending my dinners in abject silence with Nora and Watt. I suppose I could have just eaten with Corey, but I didn't want to deal with any feelings of special treatment. Still, I was glad Alia had gotten herself off the island. If the spirits were starting to appear to people other than Corey, I didn't want her to run into any of them.

I was completely exhausted. I spent my days working and researching the victims of the tragedy. My nights were restless, awakened every few hours by Corey's ghostly tormentors. Corey assured me that the frequency and length of their visits were holding steady in recent days and that I shouldn't be too worried about him dying any minute. I wanted to be reassured, but I couldn't be confident about how honest he would be on the subject, how much he was trying to just make me feel better.

I awoke early Saturday morning, or perhaps I didn't really get much sleep to begin with. Either way, I dragged myself out of Corey's bed just after dawn, groggy and bleary. Corey still slept, his brow crinkled by some uneasy dream. I dressed as quietly as I could and slipped from the room.

The sun twinkled brightly through the arched windows of the hallway gallery, and I decided a walk before breakfast was just the thing to perk me up.

I was thinking about how many names I had left on the victims list as I made my way down the stairs and out the front door. The research was taking longer than I'd expected, especially when I had to jam it in after work hours.

I think I'll spend the weekend really buckling down. Finding the right family will be the easiest part of this whole process after all.

"I knew it," Watt spat, squinting at me with disdain in the morning light. "After everything I told you, you'd still betray me with my own brother?"

I blinked at him. He hadn't said a word to me in almost a week. What exactly was he accusing me of now?

He stepped towards me, lowering his voice in a menacing tone. His amber eyes blazed. "What's your plan, huh? Was this all an act? Maybe you were after him this whole time. Were you just playing with me, and then we didn't find proof that all this was mine, so you threw me over? Thought you could get it all if you hopped into bed with him?"

"What?" I was so confused by his delusions that I couldn't muster a more coherent response.

He pointed one shaking finger at me, his nostrils flaring. "I thought it was weird that you were so willing and then suddenly so cold. That nonsense about lying about some stupid poems was a flimsy excuse. You just moved on to Bennings, didn't you? I haven't seen you leave the dorms all week, and then I find you walking out the front door like you already own the place. You would fuck my own brother behind my back?"

I curled my lip in disgust. "You've lost your mind. Whom I fuck has nothing to do with you in any way. And I couldn't care less whether Corey has money or n—"

I yelped as he suddenly grabbed me by the waist, and I pushed against him, trying to extricate myself from his arms.

"I won't let you get the best of me," he said low in my ear.

"Let me go," I demanded, struggling and failing to pull myself from his grasp.

He smiled a nasty grin, and my stomach dropped. "Maybe you were right all along. Maybe the direct approach is best. I bet he'll forgive his own brother first." Releasing me, he spoke in an unnecessarily loud voice. "You've done better than I expected, Wren. I knew you'd be too sweet to resist. So have you found proof that I'm a Bennings yet?"

I shook myself, feeling gross from having had his arms around me, and stood to my full height. "What are you—?"

"Wren?" Corey's voice called softly from behind me.

I spun around. He stood, half-dressed and unsure on the doorstep, with no shoes and a half-buttoned shirt. His dark eyes were guarded, and I knew immediately what Watt was playing at.

"Corey—" I murmured.

Watt shot Corey a very convincing look of guilt, though I didn't think he was even capable of such an emotion. "Oh… I guess we might as well come clean now. The truth is that I'm your older brother. And Wren here agreed to help me find proof. She seduced you to get close to you and have easier access to your information. We even broke into your office together that night you were away."

I scowled at Watt. "What are you even talking about?"

But when I looked back at Corey, I could see his uncertainty, that same vulnerability that made his poetry so moving.

"None of that is true, Corey," I insisted.

"Oh, so you didn't agree to help me prove that I'm his brother?" Watt pressed.

"But that was before—"

"And you didn't break into his office with me looking for a birth certificate?"

I clenched my jaw. He was twisting things to his own means. "Yes, but—"

"So there you have it. We might as well be honest with him like I wanted to from the beginning." Watt took my hand.

I snatched my hand away. My stomach rolled, and I stepped toward Corey.

He flinched away from me.

"Corey," I said earnestly. "Let me explain. He's misrepresenting everything. That's not how it happened. I really care about you, and I never planned on going behind your back. I was never with Watt to begin with."

Watt snorted. "You certainly were when you kissed me during working hours in the third-floor guest room."

I flushed.

"You both need to leave," Corey said, his expression twisted in sorrow and pain. He turned his back on us. "You're fired."

My head spun, and my knees wobbled. Pain shot through me as I sank to the ground, my knees banging on the hard surface of the brick walkway.

"Come on, you'd fire your own brother? I came clean, didn't I? I just want to know where I came from."

"I don't have any siblings," Corey said hollowly.

"Yes, you do," Watt insisted. "I have proof. A trust was put in my name by Elizabeth Bennings, and I even have a baby blanket with the initials EB embroidered on it. Why would your mother do that if I wasn't her illegitimate son?"

Corey frowned, halting his retreat back into the house.

"Because she was a kind and generous mistress," Nora said

from the path that led to the kitchen, her face pale and her lips trembling. "You aren't Elizabeth Bennings's son. Your mother's name is Eleanor Birchill."

Corey's eyes widened.

"Me," Nora clarified.

CHAPTER LVIII.

THE WORLD stood still for a moment. Nothing moved. Nothing breathed. Not even the trees twitched a leaf.

"What…?" Watt whispered, his brow wrinkling as he blinked in confusion.

Nora stood up straight, her face weary with age and burden. "When I was a new kitchen maid at my very first job, I fell in love with a man who worked on the ferry. He promised me everything—a bright future, marriage, a family—so I was happy when I found out I was pregnant."

She shook her head. "But he lied. He never came back for me. I was in a bind. What was I to do, an unwed girl of only nineteen? Mistress Bennings took pity on me. She told me that she would support my child until his twenty-first birthday. She would make sure he had everything he needed to succeed."

Nora's eyes filled with tears. "I didn't even get to see him when he was born. I didn't get to name him. I had to be satisfied that he would have a better life than I could ever give him." Her voice broke. "I didn't know what I was giving up. I didn't know how my heart would ache every day for him."

Watt shook his head. "No, this can't be right. It doesn't make sense." His eyes sharpened, snapping to Nora. "Where's your proof?"

Nora showed him her palms. "I have none. Mistress Bennings took care of everything… That blanket…the one with my initials, I embroidered an autumn birch tree on it." She searched his face and smiled warmly. "You have the same color hair as I did before it turned grey, and your eyes…they're just like my mother's were."

"Stop it," Watt snapped.

Nora flinched.

"You abandoned me as a baby, didn't even bother to know my name, and you think we're going to have some touching mother-son moment? No. For years, I've thought that I *was* someone. I thought I was the heir to a great fortune. And now you're telling me that I'm the bastard of a kitchen maid who opens her legs to the first man who smiles at her? I thought my mother was dead, and now I wish I'd been right."

Nora shook, tears streaming down her face, as he flung his abuse upon her.

"That's enough," Corey barked, moving toward Nora and wrapping an arm around her shoulders. "I won't have you speak to her that way. Instead of being grateful that your mother is still alive and right in front of you, you curse her? You have no heart, and you aren't worthy of Nora. I want you off this island before noon." His cold, dark eyes flicked to me. "Both of you. I'll call for the ferry myself."

I pushed myself to my feet, my knees stinging. I knew him well enough now to know he was hurting. And I couldn't let him believe Watt's wild accusations. "Corey, please, will you just listen to me?"

He looked me right in the face. "I don't listen to liars."

I flinched as if he'd slapped me. And there was nothing else

I could say. I had lied, lied directly to him. I'd agreed to help Watt, and I'd broken into his office. I'd sneaked around Corey's back. I'd deceived him, and I didn't deserve his trust. This was all a result of my own decisions. My vision blurred with tears. I'd hurt him. All I wanted to do was help him, but I'd caused him nothing but pain. So I simply nodded and started toward the dorms.

I couldn't see the path at my feet from the tears in my eyes, and my chest ached with every shallow breath. My mind was a mess. I didn't know how I managed to pack my things in such a state. Perhaps I left something behind without even realizing it. Then again, I didn't have many things to begin with.

I changed into modern clothes, wiping the blood from my scraped knees with a washcloth before pulling on my leggings. I didn't have a bandage, but I knew how to get whatever blood leaked out of the fabric. I folded my uniforms, stacked them on the bed, and left the dorms. The wheels of my suitcase thumped on the brick path as I headed toward the house. I parked it by the door and went into the office.

I glanced around the entrance hall. Was I hoping Corey would be waiting for me? I couldn't say. Was it better that I didn't see him again before I left?

In the office, I grabbed my camera bag and the list of victims I'd been researching. I left only one thing behind—Corey's book with a sticky note that just said I was sorry.

Though I still had a hard time taking a full breath, I was starting to feel numb. My tears stopped, and my limbs felt too heavy to carry. I knew this cycle. I knew that in a few minutes, in a few hours, in a few days, I would feel it all again. I knew the agony would come back, and I would cry for what I had lost. But for now, for this moment, I felt blank.

I barely heard the wheels of my suitcase on the bricks as I trudged toward the dock. The morning was still bright, the pleasant breeze feeling strange on my swollen face.

Before it was obscured by trees, I looked back at Moonseed Manor. My heart gave one hard thump. Was that Corey looking down at me from the tower room window or was it some specter that would bring about his end? I blinked against the sunlight, but I couldn't tell.

Watt joined me on the dock not long after I arrived. I didn't even bother to look at him.

"You ruined everything for me," he grumbled.

I didn't respond. I didn't have the energy to respond. It would have been easy to blame him for the whole thing. If he hadn't told such an outrageous lie, then I could be in Corey's arms right now, and Corey wouldn't be facing his terrifying fate all alone. But I'd had my chance to come clean, and I hadn't taken it. I shared in this blame.

CHAPTER LIX.

THE JOURNEY to the mainland was the most miserable I'd ever been on a boat. I was glad I hadn't eaten breakfast because I dry-heaved over the side most of the way, a combination of being upset and the gentle waves.

Watt could have been thrown overboard for all I cared. He didn't speak to me again, and I was grateful for it.

As I stepped onto solid ground, I realized that I had absolutely nowhere to go. I had no job and no prospects. I'd just received the security deposit from my apartment in Philadelphia, and I had gotten my first paycheck the week before, but then I'd spent some of that on Izzy's crew fees. At least I hadn't purchased her tickets to visit yet.

Maybe I had enough to put a security deposit down on a new apartment if it was really cheap, but landlords weren't keen to rent to people without jobs or at least job offers. I could stay in a motel, but that just seemed like a waste of money. *Do I have to go home to my mom?*

I shuddered. That was my last resort. Besides, even if Corey had fired me, I still wanted to help him lift his curse. Even if he never wanted to see me again, I cared about him, and I wasn't going to let him just die. *It's best that I stay close.*

A forty-minute walk later, I stood on Alia's doorstep. She opened her door moments after I knocked, her blue eyes widening in surprise.

"Is that offer to crash on your living room floor still open?" I asked.

"What happened? I thought you liked it on the island?"

Tears welled in my eyes, and my nose started to burn. "I was fired."

"What? Oh my God, honey, come in." Her sympathetic tone was just what I needed, though it only made me cry harder.

For the next hour, between sips of warm tea and hiccupped sobs, I told Alia everything—well, almost everything. I told her about Watt's schemes and how he'd roped me into them. I told her how Corey and I had gotten together—she wasn't at all surprised—and how it had all fallen apart. I didn't mention the ghosts or the curse though. It was far too complicated, and I didn't really have the words to explain. Plus, it only would have freaked her out, and she was just settling into her new life.

I rested my head on Alia's shoulder as she rubbed my back. Despite not being a touchy person, sometimes I just needed that little comfort only human contact could bring.

"So what are you going to do now?" Alia murmured.

"I don't know," I said hollowly. "Look for another job, I guess. I don't want to take advantage of your kindness for too long."

"Well, don't worry about that right now. Just take a few days to recover and set a plan. All right?"

I nodded.

"Why don't you go wash your face with some cold water? I'm going to call Phil and tell him I can't meet up today."

I pulled back. "No, don't do that. I don't want to ruin your date."

Her eyebrows puckered with worry.

"Seriously. I'm fine. I'm not just going to sit around. I'm going to go to the library and do some research."

She quirked her mouth, then sighed. "All right. If you're sure."

I gave her what probably looked like a broken smile. "I'm sure. Go ahead. Don't worry about me."

She squeezed me a little and then let me go so I could rinse my face.

Before leaving for her date, Alia handed me her spare key in case I got back before her. She also looked up where the nearest library was, and I was glad to see it was within a comfortable walking distance.

I probably should have spent the next few hours looking for jobs, but I spent it going through the list of mine disaster victims instead. I was so focused on my task that I jumped when the librarian told me they were closing for the night.

Still, I didn't have many names left. I didn't know whether that was encouraging or not. On one hand, I hadn't found a whiff of anyone named Maggie. On the other, if there was only one victim with a wife or mother named Maggie, that would focus my secondary search.

My stomach grumbled as I stepped onto the street. I hadn't eaten all day. And though I didn't much feel like eating either, I stopped at a gas station and bought a granola bar. Wondering where the nearest dollar store was, I walked back to Alia's apartment, the granola bar too dry and crunchy to be pleasant.

Alia still wasn't back from her date when I arrived, so I let myself in. I took my time getting ready for bed, showering and pulling on my pajamas, the routine comforting in its own way. The scrapes on my knees were already starting to scab over, but they still stung when I bent my legs. I lay my pillow and blanket out on Alia's living room floor beside her green sleeping bag. And then I just stared at the ceiling.

Was it really only this morning that I left Corey's bed, that he breathed softly beside me? Was it really only yesterday that he made love to me so sweetly as if we wouldn't see tomorrow? Tears leaked out of the sides of my eyes and trailed down into my ears. *I guess we didn't see tomorrow after all, at least not together.*

I wondered if he was lying in his bed trying to sleep or if he'd gone back to wandering the island, his restless steps driving him to exhaustion.

"I'm sorry," I whispered as if his warm body were still beside me. "I'm still going to help you. I want you to live a long and happy life even if it's not with me."

I rolled onto my side and squeezed my eyes shut, glad that Alia wasn't there so I didn't have to stifle my sobs.

Eventually, I cried myself to sleep.

CHAPTER LX.

ALIA WAS VERY gentle with me the next morning, all soft tones and kind words. I appreciated her sympathy, and I felt bad for having to rely on her in this way.

"Do you want to do something today?" she asked before biting into a piece of peanut-butter toast.

"I was planning to head back to the library, actually."

"You're so diligent. Are you sure you don't want to go to the park? It's supposed to be nice again today."

I did, in fact, think the park sounded lovely, exactly what I needed to fortify myself for everything ahead. But I wasn't going to give myself a break, not when there were still names on that list to be checked. "Maybe we can go this evening when the library closes? It isn't open for many hours on Sundays."

She smiled. "All right. Let's do that then. Why don't I come pick you up from the library around closing time? We can get something to eat and take a long walk."

"Sounds good."

I was standing anxiously at the automatic doors of the library the moment they opened, and I rushed to a computer before the librarian even had time to sit back down. Before jumping in, I thought I'd better check my email. I was expecting something from Cecily. She'd promised to rework the curse so that we could have a way out once we found Maggie's descendant.

An unread email from Cecily was waiting in my mailbox. I clicked on the bold text to open it.

What the hell is going on?

I called Corey to tell him about some protective measures that might slow the spirits down, and he told me not to worry about it anymore. He said you don't even work there anymore???

Did something happen between you two? Are you all right? I don't understand what's going on. Message me immediately when you get this.
C

I sighed. I didn't want to explain everything to Cecily right now, but I took the time to do so anyway. I wrote out a very long email telling her what had happened and how I was still going to help him.

Then I got back to work. A few hours later, I gnawed at my lip. There was only one page of names left, with only four names highlighted.

Is it possible that I missed one? Am I going about this all wrong?

I blinked at the last set of names, tilting my head—William, John, Harry, and David Birchill.

Why does that sound familiar?

I did a search for "William Birchill 1894 Bennings Mine disaster."

The first hyperlink led to a newspaper out of Mansfield,

Ohio, covering the disaster and listing William Birchill as one of the victims. *It must have been really big news for an Ohio newspaper to cover it even though it happened in Pennsylvania.*

The second link was to a genealogy website. I clicked it, and it brought up his entry.

William David Birchill
Birthdate: September 15, 1842
Birthplace: Forest Row, East Sussex, England, United Kingdom
Death: January 27, 1894 (52)
Mount Blessed, Allegheny County, Pennsylvania, United States
Immediate Family: Son of <u>David William Birchill</u> and <u>Ann Saxbury</u>
Husband of <u>Margaret Birchill (Walworth)</u>
Father of <u>John Birchill</u>, <u>Henry (Harry) Birchill</u>, <u>David Birchill</u>, and <u>Arabelle Birchill</u>

"This is it," I said excitedly, then ducked my head in embarrassment when the librarian smiled at me. *Maggie is short for Margaret. All their children but one died in the mine. She said she lost her husband and all her sons, but she also had a daughter.*

I clicked on Arabelle's name, and it brought me to another record.

Arabelle Birchill
Birthdate: February 13, 1886
Birthplace: Mount Blessed, Allegheny County, Pennsylvania, United States
Death: June 17, 1947 (61)
Mount Blessed, Allegheny County, Pennsylvania, United States

Immediate family: Daughter of <u>William David Birchill</u> and
<u>Margaret Birchill (Walworth)</u>
Mother of <u>William John Birchill</u>

Following the trail, I clicked on William John's name.

William John Birchill
Birthdate: November 5, 1902
Birthplace: Mount Blessed, Allegheny County,
Pennsylvania, United States
Death: January 22, 1996 (93)
Oswego, Oswego County, New York, United States
Immediate family: Son of <u>Arabelle Birchill</u>
Husband of <u>Rosalie Birchill (Wilson)</u>
Father of <u>William Henry Birchill</u>

William Henry Birchill
Birthdate: December 15, 1940
Birthplace: Oswego, Oswego County, New York, United
States
Death: July 7, 1985 (44)
Oswego, Oswego County, New York, United States
Immediate family: Son of <u>William John Birchill</u> and <u>Rosalie</u>
<u>Birchill (Wilson)</u>
Husband of <u>Sabine Birchill (Allaire)</u>
Father of <u>Eleanor Birchill</u>

I stared at the screen, the familiarity of the surname coming
back to me. "No way. Nora?" My head spun, and I lay my hands
flat on the desk to stop myself from feeling dizzy.

*Nora was a descendant of the wycche who cursed Corey's family
this whole time? Does she know? Is this all a game to her, or is it
just some cosmic setup?*

I could still hear the warmth in Nora's words when she spoke to Corey, her fierce defense of him and his family. *Could she really be that devious?*

I shot out of my seat. *I have to go. Corey could be in even worse danger than I imagined. He's alone with Nora right now.*

But then I froze. *What am I going to do? How am I going to convince Nora to give us her blood to break the spell if she's been there the whole time in order to see it through? Can I really get Watt to do it?*

"But I have to at least try," I whispered. I closed the tab I was currently on and was about to close the one that had my email still pulled up when I saw that I had another message from Cecily. I clicked it without sitting down.

That's very like you to help him even though he didn't give you a chance to explain and fired you. All right. I'll follow your lead. I've attached the spell that should reverse the curse. Best case scenario: you get the descendant to write this down for you in their blood. That's probably not going to be easy in today's world. But even a few drops should do. The most important thing is that the descendant needs to have the clear intention of lifting the curse. They need to forgive Corey and his family.

Good luck and keep me posted.
C

I opened Cecily's attachment and scribbled down the words on a piece of paper from the library's desk, not even paying attention to what they said.

Out on the sidewalk, spell in hand, I wracked my brain, trying to think of where Watt would go if he had nowhere else.

CHAPTER LXI.

ONCE I REACHED the marina, I headed for the apartment building where Lucero lived.

She said she lived on the top floor. I ran up the stairs, my scabs stinging in protest, until I reached the fourth floor. I frowned at the row of apartments that stretched out before me. *I guess I'll just have to try every one until I find it.*

The man who answered the first door I knocked on hadn't even bothered to put pants on, his boxers pushed low by his potbelly.

"Um… Does Lucero live here?" I asked, trying to keep my attention on his beady eyes.

He shook his head. "No, you're looking for 403." He pointed two doors down and gave me a friendly smile.

I blinked and returned his smile. "Oh, thank you very much."

"No problem," he added pleasantly before shutting his door.

Following his directions, I went to the appointed apartment and knocked. Lucero answered a minute later. Her expression darkened upon recognizing me. I understood that she had seen me as a rival before, but she had never looked so hostile.

I reflexively avoided her gaze. "Hey, Lucero, is Watt here?"

"You've got some nerve showing up here after what you did."

I furrowed my brow.

"Haven't you ruined his life enough?" Her voice was getting louder and louder as she went on.

Watt appeared over her shoulder.

"You get him fired, you—"

I glared at him, cutting off her rant. "Are you serious? Do you have no shame at all?"

He shrugged as if to say, "No, not really." Then he rested his hands on Lucero's shoulders. "I'll take care of this, Luc. Your sister is asking for your help anyway."

Lucero gave me one final stab with her eyes before turning on her heel and stomping farther into the apartment.

Watt crossed his arms and leaned against the door jamb, raising his eyebrows in a gesture that asked me what I wanted.

I steeled my gut. "I need your help."

Amusement sparkled in his eyes, and he grinned. "Do you?"

"Yes."

"And what's in it for me?"

I scowled at him. "The feeling you get from being a decent human being for once in your life."

He quirked his mouth. "Doesn't seem worth it. But now I'm curious."

I sighed angrily through my nose. "Corey is cursed, and we need your blood to break it."

His expression told me he clearly didn't believe me. "Okay. I'll play along. Why does your precious Corey need *my* blood?"

"Because it was your family who cursed him."

He had the audacity to laugh, a long hearty chuckle. "Oh, that's too good. Maybe the universe is just after all."

"This isn't funny. He's going to die," I snapped.

He sobered immediately. "Good. Let him."

"God! What is *wrong* with you? How can you be this cold?"

"Why would you expect me to be any different? Has anyone ever shown me warmth? Why should I help him when he's never helped me?"

"His mother took care of you most of your life."

"Yeah? Gave me the taste of a life I would never have. Actually, you know what? I will help Bennings."

I flinched at his sudden change, looking at him from the corner of my eye.

"Sure, he can have my blood if he signs everything over to me. The hotel, the island, everything."

I just stared at him, my mouth hanging open. Then I shook my head. "I don't know how I ever took you for a better man."

"Hey, a man's got to eat. That's my offer. Take it or leave it."

I sighed. "I don't speak for Corey, so how can I?"

He smirked at me. "Oh, right. Your sweet love threw you out without a second thought, didn't he? I guess that's what the better man does."

I clenched my jaw. "You're such a dick."

He didn't acknowledge my words. "Well," he said with a sigh. "I better get back to Lucero. She's been *such* a comfort in my current situation." He moved to step back into the apartment.

"Wait! I can't promise that Corey will agree to that. But if you come with me to the island, you can ask him yourself."

"Will you plead my case for me?"

I ground my teeth. "I'll do whatever it takes to save Corey's life."

Watt gave me that warm smile of his, that fake smile that I had so easily allowed to deceive me. "I'll get my shoes."

When we reached the harbor, the ferry to the island was already out making its rounds for the day. On a Sunday as pleasant as this, many of the boats were gone. I scanned the marina. There was only one other person there, an old man climbing into a small motorboat, fishing tackle in his hands.

I rushed toward him. "Excuse me, sir." I waved my arms.

He was already inside the boat when I reached him. He looked up at me from under his bucket hat.

"Hi, I know this is inconvenient, but could you give us a ride to Nightfall Island? We've missed the ferry, and we need to get there as soon as possible."

The man frowned.

"I can pay you. It's really an emergency, life or death."

"How much?" he asked, squinting at me suspiciously.

"I have thirty dollars on me, but I can send you more once I get to a computer."

"Two fifty."

My mouth dropped open. "Two hundred and fifty dollars?"

The man stared at me blandly, then shrugged.

"Fine." I pulled out my wallet and handed him all I had. "I can send you the rest."

He shook his head. "Cash only."

"But—"

He pointed at the ATM near where tickets for the ferry were sold.

I sighed. "All right." I turned to head that way, then looked back over my shoulder. "You won't leave without us?"

He snorted. "For two hundred and fifty dollars, I'll sit here all day."

CHAPTER LXII.

AS WE PLODDED out of the harbor, I thought about how little was left in my account. *It's worth it. There's no price I wouldn't pay for Corey's life.*

I looked back at the shore, suddenly remembering how Alia had said she would meet me at the library. "Do you have Alia's number?" I asked Watt, clinging to the railing of the boat.

He scowled at me. "Why would I want to call her?"

I clicked my tongue. *Jerk.* "Do you or not?"

"No."

I sighed. *I'll just have to call her from the island.*

The ride there took nearly twice as long as on the ferry, and I felt the waves much more on the smaller boat. But I didn't let myself get sick. I concentrated on the wind on my face and kept my eyes on the horizon.

It was eerily quiet as we stepped onto the dock of Nightfall Island. The day around us was pleasant with bright sunshine filtering through the new spring leaves of the trees.

Our shoes made little sound on the path that led to the

manor, and I scanned the windows for any signs of life. I found none.

"Where are they?" I asked Watt as we entered the front door.

He shrugged. "How the hell would I know?"

I bit my lip, listening hard to the silent house and clutching Cecily's spell in my hand. "Let's try Corey's office first."

The first stair creaked loudly when I stepped on it, the sound echoing despite the rug. I jumped, glancing around as if it had come from somewhere else.

Watt chuckled at me. "You really are cute," he said with a smirk.

I scowled at him and continued up the stairs.

On the second floor, we passed through the men's drawing room, stopping at Corey's office. I knocked on the door, opening it when I didn't get a response. The room was empty.

I looked to Watt, who shrugged. "Maybe he's in his room."

We headed back to the stairs and climbed to the third floor.

Outside Corey's bedroom, there was a covered tray on the floor. I bent down and lifted the lid. Nora had made him a turkey club for lunch, and he hadn't eaten a bite.

I tapped at the door, and a rustle sounded in the room beyond though Corey didn't answer.

"Corey? Are you in there?" I called.

There was more rustling, then a thump followed by rhythmic taps. Finally, the door flung open.

I frowned. Corey looked like shit. He still wore the clothes he'd been wearing when I'd left him yesterday morning. His hair was a complete mess, and his face was sallow and drawn with bruises under his eyes.

His black eyes barely had the energy to convey his displeasure at our return. "I thought I made myself clear."

I lowered my head. "You did. But I'm here nonetheless. I

found the descendant you need to lift the curse."

His expression didn't change, and he didn't speak for a few heavy moments. "Is that a thing you're still doing?"

I stood up straighter. "Yes, I made a promise to you, and I'm not going to let you die just because you don't want me anymore."

I don't know what he opened his mouth to say, but I cut him off. "Watt. Watt is the descendant of Maggie, the wycche who cursed you."

Corey's eyes flicked to Watt, who stood relaxed beside me. "You can't be serious."

"It's true," I insisted. "Birchill was a name on the list of victims. I followed the line all the way to Nora and Watt. I got the spell from Cecily, so all he has to do is write it down and give a few drops of blood. As long as the intention is there, the curse will be lifted." I held up the spell as proof.

"And why would he help me?"

Watt smirked. "I knew you were smart. I'll help you…for a price."

Corey curled his lip at him. "And what price is that?"

Watt waved his arms to indicate around us. "All this. Everything. The hotel, the island, and all your fortune over to me, and you can have my priceless blood."

Corey scoffed, laughing a sardonic huff of disbelief. "What fortune? The hotel? The island? None of it belongs to me. Everything belongs to a nonprofit. If it didn't, it would have been drained away long ago. That was part of the curse."

Watt's face flushed. "What do you mean?"

Corey shrugged. "The only money I have is what I earn from working here. My salary is the same as yours. You can have what I've saved if that will satisfy you, but you won't be getting the Bennings fortune because it's long gone."

Watt growled his frustration.

Corey continued, looking at me. "Sorry to disappoint your little scheme."

I frowned. "I had no scheme. I told you. Watt and I were never together. I agreed to help him search for his birth certificate, and, yes, I broke into your office to do that. But I severed ties with him the minute I realized he'd lied about the poems." I turned to Watt. "There. You see? There's nothing for you to gain. Will you do one decent thing in your life and just help him?"

Watt clicked his tongue. "Why should I?"

I groaned. *If it wasn't for the fact that we need his intention, I'd get that blood by punching him in the nose.*

"I don't need him," Corey said. "If it was the Birchills, I can just ask Nora."

My chest tightened. I still wasn't sure whether Nora had known about this the whole time, whether she was really on Corey's side or on the side of her great-great-grandmother. *I suppose there's no harm in asking her.* "Do you know where she is?"

He looked down at the food tray at his feet. "I haven't seen her all day. She asked me if she could stay in one of the upstairs guest rooms, said she wanted to be close to where she'd given birth to Watt…" Corey gave Watt a sharp glance. "She could be up there, or she could be starting dinner in the kitchen."

"We're closer to the guest rooms. Let's check there first."

Corey stepped over the food tray, and we started toward the stairs.

"So that's the end of the negotiation?" Watt asked, following after us. "You said you would plead my case."

I glared back at him. "I said I would do whatever it took to save Corey."

We climbed to the fourth floor and turned into the hallway with the guest rooms.

"I bet if we both gave you our blood, it would be even stronger," Watt said.

Corey ignored him and knocked gently at the first room on the left. No one answered, so he opened the door. He let out a strangled gasp and rushed in.

Nora lay on the bed, a kitchen knife in her hand, the purple of the bedspread had turned rusty—drenched in her blood.

CHAPTER LXIII.

AS I MOVED into the room, I saw everything in a second.

Nora was pale, her eyes drooping as she struggled to breathe. Her arms and hands were covered in blood, which still gushed from long slashes on her arms. The ghostly miners stood all around the room, watching as they faded in and out. But they didn't watch her with menace; it was almost as if they were there just to bear witness.

Corey had removed his shirt, and he was wrapping it around her wounds, his hands glistening in the cheery sunshine from the window. I rushed to help him, pulling a pillowcase from a pillow on the bed to bind her other arm.

"Nora!" Corey called, trying to focus Nora's glazed eyes on him. "Can you hear me?"

Her gaze shifted sleepily toward him, and she smiled gently. "Corey…" Her voice was weak and unsteady. "I…want…you to know…"

"You don't have to say anything," Corey insisted. "You can tell me whatever you want when we get you some help." Corey looked over at Watt, who stood rooted in the doorway, pale as he watched this nightmare unfold. "Call for help!"

Watt fumbled for his cellphone.

My hands were slick and sticky with Nora's blood. Still, I pressed on the pillowcase as hard as I could to try to stop the bleeding.

Nora shook her head, the motion seeming to take her too much effort. "Corey…I've…loved you…as my own… Don't… blame yourself… Live…. Live a long…and happy…life."

"They're…" Watt's hand fell to his side. His voice was uneven as he shook. "I don't think they're going to make it."

Nora turned her eyes toward Watt, but I didn't know whether she could even see him on the other side of the room. "My son… tell him… I'm…sorry…for everything… At least…"—her dull eyes seemed to lose focus, and her breathing rattled—"I got… to meet him…"

"No, no, no," Corey insisted, hovering over her. "Nora. Nora!"

But she didn't answer. She just stared at where Watt stood, not moving, not breathing.

The spirits around us faded, and I released Nora's arm.

Tears streamed down Corey's cheeks, and he shook with quiet sobs. He stared at Nora's face as if she would wake up if he looked long enough.

Watt stood away, not having moved. He didn't cry. He just stared into her dead eyes.

I sighed, rising from where I'd been kneeling on the bed, and picked up Cecily's spell from where I'd dropped it when I'd rushed to help Nora. The corner was steeped in her blood, and my fingertips left bloody prints when I handled it. *I don't think Nora knew about the curse. She would have helped him.*

I knew that now Watt was Corey's only hope. But I didn't push it at that moment. It wasn't the right time. They were both grieving in their own ways.

Folding the spell, I put it in my pocket and went to the guest room's bathroom to wash my hands. When I returned, Corey sat on the bed, his back to Nora's body. Watt was nowhere to be seen.

I went to Corey and stood before him. "Corey," I said gently. "Let's go back to your room so you can get cleaned up."

His black eyes were jagged and broken when he looked up at me, but he just nodded and stood to follow me. I led the way to his bathroom, opening doors and turning on faucets so he wouldn't smear blood everywhere. I left as he stepped into the shower.

I was planning to go back to my dorm room to change into the clothes I'd left on the bed. But as I passed through Corey's bedroom, I saw the dress I'd worn the day before—a small bloodstain where I'd scraped my knees—crumpled on Corey's bed, so I just changed into that.

I was sitting on the edge of Corey's bed when he came out of the bathroom, a towel around his waist.

"How long do you think it will take for them to get here?" I asked.

He moved to his wardrobe. "Why does it matter now?"

I stood from the bed. "I'll go make us something simple to eat. You haven't eaten all day." I started toward the door.

"Were you lying?"

I halted, turning back toward him.

"When you said all that before. Did you really cut ties with him before we ever got together?"

"I wasn't lying. The truth is that I was always a little hesitant around Watt. I fell in love with your poetry, but it never seemed to match who he was. And I was drawn to you even when I thought he had written it. I did eventually kiss him, but I thought it was because he had returned my camera to me. So you see, all the things that made me like him were you all along. I'm sorry for not coming clean. I should have told you."

His black eyes clung to mine. "Come back. When you're finished in the kitchen, come back and hold me. And don't let go even when I do something foolish like fire you."

I smiled at him. "I never did."

I left Corey to get dressed and headed downstairs toward the kitchen. But as I passed by the library, I saw Watt standing with his back to me, staring out the window.

"I'm sorry for your loss," I murmured, stepping into the library.

He didn't look back at me. "This is where I was, you know… when I first met her. I had arrived early for my interview with Bennings, and I was told to wait in here. She brought me a cup of tea."

I nodded. "She was a very kind lady." *I'm sorry to have doubted her.*

He didn't respond.

"I'm going to make us something to eat. Would you like any?"

He looked back at me. "Do you pity me now?"

"I sympathize with your loss. I know what it feels like."

He moved toward me. "Do you? Did your parents abandon you? Did they kill themselves?"

I took a step back. "No, but my dad died."

He bent down and picked something up off the floor. "Did he love you? Raise you as his precious child?"

I lowered my head. "Yes, he did."

Watt unfolded the blood-stained spell, which must have fallen out of my apron pocket. And started to read it aloud.

"On this land, bought with blood,
In this house of brick and mud,
The heir was born with hair of coal,

He's suffered in body and suffered in soul.
Now let this curse come to a cease,
And all you spirits rest in peace.
The debt is paid. Let him be free.
I release you. So mote it be."

He looked up from the paper, his gaze decidedly unfriendly. "What is this?"

"It's the spell to break Corey's curse."

He snorted. "Do you honestly think I would ever help him now? Oh, I didn't want to before, but I was willing to for money. You heard her last words. He stole my mother's love from me. He can die a slow and painful death and even that wouldn't be justice." Watt crumbled up the spell and threw it on the floor. "To Hell with both of you."

Then he stormed from the room.

My stomach rolled. I knew he was hurting, knew that it was normal to lash out when grieving. But I had no faith that that's all it was. Maybe when he had some more time, I could convince him that Nora would have wanted him to help Corey. But then, with his personality, that could make him want to do it even less.

I told myself I would let him calm down first and reassess the situation later, but I couldn't get rid of the anxiety that pressed in on me. *How much time does Corey have left? Will we be able to convince Watt before it's too late?*

My chest tight, I continued on to the kitchen. I could only concentrate on what I could do at the moment.

I was planning just to make scrambled eggs and toast, but as I entered the kitchen, the rich scent of savory stew filled the space. I walked over to a slow cooker and lifted the lid, my mouth watering at the smell of the last meal Nora would ever make.

CHAPTER LXIV.

I RETURNED to Corey's room with two bowls on a covered tray. I didn't know where Watt had gone off to, but he could go to the kitchen when he was hungry. I didn't want to press him anymore that night.

Corey teared up when I lifted the lid off the tray. "Beef bourguignon," he murmured. "My favorite."

"Nora had it simmering in a slow cooker when I went down there," I told him, sharing her last loving act with him.

He cried through the whole meal, and I couldn't help but join him.

After finishing and washing our faces, we lay together on Corey's bed. Someone would be coming soon, someone who was much too late to do Nora any good but who would want to take her body and ask a lot of questions. There was nothing we could do now but wait. So we did. We lay together, wrapped in each other's arms, and just breathed. The sky outside the window darkened as night fell, and the stars started to come out.

I thought about Watt, and I wanted to tell Corey about our exchange. I didn't want to add to his burden, but I'd only gotten myself in trouble by keeping things from him.

Just when I opened my mouth to say something, I started to feel dizzy and nauseated. I clenched my eyes against the feeling. Beside me, Corey began to gasp for breath in that now-familiar sound that said the ghosts had arrived.

"Corey." I sat up and looked down at him. "Corey, can you hear me?"

"Wren," he choked. His eyes were distant and unfocused. "I can't see you."

My gaze swept over the menacing faces of the miners, their forms pulsing with power as they glared at him. "Leave him alone!" I screamed.

But they did not relent.

I clasped Corey's hands in mine. "Can you feel me?"

He squeezed back, and I took that as a good sign. "It's so loud." He trembled and shook, gasping for breath.

The next few minutes were agony, torture for Corey and horror for me. Eventually, the miners faded out, and Corey's eyes cleared.

He squeezed his eyes shut. "I'm sorry. I'm sorry you had to go through that," he told the dissipated spirits.

"Can you see me?" I asked.

He opened his eyes and focused on me, then nodded. "It was awful, Wren. It was like I was right there. The smell, the sounds, men burned, I—"

I shushed him. "It's all right. You don't have to tell me. You're here now."

His face crumbled in an expression of fear and anxiety. "They're even stronger…"

I wrapped my arms around him, cradling his head to my chest. "I know…" *Is Watt really going to just let him die? If we show him what Corey is going through, will he really have the heart to refuse him?*

Eventually, Corey and I fell into an exhausted sleep, clinging to each other as if that would provide us with any kind of safety.

I don't know what time it was when I awoke to the smell of burning. I sniffed, then coughed. *Are they back already?* But when I looked over at Corey, he still slept peacefully. And then I heard it—the loud, insistent beeping of a fire alarm.

My heart jumped into my throat. "Corey, wake up!"

He jolted awake. "What?"

"There's a fire!"

Panic taking hold, we scrambled from the bed, not even thinking to put our shoes on. Corey grabbed my hand and pulled me toward the door, testing the knob to make sure it wasn't hot.

Once in the hallway, the smoke made my eyes burn, and I covered my mouth with the sleeve of my dress.

At the stairs, I looked up as black smoke billowed from the upper floors. Corey yanked on my hand, pulling me down the stairs. "But what about Watt?" I shouted over the ear-splitting alarms.

"We'll worry about him once you're out safely."

Still, I shouted his name as if my voice could ever alert him better than the alarms and the smoke.

Once outside, we stared up at the manor. The top floor was all ablaze, plumes of yellow and orange dyeing the night sky.

I squinted, trying to see into the flames. "There! What's that?" I pointed to a window on the fourth floor.

Corey stared. "Is that Watt?"

It was. Watt stood calmly at the window, looking down at us, Nora's body in his arms. Then he turned his back and stepped farther into the flames.

My stomach clenched, and I couldn't take a breath. *Why? Why would he…?* My mind slipped as it tried to follow his logic.

"Come on," Corey said, tugging on my hand. "We have to

get out of here. It's already starting to spread to the trees.

I followed after him with faltering steps, looking over my shoulder as the blaze moved to the tower, while the green leaves of nearby trees smoked and smoldered.

Corey led me to the boathouse and helped me into a small fishing boat. After starting the engine, he turned to me as I sat in the seat beside the driver's. "Put on your life jacket."

I did as he told me, and he drove the boat out of the inside dock.

A few hundred yards into the lake, he cut the engine and turned back to watch as his ancestral home burned.

"Will you stay with me until the end?"

I looked over at him, his black eyes reflecting the flames even at this distance. I knew what he meant. His only chance to beat the curse was gone.

I laced my fingers with his. "To the very end," I promised.

I OPENED THE front door to find Cecily in the hallway.

"Oh, hey. What are you doing here?" I asked.

"Well, I went by your studio yesterday because I wanted to get your book, but it was closed. So I came by to get it before you leave town."

I smiled at her. "Yeah, sorry. We had some stuff we had to take care of before we started to pack. Come in." I stepped to the side to let Cecily enter the apartment.

"Where's Corey?"

I shut the door behind her. "Still packing."

She gaped. "But aren't you due at the airport in like two hours?"

I shrugged. "He always waits until the last minute." I walked over to a box on the coffee table and pulled a book from the stack inside.

Cecily took it from me, looking down at the cover. "*Yearning for Darkness* by Corey and Katherine Bennings. Oh, I like this cover. How much do I owe you?"

I waved my hand at her.

She frowned. "Don't be like that. I know how hard you two worked on this poetry and photography book, and I want to support you. How are you going to get rich and famous if you just give them away?"

I snorted. "Right. I think you're only the second person to even want a copy."

"Well, you have to give it time."

She looked at the price on the back of the book and stuffed the cash into my hand. "So are you excited? You haven't had a vacation in a while. California should be nice this time of year."

"I'll be excited when I'm on the ground. I like flying even less than being on a boat."

"Alia and Phil must have been surprised when you said you'd come to their wedding then."

"Yeah—"

"Hey, Wren," Izzy called, bursting into the living room with a can in her hand, a black pug at her heels. "So Edgar gets one scoop of dry food in the morning and one can of— Oh, Cecily's here."

Edgar ran to Cecily, remembering that the vet always gave him the very best belly rubs.

"Is your auntie going to watch you while your mommy and daddy are away?" Cecily asked the dog. She smiled up at Izzy. "Are you on break?"

Izzy nodded. "Yep. And it's just me and Edgar here for a whole week."

"Sounds like paradise," Cecily said.

"It will be if they actually leave."

"Hey," I protested. "That's not very nice."

Izzy sighed and flung her arm over my shoulders. "I'm just worried about you, sis. You guys haven't had a vacation in nearly a year."

"Well, Corey has been busy with work."

"How is it at the UMWA?" Cecily inquired.

I picked up Edgar, who was pawing at my pant leg. "Good. He just helped some miners in West Virginia bargain for better health insurance. So he was pretty excited about that. Here." I handed Edgar to Izzy. "Why don't you take him for a walk before we go?"

"Edgar, you want walkies?" Izzy asked.

The pug wiggled wildly in her arms, and she clutched him to her so he wouldn't fall.

"I better go, too" Cecily said. "You're clearly going to have to help your husband pack if you want to leave on time."

"Hang on a second." I waited for Izzy to put Edgar's leash on and head out the door. Then I looked around and dropped my voice. "You know, this book has brought up a lot of questions for me. And I wanted your opinion on something, but I know Corey doesn't like to talk about it."

Cecily nodded, telling me to go ahead.

"The curse…" A shiver ran over me despite myself. "We still have no idea how it was broken. Even when we went back to Nightfall Island and stayed in the dorms for those few weeks, the spirits never came back."

Cecily pursed her lips. "I thought about that for a long time. You said Nora's last words to Corey were ones of good will. I think that was the intention that, when mixed with her blood, broke the curse."

I scrunched my brow. "But we saw the ghosts after that."

She nodded. "Right. You said Watt crumbled up the paper and later burned the place down. Fire is one way to activate a spell. So I think a combination of her good will, the words you wrote, and the fire releasing it is how the curse was broken."

I frowned. *I guess that makes sense.*

Cecily smiled. "Don't worry too much about it. It's over now. There's nothing else to worry about except getting on that plane on time."

I snorted. "You're right. I'll go get him moving. Thanks for coming."

Cecily held up the book. "Congratulations. I'm looking forward to it."

Once I'd seen Cecily to the door, I went to our bedroom, where Corey was staring down at some clothes he'd laid on the bed.

Coming up behind him, I wrapped my arms around his stomach, resting my cheek on his back.

He placed his hands on mine. "Who was that?"

"Cecily. She came to pick up a copy of our book."

"Oh, that was nice of her."

I nodded. "Are you almost ready?"

I could hear his frown. "I'm still not sure what suit to wear to the wedding."

I released him and moved to stand beside him. I pointed. "Black. You look good in black."

"Do I?" He smiled over at me.

I shrugged. "When I fell in love with you, you always wore black."

He turned to me and grabbed me by the hips, leaning down to press a kiss to my lips. His hands slid to my back, and he pulled me against him.

My body flushed. "Don't get yourself all worked up. We're going to be late."

"Who's worked up? Me?" He trailed kisses down my neck.

"*Me* if you don't stop."

He paused. "Do you want me to stop?" he whispered, his breath hot on my shoulder where he'd already slipped my tank top strap down my arm.

"We can't right now. We don't have time." My voice was breathy and not at all convincing.

I could feel him smile against my skin. "We have enough."

AFTERWORD

Thank you for reading! I do so hope you enjoyed it. If you have a moment, I would very much appreciate a review. Tell other readers what you thought, and help them make a decision on this book.

If you'd like to stay updated on news about my books and events, you can subscribe to my newsletter on my website: www.dlieber.com

On my site, you will also find my blog, where I post all my fun little tidbits.

Thanks again! I hope you will travel through my worlds with me again in the future.

D. Lieber

ABOUT THE AUTHOR

D. Lieber has a wanderlust that would make a butterfly envious. When she isn't planning her next physical adventure, she's recklessly jumping from one fictional world to another. Her love of reading led her to earn a Bachelor's in English from Wright State University.

Beyond her skeptic and slightly pessimistic mind, Lieber wants to believe. She has been many places—from Canada to England, France to Italy, Germany to Russia—believing that a better world comes from putting a face on "other." She is a romantic idealist at heart, always fighting to keep her feet on the ground and her head in the clouds.

Lieber lives in Wisconsin with her husband (John) and cats (Yin and Nox).

LINKS

Website: www.dlieber.com
Goodreads: www.goodreads.com/dlieberwriting
Bookbub: www.bookbub.com/profile/d-lieber

9 781951 239299